KT-230-028

Libraries and Information

This book should be returned by the last date stamped above.
You may renew the loan personally, by post or telephone for a
further period if the book is not required by another reader.

wakefieldcouncil
working for you

www.wakefield.gov.uk

THE NIGHT BOOK

RICHARD MADELEY

SIMON &
SCHUSTER

London · New York · Sydney · Toronto · New Delhi

A CBS COMPANY

First published in Great Britain by Simon & Schuster UK Ltd, 2016
A CBS COMPANY

1 3 5 7 9 10 8 6 4 2

Simon & Schuster UK Ltd
1st Floor
222 Gray's Inn Road
London WC1X 8HB

www.simonandschuster.co.uk

Simon & Schuster Australia, Sydney
Simon & Schuster India, New Delhi

A CIP catalogue record for this book
is available from the British Library

Paperback ISBN: 978-1-4711-4058-7
eBook ISBN: 978-1-4711-4059-4

Typeset in Sabon by M Rules
Printed and bound by CPI Group (UK) Ltd, Croydon, CR0 4YY

Simon & Schuster UK Ltd are committed to sourcing paper
that is made from wood grown in sustainable forests and support the Forest
Stewardship Council, the leading international forest certification organisation.
Our books displaying the FSC logo are printed on FSC certified paper.

To Judy, for tolerating my near-incommunicado state over the four months it took me to create this story, and also to my wonderful colleagues in newsrooms, on papers, television and especially at BBC local radio in Cumbria. And, of course, to the lakes and fells themselves; a stunning revelation of natural beauty to a young city boy. Salad days, and happy times.

PROLOGUE

JULY 1976

It was still early but the lake was warm. Unnaturally warm, she thought, as she walked steadily into its shallows, her bare feet casting the first disturbance of the day across the glassy surface. In all her solitary visits here over the years, she had never known the water to be as smooth and balmy and as welcoming as this.

Beyond the immediate shimmering ripples she had created, the reflection of the parched, sun-baked hills surrounding the lake had extraordinary clarity. She could have been looking into a vast, perfectly polished mirror. The sky, waiting for the sun to make its entrance from behind a brooding shoulder of scorched mountain to the east, was the same vivid blue in these still waters as in the cloudless bowl above her.

But there was something wrong with the lake this year.

It was shrunken; diminished; humbled by the pitiless sun.

She had to hobble across unfamiliar flat rocks that were normally hidden beneath the surface, before at last reaching a strange new shoreline. She considered it for a few moments and then quickly undressed.

There was no one else in sight; it was the lake in the next valley that was attracting curious visitors this extraordinary, stretched, unprecedented summer. The waters there had now receded so far that the roofs and walls of a long-drowned village were beginning to emerge. She hadn't driven over yet to see it herself, but those who had reported that it looked eerie, like the bones of a corpse slowly rising, dripping, to the surface. Some said that the crooked medieval church steeple, which had been the first ruined fragment to silently reappear, resembled a witch's hat. The place was oddly unsettling and almost everyone drawn to the banks of the dark, shrinking waters found themselves increasingly uneasy. Few loitered there.

She waded further out into the lake so that it began to rise above her thighs. It remained tepid, even this far from the shore. Today, swimming naked would be an uncomplicated pleasure and not the physical challenge it usually was; one that, if she was honest, she only enjoyed afterwards as she towelled herself dry, glowing with puritanical pleasure.

She flexed her knees slightly and stood on tiptoe, pushing her body forward and down. The lake caressed and upheld her. Slowly she swam, breast-stroke, moving further and further away from the shore, revelling in the Mediterranean warmth. She dipped deeper beneath the surface.

Ten seconds later, she began to drown.

CHAPTER ONE

'Bugger . . . oh, *shit*.'

Seb Richmond stabbed helplessly at the pause button on the big steel tape deck and watched in dismay as the twin spools of recording tape twirled and bunched into a glistening cat's cradle.

The machine juddered to a halt with an ear-splitting metallic shriek and the radio station's technical engineer put his head around the editing suite's door. 'Problems, Seb? Again?'

The younger man sighed. 'How do you always bloody know when I screw up, Jess? I thought this studio was meant to be soundproof.'

'Thirty years at the BBC gives you an ear for trouble, son. Especially where new boys like you're concerned, and it's no different here in commercial radio. Not exactly suited to the life of a radio reporter, are you? Should have stayed on that London paper of yours.'

'Yeah, tell me about it.' Seb hesitated. 'Between you and me I phoned up my old editor yesterday, asked if they'd have me back. Not a chance. They haven't even replaced me – cost-cutting. I'm stuck up here on Lake District FM. Well, until I get the chop, that is; my three months' probation's almost up. Even I wouldn't keep me on.' He tugged ineffectually at the tangle in front of him. 'Jesus, Jess – look at this mess.'

'Wow, and he's a poet, too. What was on it?'

'Only my bloody interview with Thatcher at the Cumbria Conservative fete earlier. The network's meant to be taking it down the line on the news feed at midnight. It's for Good Morning UK tomorrow. Fat chance now. I could untie the Gordian knot quicker.' He kicked back his chair on its castors and rubbed at his eyes with both fists. 'Never mind probation – it'll be the sack for Seb this time.'

The technician eased himself further into the tiny room and looked calmly over the reporter's shoulder, trying to conceal his natural sympathy. The new boy was young enough to be his son. 'Yup, it's a grade-A foul-up,' he said cheerfully. 'Looks like one of my kids' fishing lines when they'd cocked up a cast on Windermere. Tell you what – you go get me a coffee – milk, one sugar – while I straighten it out. How many edits does it need?'

Seb stared at him in disbelief. 'You mean you can actually save this? Jess, you're a walking miracle.' He scrambled out of his chair and stood for a moment, considering.

'Let's see ... about three cuts, that should do it. Lose my opening question to her completely – I was all nervous gabble. I'll write the sense of it into the presenter's live studio cue. Start with her first answer.' He scratched his chin.

'Then take out the whole bit about whether she thinks she'll be our next PM,' he continued, as the engineer began to untangle the mangled tape with practised deftness. 'She completely stonewalled me. Eyes like bloody chips of ice. Oh, and cut the end part completely: Maggie wouldn't talk about her husband Denis or the kids or how she *really* got to be Tory leader. I come across as whiney and desperate and she just sounds irritated. I don't blame her.'

Seb sighed. 'I thought that this radio lark would be easy, but I just can't do it. I was fine with my notebook and pen, but stick a mic in my hand and I completely lose the plot ... Christ, Jess, how are you *doing* that?'

The tape had been efficiently re-spooled and was winding smoothly back to the start on fast return.

'Your problem is that you're too impatient, Seb. I've been watching you. You busk everything, don't take time to learn. Now ... let's have us a listen.' Jess punched play and after some hissing white noise, a nervy, breathy voice could be heard, stammering the opening question to the leader of Her Majesty's Opposition.

The reporter closed his eyes. 'Christ, listen to me ... see what I mean? I sound about seventeen.'

'You *are* about seventeen.'

'I was twenty-eight last week.'

'If you say so, punk ... actually, forget that coffee; go nick us both a cold drink from the station manager's fridge while I edit this. It's stifling in here.'

'And out here,' Seb said as he moved into the corridor. He paused. 'I thought it was supposed to be cooler up in the frozen north. Since I got here it's felt more like Greece. Thirty-two degrees again tomorrow.'

'Yup. Ninety in old money.' The engineer nodded and reached for a razor blade to start slicing the tape. 'I've never known a summer like it. Haven't seen a cloud in weeks, have you? My lawn looks like a piece of toast. Still, not as hot up here as your precious London, eh? They're dropping like flies on the pavements down there. At least that's something to make you glad you quit Fleet Street for us hicks in the sticks, eh?'

Seb gave a short laugh.

'You have to be bloody joking, Jess. I wish I'd never left.'

CHAPTER TWO

No one could remember a heatwave like it. People old enough to have lived through the legendary Spitfire Summer of thirty-six years earlier, when snarling British and German fighter planes left their gleaming white contrails twisting against endless china-blue skies, agreed that 1976 was in a league of its own. Weeks of uninterrupted sunshine had blazed unbroken from sunrise to sunset and still there was no sign of the great heat breaking.

Cloudless day followed cloudless day. There hadn't been even a single thunderstorm to break the pattern. True, once in a while a scattering of mackerel-shaped clouds would appear high over-head, like a sparse shoal of fish moving slowly through a barren ocean. Far below them the brilliant sunlight dimmed a little, briefly filtered and denied its full strength. But soon, always, the skies became spotless again and the faint promise of relief quietly evaporated.

It was hot, hot, *hot*.

To begin with, almost everyone was ecstatic that a Mediterranean summer had banished Britain's Atlantic depressions far from its shores. Roads to the coast around the country were jammed, especially at weekends. Car dealers couldn't lay their hands on enough convertibles. Barbecue sales rocketed. Air-conditioning units, long seen as a pointless extravagance on a mostly rainy, cloudy island, were suddenly in demand for the first time and quickly sold out. Fresh units were hastily flown in from America and went for absurd prices.

Ancient shibboleths and customs melted away like an iceberg drifting on a summer sea. In the City, gentlemen's clubs relaxed their 'jacket at all times' code. During a celebrated trial at the Old Bailey, the judge allowed barristers to remove their horse-hair wigs, from under which perspiration had been dripping steadily onto their case notes. His Lordship, too, gave himself permission to hear the case bare-headed.

In the countryside, dust-devils danced like tiny tornadoes across the parched wheat fields. Trees seemed to pray for rain and for some reason the birds fell strangely silent. Perhaps it was just too hot for them to sing. Pig farmers reported that their stock was suffering from severe cases of sunburn; if the animals could not be kept indoors, their backs were slathered in sunscreen bought in bulk from the nearest chemist. One Fleet Street wag dubbed it 'swine-tan lotion'.

Out in the meadows, the shallow horse ponds shrank and dwindled and eventually evaporated completely. Dry, cracked mud greeted thirsty cattle desperate to drink; they bellowed and stamped the ground in frustration. Farmers rigged up metal drinking troughs, filling them with water from milk churns dragged clanking across the parched fields by tractor.

All this – the discomfort, the inconvenience, the sleepless nights with windows flung open onto airless streets and gardens – was at first, in that peculiarly British way, almost perversely celebrated. But after weeks of Roman-hot days and nights, the mood began to shift, subtly, but distinctly. This endless, glorious sunshine was all well and good, but . . . it wasn't *natural*, was it? A decent fine spell was one thing: this was starting to feel like something far more profound, an endless gavotte with the sun and the moon and the stars that meant . . . well, *what*, exactly? A fundamental shift in the planet's weather patterns? Why not? It had happened before, hadn't it? Look at the Ice Age, or even the mini-ice age of a few centuries earlier, when winter fairs were held on a frozen Thames.

Such speculation, idle at first, gradually took on an unmistakable edge of seriousness, even panic. Science writers aired increasingly crackpot theories in the newspapers. Perhaps the Earth had somehow deviated from its usual course through the heavens. Could it have wobbled on its axis, effecting a small but crucial shift in the planet's aspect to the sun?

In other words, was this thing going to be *permanent*?

It had certainly become lethal. Deaths from sunstroke were multiplying, which was to be expected. That was a problem mainly affecting the south.

But hundreds of miles north, in the beautiful shining waters that lapped scorched screes and sparkled under bone-dry mountain tops, there was another penalty to be paid for such implacable, sweltering heat.

The drownings had started.

CHAPTER THREE

She didn't mean a word of it, of course. Not a word. God, she wasn't some kind of homicidal maniac. Far from it – she even had trouble killing flies; if she could shoo them out of a door or window instead, she would. She was terrified of wasps but it troubled her conscience whenever she swatted one. Which was stupid, really; she'd once read that wasps serve no useful function whatsoever in the chain of life. Nature would be quite undisturbed if the horrible things became extinct overnight.

But if anyone ever found her diary – the secret one; the one she wrote every few months, always late at night when her husband was asleep, and which she kept hidden under an old towel at the back of the airing cupboard – well, God knows what they'd think. They'd assume that either she was a frustrated horror writer, a sort of Stephen King *manqué*, or a total psycho.

She was neither. She was just … *what*, exactly? Bloody miserable, obviously, in her fucked-up, god-awful marriage to Cameron. Even after eleven years she still couldn't quite believe the levels of psychological cruelty the man was capable of. My God, how well he hid all that during their courtship and early days of marriage. And from her, of all people! Meriel Kidd, the famous, award-winning, feminist agony aunt, with her own weekly radio show and a column in one of the more upmarket Sunday tabloids. The expert on standing up to abusive men and cutting control freaks and bullies down to size – or efficiently out of your life.

It would be almost funny if it wasn't so tragic. But her listeners and readers must never, ever know the truth about Cameron and what she routinely had to put up with from him. Her credibility would evaporate overnight and she would become a national figure of pity, perhaps even contempt. Because how many times over the airwaves or in print had she counselled women in marriages *exactly* like hers – tied to abusive, mean-spirited, boorish and supremely selfish men like Cameron? Her advice to them was always firm, always unambiguous.

You give him one ultimatum to change his ways. ONE. If he doesn't? LEAVE. HIM. Get out from under and start again. You're worth much more than this. You can do it. You know you can. You're a lot stronger than you think.

14

Her public would demand to know why she couldn't follow her own counsel.

In her defence, it had been a gradual descent into the nightmare with Cameron. She hadn't woken up one morning in their sprawling Victorian house at the foot of the Cumbrian fells to find that her husband had metamorphosed overnight into a controlling monster. It wasn't as if a bad fairy had hovered over their bed as they slept and cast an evil spell over the union.

No, the depredations had been subtle, almost unnoticeable to begin with. The occasional sneering comment directed at something she had just said or done, swiftly followed by a contrite apology.

But the put-downs gradually grew more frequent and the apologies less so. Then the dominating behaviour began to emerge. Especially over money.

Cameron was not only much older than her – she was thirty-one, he was fifty-nine – he was wealthier, too. A *lot* wealthier. By the time he was forty he'd made his first million and he was worth many times that today after making a series of killings on the stock market. As soon as they married, in what seemed to her at the time to be a sincere and generous act, he'd insisted on adding her name to all three of his private bank accounts.

'But I earn a fraction of what you do,' she protested. 'It doesn't seem fair.'

'What's mine is yours,' he told her firmly and, with a mixture of guilt and gratitude, she had agreed.

Now, the joint accounts were joint in name only. Cameron had slowly asserted complete control over every aspect of their financial affairs. What had begun as the occasional good-natured question from him at the breakfast table when he opened their bank statement ('Hello, what's *this* about? I don't remember taking out a hundred pounds from the cashpoint in Kendal last Thursday. That must have been you, darling. What did you need it for?') had become a forensic weekly inquisition.

He went through their statements line-by-line, using a clear Perspex ruler, peering over rimless reading glasses at each entry as he moved remorselessly down the page. He insisted she account for everything. Last year she'd made a short local speaking tour around the Lakes and the Scottish borders and had quietly asked the organisers to pay her expenses in cash. The fees weren't much more than token payments but at least, she thought, she'd have a few pounds of her own to spend how she liked without being grilled.

But Cameron had found the money – he went through her purse one evening when she was in the bath – and there'd been a terrible row. 'You can't have it both ways, you deceitful bitch!' he'd roared, waving the pathetic handful of banknotes in her face. 'If what's mine is yours, what's yours is mine. I'm putting this straight in the bank tomorrow. Actually, I'm not. *You're* going to. And I've bloody counted it so you'd better not keep any of it back. I'll know if you do.'

Belatedly she'd realised that Cameron's insistence on adding her name (and of course her income) to his bank accounts had nothing whatsoever to do with generosity of spirit. From the start his motive had been to keep her under constant observation, supervision and constraint. It begged the question she knew would mystify any dispassionate observer: why on earth was a strong, self-confident woman like Meriel Kidd sticking with her marriage to a total shit like Cameron Bruton?

She knew the answer and it shamed her. She was doing it to preserve her career. There was no lie she wouldn't tell to preserve the public fiction that she enjoyed the happiest of marriages. 'I'm very lucky,' she'd told *Woman's Own* only last month. 'I know it sounds like a terrible old cliché, but Cameron and I were quite simply made for each other.'

Perhaps if she had left him years ago, as soon as she realised the kind of man he really was, it would have been all right. More than all right; it would have demonstrated that she practised what she preached.

But divorce him now? It was simply too much for her to risk. Her career gave her self-worth and public standing and respect. It was the only thing she had left (Cameron had made it clear he had no interest in becoming a father) and she was damned if she was going to risk losing it. She'd just have to carry on, chin up, smile firmly in place.

For now.

Always that caveat at the back of her mind. *For now.* One day, she *knew* she'd find a way out. It was that quiet certainty, unsupported by any actual plan of action, which kept her going.

That, and the secret diary.

She'd bought it on impulse years before from a second-hand bookshop in Windermere. God knows who it had originally belonged to, but whoever it was, they hadn't written a single word on the thick white pages that were bound inside an expensive-looking supple black leather jacket. A red silk ribbon was attached to the spine to mark entries and, just beneath it, a hollow leather tube, a sort of holster, to hold a pen.

There were no lines on the pages, no margins, no dates. The diary was perfectly blank. Meriel couldn't help thinking that it had been waiting for her, and her alone, to buy it. She couldn't really understand her compulsion to do so, but it was absolute and not to be denied.

Her marriage to Cameron had yet to descend into the abyss; she was still relatively happy on the day she bought the diary.

But for some reason, she didn't tell him about it. She hid it from her husband right from the start.

*

Cameron never listened to Meriel's show – he made a point of telling her that, pleasantly describing it as 'your brainless apology for a programme' – but if he had, how he would have laughed. 'Healer, heal thyself,' he would surely mock when she arrived home (Cameron was fond of Biblical aphorisms). He knew exactly how unhappy she was with him. Of course he did. Her misery was his hobby.

Her hobby was her secret.

She'd begun writing the diary five years earlier, when she'd finally admitted to herself her catastrophic mistake in marrying Cameron. The first entry was inspired by a letter from one of her listeners, a woman who had poured her heart out to Meriel in half a dozen anguished pages that described the emotional abuse she was suffering at her husband's hands.

Meriel had identified with the woman's wretchedness, but it was what was scribbled below the signature that had caught her imagination.

PS. Thank you for reading this. Even if you are unable to reply, I can't tell you what a difference it has made just to write all of it down. I feel so much better for it. I think I might start keeping some sort of a diary. I believe it could help, whatever I eventually decide to do.

That very night Meriel made her first entry in her diary, while Cameron slept upstairs.

It was an extraordinarily vicious fantasy. When she'd finished, Meriel could scarcely credit herself with writing it. It was practically pornographic; an outpouring of graphic, almost maniacal violence.

And it was utterly, wonderfully cathartic; a calming effect that lingered for weeks.

She wasn't entirely sure what would happen if Cameron ever caught her making one of her entries. He'd certainly snatch the black, leather-bound book from her grasp and read its explosively angry pages.

He'd realise immediately that it was about him, his wife's secret outlet for her fantasy revenges on him.

And what revenges they were.

Would he strike her? She doubted it. He'd never actually hit her; she'd go straight to the police if he did. In fact, she sometimes found herself perversely wishing that he'd punch her in the face, kick her kidneys, tear out her hair, try to throttle her. Because then she'd have him. By God, she'd have the bastard. It would be her ticket out of the impasse she'd got herself into. Worth a few cuts and bruises to see Cameron hauled off by the scruff of his neck to a police cell, and later hanging his head in the dock.

'It came as a total shock,' she'd tell her earnestly sympathetic TV hosts as she did the obligatory round of talk shows. 'Of course, I divorced him on the spot.

No woman should *ever* put up with abuse, be it mental or physical. I just hope that my experience acts as a positive example to others.' There might even be a book deal in it.

But Cameron was clever. He never hit her. He had far too much to lose, a man of his public status, the brilliant businessman with the younger, foxy wife.

The only book she looked like writing any time soon was a diary that no one would ever be allowed to read.

I take the breadknife from the drawer and hone it one last time on the whetstone that hangs from a hook above the sink. The knife's keen edge is already glitteringly sharp but I want to be absolutely sure. One stroke must be enough. I don't want him to wake in time to fight me off before I open his throat with a single, deadly slash.

I make a few final light, upward strokes, unconcerned by the squeal of metal on stone. He's asleep up in our bedroom at the back of the cottage. Even if he were awake, he couldn't hear this.

I climb the stairs quietly as I can, taking care to keep close to the side of each tread, next to the wall, so they don't creak. I oiled the hinges of the bedroom door this morning so when I gently push at it now, it slowly swings open in complete silence.

There he is. He insists on a nightlight, the big baby, so I can see him quite clearly, snoring on his back, duvet pushed down all the way to his horrible, hairless knees, his revolting potbelly sticking up towards the ceiling. Beneath the swollen stomach the penis is shrivelled and shrunken. It looks like a button mushroom. It only ever feeds and grows on his cruelty; he can never manage it unless he declares all my perceived faults and failures, aloud, to my face, which he holds between his fat, sausage-like fingers. The exact opposite of a love song.

I tiptoe to his side of the bed. I can't believe how calm I am feeling. I steady myself, allowing him to take his last breath. His last breath. What a wonderful thought.

And then I do it. I bend down, cup his stubbly, fat-folded chin in my left hand and force his head up and across to one side. He starts to mutter something but I'm much too quick for him. The knife is ready in my right hand and I press the hilt hard against his throat, just below the Adam's apple, and then pull it back and down as fast as I can and with all the strength I have.

A fountain of blood – it looks black in this dim light – explodes from the scimitar-shaped, gaping incision I have just made and he makes exactly the same kind of stupid gargling noise I hear coming from our bathroom every morning when he brushes his teeth. I step back, trying not to laugh; this is incredibly funny. I wasn't prepared for that.

Now he's thrashing about with his arms and legs, and the gargling turns to gurgling, along with a weird, high-pitched whistling noise. I never hear that when he brushes his teeth. Then he abruptly goes into convulsions – proper, full-body convulsions – before giving a long, tip-to-toe shudder which goes on for a surprisingly long time. Eventually it subsides, and at last my wonderful husband lies utterly still.

I'm pretty sure he didn't actually wake up before he died.

Pity.

CHAPTER FOUR

The coroner's clerk moved grumpily down the windowed side of the impossibly stuffy little courtroom, methodically opening each top panel with the long-handled winding rod that his own father had used half a century before.

He cursed under his breath as the small hinged Victorian rectangles of glass crowning each bay grudgingly squeaked open by their regulation few inches. Call this ventilation? The inquest about to begin into that poor girl drowning in Buttermere had better be an open-and-shut case, or the next one would be about a mass suffocation right here in this room. He half-hoped the old boy would adjourn the hearing to a later date when this ruddy heatwave had passed, if it was ever going to.

A side door opened behind him and several men in shiny suits, and one woman with a shiny face, sauntered in, talking and laughing. Bloody press. No respect. Ghouls, the lot of them. What if it was their kid what drowned? They wouldn't be so bloody pleased with themselves then.

He turned his back on them in disgust and walked over to the old boy's raised desk to make sure the case notes were in order. They'd be starting soon.

Dr Timothy Young was probably over-qualified to be the Kendal Coroner. He'd got a first in medicine from Bristol and went on to qualify as a consultant neurologist, practising in one of the big London teaching hospitals.

But to his surprise, he found he was slightly bored there. Of course, the job was demanding, sometimes exceptionally so, but still, still ... He missed the intellectual rigour of the university's union debates, and the semantic arguments that sometimes carried on well into the night long after the official jousting had ended. He was naturally opinionated, even disputatious, and enjoyed a good wrangle.

He began to realise that he'd taken the wrong career path, and when he was in his mid-thirties he made his decision. Ignoring his father's warnings about 'changing horses in mid-stream, Timothy', he quit his post at the hospital and went back to university, this time to study law.

He qualified as a barrister in time for his forty-first

birthday and moved back home to his beloved Lakes. The work in Carlisle Crown Court wasn't as high-profile as the Bailey (where during his pupillage he'd been quietly told he was assuredly destined) but he didn't care. A good argument was a good argument whichever court you were in, and when his cases adjourned for the day he could be at his beautiful wood-framed house overlooking the lapping waters of Bassenthwaite in less than an hour, in time for dinner with his wife.

Now in his early sixties, Dr Young had been happy to slow the pace down a notch or two. He wanted to spend more time sailing his boat on Windermere, so he'd gladly accepted the local council's offer the previous year to take over as Kendal Coroner.

Thus far, there had been nothing particularly complicated or unusual about the deaths he'd examined. A couple of shotgun suicides, one case of carbon monoxide poisoning from a faulty farmhouse boiler, a dairyman crushed to death by an ill-tempered heifer. Routine stuff for a country coroner.

Until this morning.

There was something about this one he didn't like.

'. . . and therefore my conclusion is that Miss Winterton suffered death due to cardiac arrest caused by the inhalation of water.'

'In other words, she drowned,' Dr Young prompted the nervous young pathologist giving evidence.

'Er, yes, sir,' the young man replied, going rather pink. 'She drowned.'

'Hmm.' The coroner tapped his desk lightly with a pencil. 'Doesn't that surprise you somewhat, doctor? We've heard that Miss Winterton was a physically fit young woman of twenty-four, an experienced swimmer. Indeed her father has told us that his daughter had swum in Buttermere almost daily since childhood. We also know that conditions on the lake on the day in question were flat calm. Do you have any theories as to how she could have inhaled enough water to incapacitate and kill her?'

The pathologist looked slightly hunted.

'Er . . . no, I'm afraid I don't, your honour.'

The older man suppressed a smile. 'I'm not a judge, Dr Bullen. "Sir" will do.'

'I'm sorry, sir.'

'That's quite all right.' The coroner paused for a moment before continuing: 'Am I correct in thinking you appeared before me earlier this month to give evidence in another case of drowning? That of a middle-aged man? He was swimming in Bassenthwaite Lake, as I recall.'

The pathologist appeared surprised, but nodded. 'That's correct, your hon— . . . sir.'

'I thought so. Could you refresh my memory of that particular case? I can adjourn if necessary.'

The man opposite relaxed a little. 'There's no need

for that, sir. I believe I may have my notes on it here with me. Bear with me a moment, please.'

He bent to pick up his briefcase and rummaged briefly through it before removing a slim brown file. 'Yes, I thought so. Here we are. What exactly do you wish to know, sir?'

'The cause of death, please.'

The pathologist relaxed even more. 'Oh, I can remember that easily enough. It was cardiac arrest.'

'Caused by inhalation of water?'

'No. There was no water in the deceased's lungs. It was straightforward cardiac arrest – a heart attack.'

'Ah, so I was wrong just now. It wasn't a drowning.'

'No, sir, technically it wasn't, although death did occur whilst swimming.'

Timothy Young thought for a moment before leaning forward slightly. His instincts were telling him he was close to the edge of something.

'If memory serves, Dr Bullen, your autopsy found no signs of associated heart disease.'

The pathologist examined his file and then looked up. 'That's correct, sir. My examination of this . . .' he paused again, looking back down at the papers, 'yes, this forty-four-year-old male, showed the heart and surrounding arteries to be in excellent condition.'

'Can you pass any conjecture, then, as to why this gentleman should suffer a fatal coronary whilst swimming in Bassenthwaite?'

'I'm not a heart specialist, sir. I'm afraid you'd have to consult one of them.'

The coroner nodded. 'Of course. You have been most helpful, doctor. You may stand down.' He glanced up at the clock on the opposite wall.

'I see it is approaching half past twelve. I'll take an adjournment for lunch and this hearing will reconvene at two o'clock. Mr Armstrong?'

His clerk looked up from the desk below. 'Sir?'

'I would like to see you in my room. Now, if that's convenient.'

'Sir.'

'Thank you. This hearing is adjourned.'

Back in his cramped office directly behind the court-room, Timothy Young poured himself and his clerk a glass of chilled water from a jug kept in a little fridge.

'Bloody hot in there this morning, eh, John?'

'Too right, sir,' Armstrong replied, before grate-fully gulping down the water in one long swallow. 'I'll bet my old man never experienced one like it in all his days here. I was with the Eighth Army in North Africa during the last lot and this is almost as bad. For the heat, I mean.' He wiped his mouth with the back of his hand. 'What did you want to see me about, sir?'

Young drained his own glass before replying.

'It concerns the period I was on holiday last month – towards the end of June. Didn't I read in the paper that you'd had an inquest into another drowning? It was a young mother, wasn't it? She got into difficulties in Thirlmere.'

Armstrong nodded. 'Absolutely right, sir. It was very sad. The woman had two kiddies and the poor little blighters saw the whole thing happen from the shore with their grandmother. Quite dreadful. The visiting coroner recorded it as accidental death.'

'Was it actual drowning or an unrelated cardiac arrest? Can you remember?'

His clerk looked faintly offended.

'Course I can remember, sir. It was just like the poor young lady we've been hearing about today. Lungs full of water. She drowned.'

Timothy Young steepled his fingers and closed his eyes, thinking hard. After a minute he opened them again.

'John, how long have you been clerk here?'

'Thirty-one years, sir.'

'Do you ever remember so many deaths in the water happening in such a short space of time?'

The clerk shook his head. 'Not separately, no. We had a ferry go down once, September 1948, I think it was. Five souls lost that afternoon. But I don't recall three unconnected fatalities in as many weeks, no.'

'And neither of us recalls a summer as fierce as

this one, do we?' The coroner began tapping with his pencil again. 'I think there *is* a connection here, John.

'In fact, I think we may have a problem.'

CHAPTER FIVE

AUGUST

Seb Richmond hadn't been sacked, but he was still on thin ice. His interview with Margaret Thatcher, thanks to skilful editing by Jess, had been just enough to win him a grudging extension to his probation at Lake District FM – three more months, one last chance to prove himself.

'It's like living under the fucking Sword of Damocles,' Seb grumbled on the phone to his girlfriend in London. 'Honestly, Sarah, if I didn't have you to talk to, I don't know how I'd stand it. When can you next come up here?'

The line crackled.

'Sarah? You still there? Sarah?'

The voice at the other end had been distinctly

subdued since the beginning of the conversation. Now it was almost inaudible.

'Yeah, I'm still here, Seb.' The line crackled again. 'The thing is ... about coming up ... the thing is ... look, Seb, I've got something to tell you ...'

He'd never been dumped before. A week later, as he drove in for the morning news conference, Seb still couldn't quite believe it had happened to him. He'd always been the one to move on, with all the usual honeyed, hackneyed words and expressions.

'It's not you, it's *me* ...' 'It's *because* I love you that I want you to be *free* ...' 'You deserve someone so much *better* ...'

He had to admit that, after her initial hesitancy, Sarah had certainly got into her stride. She'd been impressively blunt.

'We're three hundred-plus miles apart, Seb, I hardly ever see you, the last time I came up you *slept* most of the bloody time – yes, I know you were on breakfast-show shifts, but still ... All you can talk about is your rotten job and how much you hate it, and anyway, to be quite honest I've met someone else and d'you know what? From time to time he actually asks *me* how *my* day's been. Can you believe that? I'm sorry, Seb, but I've had enough. Oh, and another thing, you never even *think* to—'

Fortunately, he'd called her from the pub.

Now, Seb parked his Triumph Spitfire two-seater sports convertible in the radio station's car park and regarded it sadly as he pointlessly locked the door. It was the easiest car in Britain to break into or steal. Back in London he'd thought it looked fashionably urban with a sort of scruffy-to-naff chic about it. Up here in the Lakes it just looked naff. He sighed and made his way through the building's front doors.

The news editor was busy handing out the morning's assignments when Seb walked into the office.

'Ah, Seb. How kind of you to join us. About bleedin' time. I want you to go down to Kendal. Take the radio car. You're probably going to be doing a live voice piece into the lunchtime news and I want speech quality, not a crappy phone line.'

The station only had one radio car. Actually it wasn't a car, it was a big Ford Transit van with an extendable twenty-foot radio mast on the roof and if you were assigned it, it meant you were on a decent-sized story. Seb brightened up.

'Great. What's the job?'

Bob Merryman, a chain-smoking ex-newspaperman from Birmingham, shook his head. 'Not exactly sure but I've got a feeling about it. There's a press conference at the town hall. It's at eleven-thirty, which is why I'm pissed off you're in late again. You'll only just make it even if you leave now. Get weaving.' He tossed the van's keys across the newsroom and Seb caught them one-handed.

'But what's it about?' he asked. 'You must have some idea.'

'Not a lot. It's something to do with these drownings in the lakes this summer. The local freelance guy down there says he's heard they're linked in some sort of way and that's what the press conference is about. The coroner and some hydrographer from Lancaster University are going to make statements. Make sure you record them and take Jess with you to do the edits while you write your script.'

'I can do both.'

'Maybe you can and maybe you can't. But like I say, I've got a feeling about this and I don't want any fuck-ups, OK?'

Seb hesitated. 'Why are you sending me, then? I thought you thought I was still—'

Merryman lit a fresh cigarette. 'I'm sending you, Sebastian old chap, because, believe it or not, I actually have the teeniest tiniest fragment of faith in you.' The Brummie accent was very pronounced. 'You covered some big stories when you were in London and you did OK. I've seen your cuttings. I think you just need something to get your teeth into and get your confidence back. You did good with Thatch the other day.

Now piss off before I change my mind. I want you to—'

Seb was already running down the corridor to find Jess.

CHAPTER SIX

Jess pushed the ageing Transit to its limits as they thundered down the M6 towards Kendal. All the windows were rolled down in a futile attempt to combat the heat, and the roaring slipstream made it almost impossible for the two men to talk. The needle on the van's temperature gauge was moving into the red band as they raced past the pretty little market town of Penrith and into the wide, deepening valley that separated the steadily rising Yorkshire Dales to the east from the brooding Cumbrian fells to the west.

A fretting Seb had neither the time nor inclination to appreciate the savage grandeur that was beginning to unfold around them. 'D'you still think we'll make it for eleven-thirty?' he yelled at the engineer, as Jess indicated for the Kendal turn-off.

'Bloody hell, Seb, how many times? I keep telling you, *yes*! Only just, though ... are you all set up?'

The reporter tapped the compact reel-to-reel tape recorder nestling in his lap and checked the mic connection yet again before giving the thumbs-up.

'Yup. Good to go.'

To their relief the noise level dropped appreciably as Jess slowed for the exit roundabout.

'Right,' he said, in a more normal voice. 'Let's go through it one more time. When we get to the town hall you run in while I get the mast up and establish the live link to base. When the press conference is over, give me the tape, tell me the sound bites you want, and I'll get editing while you write your script. Then when we go live, I'll play them in on your hand cues – just point at me *very clearly* each time. Got it?'

'Er ... I think so. I've never done a live news insert before, Jess. Hope I don't screw up.'

'Not with your Uncle Jess with you, you won't. Ah, here we are – town centre coming up. Out of my way, matey.' Jess performed a hair-raising overtaking manoeuvre around a lumbering livestock lorry full of bleating sheep, and suddenly Kendal was before them, the pale stonework of the town hall's Victorian clock tower rising above the old rooftops, its spire gleaming dully in the baking heat of an already aggressive mid-morning sun.

Directly beneath it, a story was about to break.

*

Timothy Young had toyed with the idea of issuing some kind of public warning about swimming in the lakes, but in the end he decided against it. He only had a hunch that the cluster of deaths that summer were somehow connected, and that was hardly evidence.

But as soon as he recorded his verdict of accidental death on the girl who had drowned in Buttermere, he phoned his daughter in London.

Christine was a systems analyst in the City (she'd explained her job to him many times but he still didn't really understand what it was she did) and after a few minutes of father–daughter banter he came to the reason for the call.

'Do you remember that professor when you were a student at Lancaster? You know, the one with a bit of a thing for you, the old devil.'

Christine laughed. 'He wasn't old and he wasn't a devil either, Dad. But yes, of course I remember Brian. We went out for a few months. He was only about ten years older than me. He was nice.'

'Didn't he try to get you to switch courses? Study under him, if that's the right expression.'

His daughter laughed again. 'He certainly did. It wasn't entirely self-serving of him, though. I was fascinated by his subject – hydrography. You know, the study of seas and rivers and lakes. When Brian discovered our family lived above Bassenthwaite he was incredibly interesting about it and the Lake District

41

generally. He used to joke that at least it couldn't possibly be a *dry* subject.'

'Yet you drifted apart.'

'Oh, very funny, Pops, ha-ha! Anyway, why are we talking about Brian? It was years ago. Water under the bridge – *there*, gotcha back!'

Her father smiled. 'One-all ... Look, Chrissie, I need to speak to him, or someone like him. An expert on lakes. Something's going on up here that's not right. Do you still have his number?'

'Gosh, how intriguing! Yes, I think I do. Give me a sec.'

Half an hour later Kendal's coroner was talking to Professor Brian Parker of Lancaster University.

And, like the coroner's daughter, the professor was intrigued.

'Thanks so much for this, Brian. I'm amazed you've turned things round so quickly – it's less than a fortnight since we first spoke.' Timothy smiled gratefully at the professor as they prepared to go into the press conference together. The chief executive of the county council was with them.

'Well, these guys helped,' Parker said, nodding at the official. 'They came up with the boats and paid for most of the equipment I needed. And it wasn't that difficult to do, technically. The results were a hell of a surprise, though, in this country and this far north.

Not what I was expecting at all. Just goes to show how profound this summer's effects are becoming on surface-water temperature. Everything's being influenced – human behaviour, aquatic reproduction cycles ... I'm going to write a paper on it.'

The coroner turned to the council boss. 'And you're happy, Peter, with the public warning I want to give? You don't think it'll hit the tourist trade here?'

The executive shook his head. 'No. Bookings are solid and this thing in itself won't stop people coming. Anyway, we have a duty to get the information out there. We've *got* to do something to stop these drownings.'

'Right.' The coroner looked at his watch. 'It's exactly half past. Let's get in there.'

Ninety minutes later, inside the radio car, Seb was ready. Just. The press conference had only wrapped up a quarter of an hour ago – it had overrun due to an unexpected development – but somehow he'd managed to scribble down his script while Jess edited the tape in an incredible blur of razor blades and spinning spools.

As if he wasn't nervous enough, Seb had just been told that the network's main lunchtime news was going to take his report simultaneously along with his own station. He'd be broadcasting live from Land's End to John o' Groats.

He swallowed and held his handwritten script a little tighter.

In his earphones he could hear the final words of the introduction to him from the presenters in both Carlisle and London. They were synchronised to the second and suddenly the two voices – one male, one female – were simultaneously saying his name.

'. . . live from the Lake District, Sebastian Richmond.'

Bugger. He'd *told* them he wanted to be catch-lined 'Seb'. Too late now. He took a deep breath and suddenly, miraculously, his nerves evaporated.

He had a story to tell.

'Thank you . . . Today's press conference was called by local coroner Dr Timothy Young in the wake of a spate of drownings here in the Lakes. Dr Young has become concerned at the unusually high number of summer deaths in the water and took it on himself to commission an emergency survey of all three lakes involved, looking to identify any possible connection.

'As if to underline his concerns, and in a moment of extraordinary drama here this morning, news came of a fourth drowning that took place earlier today. Here's how that story broke as Dr Young was about to introduce expert testimony about the previous tragedies.'

Seb pointed with a chopping motion at Jess and the engineer instantly fired off the first tape. Timothy Young's clear, confident tones could be heard being interrupted mid-sentence by a low, almost inaudible voice and the faint crackling of paper.

'… *without further delay I'd like to hand you over to Professor Br— I'm sorry … bear with me for one moment, please, I'm being handed a note.*'

After more rustling and what sounded like a sharp intake of breath and a muttered '*Good Lord,*' the coroner continued, more slowly this time.

'*I have just been informed that the body of a man, believed to be aged between thirty and forty, was recovered earlier this morning from Derwent Water, several hundred yards from the shore near Portinscale. Early indications are that the victim had drowned, but of course there will need to be an autopsy followed by an inquest to establish the full facts.*'

A low murmur could be heard sweeping through the roomful of journalists, and then the tape spooled out and Seb was back at the mic again.

'*If, as seems likely, the latest death turns out to be drowning-related, it would bring the number of such incidents in the waters of the Lake District during this long, hot and unprecedented summer of '76 to four. This represents a record number for a single season. Causing increasing concern is the fact that the frequency of the tragedies appears to be accelerating – and that was before this morning's shock news. Meanwhile Dr Young told the press conference that recent expert surveys of three lakes – Buttermere, Bassenthwaite and Thirlmere – appear to show a hitherto hidden and sinister cause. The scientist conducting those surveys, leading hydrographer Professor Brian Parker, had this to say.'*

Seb pointed almost fiercely at Jess and the second tape began to play. Parker's flat, Lancastrian vowels filled Seb's earphones as they simultaneously rippled across the entire nation.

'Morning, ladies and gentlemen, I'll keep my remarks as free of jargon as I can. As you know, the entire UK has been enduring – I think we can all agree that's the appropriate word for it now – exceptional high temperatures for many weeks. Not only has there been no rainfall, there has been virtually no cloud cover. So the sun has been shining more or less unbroken from sunrise to sunset, and at a time of year when it is at its highest point in the sky.

'As you would expect, this has directly resulted in a rapid warming of the lakes, which to some extent is normal at this time of year. However, the heat, which as I say has continued without even the briefest of interruptions, has resulted in an exceptional effect – one I doubt has occurred here in living memory.

'The entire upper surface of these waters has now been superheated to a remarkable degree. The lack of any significant breeze has denied the possibility of any wind-chill effect and nights have been exceptionally warm. Each successive day the sun's rays strike the waters, for hours at a time, so the temperature inexorably rises a little further.

'This produces a dangerously misleading effect for swimmers, because however far they venture out into the lake, they feel they are surrounded by pleasant, balmy water. As indeed they are.

'But, what they do not realise is that these conditions are what we might describe as skin-deep. Directly beneath the superheated layer lies a body of water that is almost as cold as it is in mid-winter. In itself, that is not necessarily dangerous. Many hardy swimmers take to the lakes in winter and are invigorated by the experience. The danger comes in the absolute contrast between moving from the unprecedented surface warmth to the freezing cold just beneath it.

'It is the coroner's belief – and I concur – that these deaths are occurring when strong, confident swimmers decide to dip down deeper below the surface and encounter the intensely cold water that lies there. They may gasp in shock – hence the inhalation of water and subsequent drowning – or, in other cases, suffer a cardiac arrest.'

The second tape spooled out and Seb was speaking again.

'The coroner acknowledged that swimmers, particularly strong ones, might still be tempted by the unprecedentedly warm waters to venture further into the lakes than is usual. He had this message for them.'

He pointed towards Jess for the last time, and Timothy Young's calm, clear tones returned.

'*It doesn't matter how good a swimmer you may be: if you move from the upper warmth into the deadly cold immediately beneath, it could be the last thing you ever do; your body will respond automatically to the shock. As coroner for Kendal, and all the beautiful Lakeland countryside that surrounds it, I have no wish to preside over one more of these immensely sad incidents. I implore* all *swimmers – please, stay close to the shore.*'

Seb was back at the mic.

'*This is SEB Richmond reporting live from Kendal for Lake District FM, and Network News.*'

The red transmission light winked out and Jess grinned at him.

'What did I tell you? Piece of piss.'

CHAPTER SEVEN

'This is Seb Richmond reporting live from Kendal for Lake District FM, and Network News.'

Meriel switched the Mercedes' radio off as she pulled into the railway station car park and nosed slowly around for a space. Seb Richmond. Yes, she was aware of him; the new boy in the newsroom, having a bit of trouble settling in, apparently.

Not judging by what she'd just heard. She thought he had an attractive voice – in fact, it was rather sexy – and it had been an interesting piece.

Fascinating, in fact. She and Cameron had a two-berth motorboat moored on Ullswater and every other weekend in the summer they took it out on what was still one of the Lake District's quieter stretches of water.

Meriel had never learned to swim and always stayed on deck while Cameron clambered down the little chromed ladder at the back of the boat – he insisted on calling it 'aft' – and slowly paddled around in the lake, never moving far from the vessel. He wasn't the strongest of swimmers, but he enjoyed these expeditions and so did Meriel. The waters seemed to have a strangely pacifying, moderating effect on her husband. He invariably emerged from them in an improved mood and generally more cordial frame of mind towards her than was usual.

They always took a picnic lunch on board, and some wine in the boat's cool-box. If it was a Sunday they'd browse through the newspapers on deck together, gossiping over the headlines and articles. For Meriel, these were almost like the old times with Cameron. His genial mood sometimes continued all day. In fact, the last time they had made love was after just such a trip. But that was back in the previous summer.

It had been more than a year now.

Meanwhile, after that last horrendous Christmas they'd spent together – one dreadful row chasing hard on the heels of another, and then Cameron getting completely drunk and trying to force himself on her in the middle of the night – she'd moved into the largest of the guest bedrooms. They hadn't shared a bed since.

But somehow, their weekends on the lake survived as unusual oases of compatibility. Listening to Seb Richmond's report just now, Meriel had been

reminded of Cameron's delight in recent weeks whenever he entered the water.

'Christ, Meriel, it's warm as a bloody bath in here
again!' he'd called up to her last Sunday, as he slowly
circumnavigated the boat using his habitual breast-
stroke. 'What a shame you can't swim! You'd love it.
We must find someone to teach you!'

She'd have to remember to tell him about the danger
that lay beneath.

Then, recalling the way he'd spoken to her only
that morning, when she'd reminded him of this trip
to London to have dinner with her agent, she changed
her mind. He could do with a scare. Cameron never
dived or swam under the surface so he wouldn't be in
any real danger, but he might encounter a pocket of
icy water that would give him a nasty fright.

He'd been absolutely vile to her at breakfast when
she'd come downstairs with her overnight case and
her evening clothes neatly folded and zipped away in
a smart black nylon clothes bag.

'Where the hell d'you think you're off to, then?'

'You know perfectly well, Cameron. I'm having
dinner with David at Claridge's this evening. I told
you, he has a book idea he wants to talk to me about.'

He snorted. 'That'll be a new outfit you've got with
you, then. I know you. Same formula every time: we're
buggering off to London, so let's buy ourselves a new
frock. With my money. How much did that one cost?'

Meriel managed to keep her temper.

'It's not new. I got it last year. Anyway, I earn money too. Not as much as you, but I'm perfectly entitled to—'

He cut her off. 'Liar. It's new. I told you, I know you inside out. Well, not inside, not any more.' He leered. 'That's David's little treat tonight, I'll bet. In lieu of this month's fifteen per cent, eh? Commission in kind?'

'You're completely disgusting.'

It was strange, she thought as she walked down the London platform towards the first-class carriages at the front of the train. Exchanges like that with Cameron used to leave her trembling with fury. Now, she'd become almost indifferent to them. Was that because of her secret, fantasy diary? Had she stumbled across a therapy that really did channel her anger into a safe, neutral place? Perhaps one day, when she had somehow found a way to escape this mess of her own making, she could incorporate it into her portfolio of advice to others.

As she found her seat and placed her bags on the overhead rack, her thoughts returned to the new reporter. What was he called? Sam … Seth … no, Seb, that was it. Meriel rarely went into Lake District FM's newsroom; she had a desk in the open-plan production office at the other end of the corridor where she spent two days a week, one preparing her programme with her researcher and the next on the actual day of broadcast. The show was syndicated to most of the other commercial stations around the UK and as a result Meriel Kidd was becoming that most contemporary of social oddities: a household name.

The only time she put her head around the newsroom door was when they wanted a quote from her on something; a new report on depression, or research into eating disorders, or the latest celebrity infidelity.

But the other day she'd overheard some of the secretaries in her office discussing Seb. They seemed intrigued and concerned for him by turns.

'He's got a girlfriend in London and she came up to see him the other weekend. Philippa saw them in the String of Horses together. Phillie says she's gorgeous – looks like one of Charlie's Angels, apparently. The blonde one.'

'No, no, they've split up now, didn't you hear? He's ever so upset. Wants to go back to London to try and win her back.'

'Really? She must be completely loopy. He's lovely. Reminds me a bit of that bloke in *Upstairs Downstairs*, you know, the young lord or earl or whatever. Except he's fairer and he doesn't have a stupid tash.'

'Well, you'd better make your move on him soon, Denise. Everyone says he's headed for the chop.'

Hmm. Unlikely, based on the report I just heard, Meriel thought now as her train pulled smoothly away from Carlisle station. He's good. In fact, I must remember to find an excuse to drop by the newsroom when this Seb is on the news-reading rota. See what all the fuss is about.

She was surprised to find herself blushing.

'I don't understand you, Meriel. I've worked really hard to make this happen and now you ... well, you just chuck it back in my face. I honestly thought you'd be biting my hand off, not my head. What on earth's wrong?'

David Weir wasn't the biggest media agent in town but he was getting there. Meriel Kidd wasn't his biggest client either, but he had plans for her. Big plans. As far as he was concerned, she was the complete package. Most agony aunts were knocking on a bit, or a lot, but at thirty-one Meriel stood out from the crowd, and not just because of her relative youth. She looked a knockout, with long chestnut hair that tumbled past her shoulders, enormous brown eyes set in a flawless oval face, and a figure kept trim from regular walks among the Lake District's fells.

Put all that together with a honey-toned voice and a mind as sharp as a whip and you had – well, as he kept repeating to anyone who'd listen, you had the complete package. Especially in broadcasting. David Weir had all kinds of plans to grow and develop Meriel into a TV star, but he was in no rush. He was a canny agent and he knew it was important to build clients a solid base from which they could securely advance.

Which was why he was so pissed off now.

'It's a book deal, for Christ's sake, Meriel! A *book* deal! I can think of five women – clients – *right this minute* who'd be fighting each other off to sign up to something as good as this.'

'I'm not going to work with my husband.'

'But why not, Meriel? Look, maybe I put it across wrong. Let me try again. It's ridiculously hot in here, you're probably having trouble focusing.

'The working title's *Mrs … and Mr.* You and Cameron have the perfect marriage, but you're a *modern* couple. He has his career, you have yours. He doesn't take any crap from you, and you don't take any crap from him. It's a marriage of equals.

'Jesus, Meriel, you know all the balls married women have to put up with about daring to go out to work! You're helping to change that. No one's done more than you to champion the cause of working women within marriage. So why not explain how it works from the inside?

'I see it working as alternate chapters. Cameron has his – hell, you can write them for him, who cares? – and you have yours. *You* top and tail it with an introduction and a postscript. Throw in some great photos of you and the old man at your rustic idyll and on the boat – Bailey will come up to Cumbria to shoot them, I've asked him already, he's a mate – and Bob's your uncle. We can tie in a spread in one of the upmarket glossy magazines, too. It's perfect.'

Meriel opened her mouth to speak, but Weir flapped his hands at her.

'Wait. I haven't got to the best part. I've got two publishers fighting like cats in a sack for this and they're *both* prepared to fund a TV advertising campaign to support publication. I'm not even going to tell you what the advances they're offering are: I don't want you fainting on me. Meriel, *please* – we get a book like this away, and it's next stop television. The book will give you the kind of credibility that money simply can't buy. Meriel! Come on! What's the big problem here?'

Oh, what the hell, thought Meriel, draining her fourth glass of sauvignon blanc. I might as well tell someone the sodding truth.

So she told him.

David Weir was a good listener. He gave his client his full attention as she unburdened herself of the dead weight of her dead marriage. He didn't interrupt as Meriel described the daily humiliations and accommodations she had to endure and contrive. He merely nodded occasionally, and waited for her to finish. When she finally ran out of words, he took her hand and squeezed it gently.

'Meriel ... have you told anyone else about this? Does anyone else know how awful things are at home?'

Meriel gulped and shook her head. 'No. You're the first person I've confided in. God, David, I feel *so* much better for it. Thank you for listening. As far as divorce goes, I suppose I—'

'Shut up. Shut the fuck *up*, Meriel. I don't want to hear any more – especially about divorce.'

Meriel stared at him in shock. '*What?* But I thought—'

'Well, don't. I'll tell you what to think. Just be quiet. Give me a minute.'

A waiter arrived with coffee. The agent waved him away.

'Right,' he said at last. 'Right.' He spread his hands, palms down, on the table, before lifting his head to stare directly at her.

'*Jesus*, Meriel! What the *hell* do you think you're playing at? Do you want to lose *everything* we've built up together over the last five years? So your marriage to Cameron is a sham, is it? Do you think you're the only woman married to a shit? You need to get with the programme, honey, and in case you've forgotten what that is, let me spell it out for you.'

The waiter hesitantly approached the table again with their coffees. 'Forgive me, but I thought sir ordered—'

'Fuck off.'

The man melted away.

Weir continued without missing a beat.

'The programme runs like this. Meriel Kidd is the acknowledged expert on modern marriage. Why? Because she's got one. A modern marriage, that is. Meriel Kidd wouldn't settle for anything less. How many times have you said that, when you're telling some snivelling loser how to put the skids under the tosser in her life?

'Women look up to you, Meriel. You make them realise that they don't have to take the crap any more. This is 1976. You empower them. You lead by sodding example, for Christ's sake.'

He took a deep breath. 'Look. You even *hint* that you've been hiding the truth about your piss-poor marriage, and you're finished. Your fans would never forgive you. They might feel sorry for you; hell, some would probably even feel superior to you, but they'd never trust a word you said again. Meriel Kidd. Turns out she's just like the rest of us. Marriage fucked up to buggery and, what's more, lying through her teeth to everyone about it ... I mean, *Christ*, Meriel! It's the kind of confession you might consider coming out with twenty years or so down the line, if you were on your uppers and looking for a last big payout.'

There was a long silence. Meriel had turned very pale. When she eventually spoke, it was in a voice barely above a whisper.

'Do you think I don't know all that, David? I live with it every single day. And yes, I manage it. Somehow I manage the whole, horrible, sordid mess. But there are some things I can't do. Such as writing this book. It's out of the question. I think it would send me mad, actually.'

David Weir always knew when to give ground and he did so now. In a gentler voice, he said, 'Yes, obviously I see that, now you've explained how things are with Cameron. I'll go back to the drawing board with the book idea, come up with something else, don't worry. But, Meriel, listen to me. Listen carefully now.'

He glanced around them, instinctively checking that no one was eavesdropping on their conversation.

'You must never, *ever* confide in anyone else about this. I don't want to see one of your so-called friends popping up in the News of the Screws with a tell-all exposé on the devastating truth behind the Kidd–Bruton fairy tale. You want someone to unload on, you come to me, and only me. Understand?'

She nodded. 'I think I only told you because I've had too much wine.'

'Whatever. This is our secret and I want to keep it that way. You're right on the edge of big things, Meriel, and it'd be a tragedy to see everything you've achieved so far go to waste because of a prick like Cameron.'

Meriel managed a small smile.

'I reckon you'll have your own television show by

this time next year. I wasn't going to tell you this, I wanted to wait until I had something more solid to offer you, but I've been in talks already with BBC1 and Granada. They both think the time's right to move your radio phone-in format to TV. The Beeb's even got a working title: *Meriel Matters*. Your name on the tin, honey.'

She tried and failed to look enthusiastic. 'I'm sorry, David, obviously that's wonderful news, I'm just not in the mood to celebrate tonight.'

'Sure, I get it.' Her agent hesitated. 'Can I ask you a personal question?'

'Of course.'

'What are you doing for sex, Meriel? You're only thirty-one. It's not healthy for a woman your age to be sleeping alone every night. You must be incredibly lonely. Haven't you been tempted to have a discreet affair? Not that I'm suggesting it. Kiss-and-tell, remember?'

Meriel sighed. 'To be honest, David, I seem to have switched off as far as sex is concerned. I can't remember the last time I fancied someone. It must have something to do with living under the same roof as Cameron; he's so unutterably dreary when he's not busy being a bastard. He just sucks all the atmosphere out of a room.'

Weir gave a short laugh. 'I suppose what I'm trying to say, Meriel, is be very careful. You're only human.

We all have our urges. If you do end up giving in to one, just be damn sure not to get caught out. That would be a disaster, too.'

Meriel beckoned their sulking waiter over. 'We'd like our coffees now, please ... Don't worry, David, it's not going to happen. As I say, I'm simply not interested. Anyway, I can't think of a single candidate for an affair. There's no one even remotely on the horizon.'

Her agent gave a tight smile.

'Good. Let's keep it that way, shall we?'

CHAPTER EIGHT

Seb's live report from Kendal had been the turning point, no question about that.

The network sent a herogram to Lake District FM saying they'd prefer Sebastian Richmond to be their pointman on all future stories from the region, and his news editor received a handwritten memo from the station manager, congratulating him on keeping faith with the new boy.

Everyone was happy.

Not least Seb and Jess. When they returned from their assignment, the reporter insisted on taking the engineer to the pub across the road, where they both ended up getting spectacularly drunk. 'You're a good lad, Seb,' the older man slurred several hours later as he stumbled into a taxi. 'You'll be all right, now you've made your mark.'

Seb didn't hear a word. He was too busy throwing up into a flower tub outside the pub's front door.

Next morning he was on early shift, reading the headlines during the breakfast show, and staying on afterwards to help put the main lunchtime news show together. That included presenting bulletins at the top of each hour, including the one at eleven that fed in to Meriel Kidd's live phone-in programme.

Meriel, who had caught the first train from London and gone straight to the radio station, waved cheerfully at him through the soundproofed glass of her studio as he entered the little adjoining news cubicle. Seb recognised her from newspaper and magazine photographs, but this was the first time he had seen her in the flesh. She was illuminated by the sunshine that streamed through the huge window that looked out onto the distant mountains away to the south.

Seb swallowed, hard. This woman was beautiful.

He was so distracted he made at least three verbal slips in the short two-minute bulletin, pronouncing 'Buttermere' as 'Battermere', struggling with 'unsubstantiated' (eventually giving up, replacing it with 'unproven') and cocking up the time check, telling listeners it was just past midday when it was actually two minutes past eleven.

'What the bloody hell happened to you in there?' his editor demanded when Seb returned, damply, to the newsroom. 'Not still pissed from yesterday?'

Seb laughed sheepishly. 'Course not. Sorry ... it was ... Meriel ... I had no idea she looked quite like that. She's a complete knockout. I couldn't take my eyes off her. You should have warned me.'

The news editor grinned. 'Ah, the comely Miss Kidd. Well, not Miss, actually – she's a Mrs. Married to Cameron Bruton. Heard of him?'

'Of course I have. The businessman. Major player. Isn't he much older than her?'

'Yes. He's also probably the richest man in the Lake District.'

'Oh well, no chance there then. Pity. She's gorgeous. What's someone like her doing stuck up here?'

His boss frowned. 'Less of the *stuck up here* if you don't mind. We were radio station of the year last year, I'll have you know. And Meriel's show doesn't just go out locally – it's syndicated. I think everywhere except London takes it now. Anyway, you'll just have to worship from afar, matey. Like I said, she's taken – and by a bloke with more money than you'll earn in a hundred lifetimes.'

Seb shook his head. 'Money isn't everything. Poverty has its virtues. And I have youth on my side. Maybe I can persuade her to give someone closer to her own age a look-in.'

'Stroll on, sunshine.'

Meriel immediately understood why the girls in the office kept going on and on about Sebastian Richmond.

He was quite the package. Probably five or six inches taller than her – she was five-eight – and slim-hipped in black Levis and matching black trainers. He was wearing a tight-fitting, off-white cheesecloth shirt, and dirty-blond hair hung in a ragged fringe above intelligent blue eyes.

He was making a complete idiot of himself reading the news, mispronouncing everything and getting the time check all wrong, and she was pretty sure that was because of her. She was perfectly aware of the effect she could have on men, and the truth was that she'd made a special effort.

When she got into her car that morning and heard him on the breakfast show, she realised he'd be the newsreader for her segment later, so she'd found time to dash into the bathroom on her way in.

This is ridiculous, she thought to herself. You're behaving like a bloody schoolgirl with a crush, Meriel. You don't even know what he looks like.

But that hadn't stopped her from reapplying lipstick, adding some extra mascara, and spraying Yves St Laurent's Rive Gauche behind her ears. Not that anyone outside her studio would be able to tell she was wearing it.

Still . . .

Seb's shift ended at one o'clock but he stayed on to listen to the lunchtime news. He'd written four or five of the stories and he wanted to hear them go out.

When the early afternoon music and talk show began, he stuffed his things into his shoulder bag and headed for the lifts. The sliding doors were just closing as he got there and he thrust his arm into the narrowing gap. 'Hang on! Room for one more inside?'

The doors juddered before slowly reopening.

He found himself looking into the dark-brown eyes of Meriel Kidd.

CHAPTER NINE

Bob Merryman slammed the phone back down and swore out loud as he looked around the empty office. The lunchtime news team had gone to the pub and it would be almost an hour before the next shift came in, working on the early-evening bulletin and the following day's breakfast show. He was on his own.

Then, remembering that Seb had only just left, he ran to the window that looked out over the car park below. Yes, there he was, leaning against his sports car talking to Meriel Kidd. The crafty bugger didn't let the grass grow, did he?

Heaving the window up, the news editor stuck his head out.

'Seb! *Seb!* Up here!' he yelled as the startled reporter looked confusedly around him.

Seb squinted up against the sun.

'Bob! What is it?'

'There's been another of these bloody drownings,' his boss called down to him. 'Two, in fact – it's a double one this time. Mother and daughter. Get your arse up here so I can brief you. I need you to get down to Windermere, *prontissimo*.'

Seb turned back to Meriel. He'd been working up to ask her to join him for a drink or even lunch at the radio station's adopted pub in the city centre, but that would have to wait now.

He smiled ruefully. 'Duty calls. I was going to suggest we adjourn to the Prince of Wales for a post-programme bite of something, but ... well ...'

Meriel smiled back at him. 'That would've been nice. Really. Maybe next week, after my show. I can give you the inside story on what goes on at Lake District FM. Your newsroom's so busy chasing down stories they don't see what's happening in their own back yard.'

Seb extended his hand. 'I'd like that. It's a date – lunch this time next week.'

His palm and fingers felt warm and dry, Meriel thought, and the ball of his thumb on the back of her hand was firm. A distinct tingle ran up her spine and she caught her breath.

For the first time in as long as she could remember, she was feeling the faint but unmistakable twitch and pull of desire.

*

Seb cursed under his breath as the lift rumbled its way back up to the top of the building. After the initial surprise of seeing Meriel Kidd up close and in such a confined space he had rallied, making her laugh with self-deprecating references to his blooper-strewn bulletin earlier.

Outside in the sun-drenched car park she'd seemed happy to stand and chat with him, and Seb began to think she might be open to joining him at the pub. Then Merryman had put the kybosh on everything.

Mind you, it sounded like a hell of a story. Two more drownings – and barely twenty-four hours after the appeal to swimmers to stay in the shallows. The papers had been full of it that morning. He'd have to check with Bob, but he was pretty sure Windermere was the biggest of all the lakes, and it was definitely the busiest. And what if there were more deaths to come? This was rapidly turning into the news sensation of the summer.

The lift doors opened and Seb walked, then jogged, down the corridor towards the newsroom.

The long drive down to Windermere had barely left him enough time to establish the basic facts of the story. There'd been a police press conference on the banks of the lake at four o'clock, but all the eye-witnesses to the tragedy were holed up in the police station making statements, so there were no worthwhile interviews to be done yet.

71

Now it was almost five and Seb was about to go on air. It was far too late to script anything; he'd just have to busk it as a two-way ad-libbed conversation with the programme presenter up in Carlisle. Once again the network had muscled in on the act and London was taking the interview, live.

With perfect timing the radio car was off the road having its annual service, so Seb had been forced to find a phone. He'd talked his way into a Bowness-on-Windermere hotel. The manager had been most helpful, guiding him through to a little office behind reception.

'Here you are, Mr Richmond, I'll make sure you're not disturbed. This is quite becoming *your* story, isn't it? I heard you on the wireless yesterday.'

Seb, receiver jammed to one ear, listened to the programme's headlines being read out and then it was his cue.

'*But first, breaking news this afternoon: another drowning in Cumbria's lakes, a double tragedy that takes the death toll this heatwave summer to six in as many weeks. Over to our reporter Seb Richmond, live from Lake Windermere. Seb, what can you tell us?*'

Seb had made a brief list of bullet points on the back of a hotel beermat, but he didn't really need them. The story virtually told itself.

He took a deep breath.

'*Thanks, Graham. Shock and grief are the*

dominant emotions here in Windermere this evening as the community struggles to come to terms with yet another tragedy. As you say, this time not one but two lives have been simultaneously lost to this summer's extraordinarily treacherous waters – seemingly so inviting, and yet proving to be so deadly.

'This afternoon Cumbria police confirmed the deceased as Keswick teacher Mrs Brenda Whately and her nine-year-old daughter, Karen. Details are still being established but it appears that the little girl had ventured some distance from the shoreline and was being summoned back by her mother when she, Karen, got into difficulties and disappeared beneath the surface. Mrs Whately, who police say was a strong swimmer, went to her daughter's rescue and made an attempt to dive down to find her, but then also got into trouble. A boat launched from a nearby pier eventually located both mother and daughter, but all attempts to revive them were unsuccessful.'

The presenter's voice broke in again.

'I appreciate that it's very early to speculate, Seb, but is the feeling there that this is another case of people being lured into water that may feel invitingly warm on the surface, but remains dangerously cold just a little way down?'

Seb considered his answer.

'Well, it's hard to avoid that thinking, isn't it? The specific warnings to the public about the treacherous *state of the lakes this summer – this unprecedented summer – were only issued yesterday and perhaps Mrs Whately and her daughter were unaware of them. Cumbria Police say hazard signs will shortly be erected along stretches of shoreline popular with swimmers, and they have requested that the media play its part by giving regular reminders of the dangers. I understand that Lake District FM will itself be broadcasting explicit warnings after every hourly news bulletin until conditions in the lakes are judged to have returned to normal. However, with long-range weather forecasts predicting no let-up in the heatwave conditions, that's unlikely to be any time soon.'*

'Seb Richmond in Windermere, thank you.'

CHAPTER TEN

Meriel loathed her marriage, but she loved her house.

It was built as a rectory in the late 1880s by a Church of England priest, who lived comfortably on a substantial private income from his family trust.

The building was beautifully placed. It nestled like a bird beneath its mother's wing, tucked as it was under a giant shoulder of ivy-clad rock, one of a series of ascending outcrops that stacked their way upwards like a towering natural cathedral. Indeed, the mountain had been known locally as Cathedral Fell long before the clergyman chose to build his home there, naming it Cathedral Crag.

The Reverend Thomas Bolton had sired a large family. Three sons and five daughters grew up in the rambling rectory. There were ten bedrooms – twelve, if you counted the servants' quarters at the back of the house – and three enormous reception rooms. The largest of these looked directly east across Derwent Water and towards the distant rooftops and spires of Keswick, which lay to the north.

When Cameron Bruton had bought the house it was in an extremely run-down condition. He planned to convert it into a hotel, but had never quite got around to it. Soon after he married Meriel he brought her to Cathedral Crag to show her the place. She fell in love with it on the spot.

'Oh darling, can we live here?'

So for six months builders and decorators had swarmed over the rectory, transforming it into a luxury home. Windows were subtly heightened and widened to make the most of the stunning views over mountains and lake; ceilings were raised and their ornate plaster cornices and mouldings restored to past glories. The woodwormed oak banisters running up both sides of the wide stairway that climbed all the way to the top of the house were ripped out and replaced with expensive teak. The decaying cellar was transformed into a gymnasium and swimming pool and, outside, the mossed and lichened brickwork was sandblasted so that the front of the house glowed rosy red in the rays of the rising sun, just as it had nearly a century earlier when the rector and his family had lived there.

Meriel adored it.

She'd been sunbathing on the elevated terrace to the

southern side of the house when she realised it was approaching five o'clock in the afternoon, and the breaking story that had robbed her of lunch with Seb Richmond was about to air.

Meriel was curious. She went inside, switching on the expensive sound system as she passed through the kitchen. Immediately, discreetly hidden wall speakers popped and crackled into life, and she heard the voice of the man she'd been talking to – no, come on now, Meriel, be honest with yourself, *flirting with* – just a few hours earlier.

He communicated an unfolding sense of tragedy and she found herself genuinely moved. Mother and daughter. Dear God. How awful.

When Seb's report was finished she poured herself a gin and tonic from the drinks tray on the sideboard, added ice from the huge crimson American fridge-freezer in the kitchen, and went back outside to enjoy the last of the sun. Cameron would disapprove of her drinking so early, but he was up in Edinburgh nego-tiating a property deal so she could do as she pleased.

As she sank back in the recliner, her thoughts flick-ered around a triangle formed by three men – David Weir, Cameron, and Seb Richmond.

She mentally replayed her agent's acid analysis of the consequences if people discovered she'd been lying through her teeth about her marriage. David had been absolutely right, of course, but he'd merely confirmed what she already knew. If she wanted to keep her career – and the increasingly bright prospects that were now coming into view – the charade of her relationship with Cameron must continue.

So, for now, her secret diary would remain a work in progress. Although she was beginning to understand that it was not simply a release for her humiliation and anger.

It was more; it was wish-fulfilment, if in a distorted form. Of *course* she didn't want Cameron to die in the grotesque ways she graphically described. She wasn't a monster.

But she was coming to realise that deep down, in her secret heart, she *did* want him gone. She really, really did. It would solve everything. The quicker and cleaner the better. A heart attack, say.

Actually, that wasn't entirely out of the question.

Cameron's father had succumbed to a fatal coronary some years before, as had an uncle and a first cousin. Heart disease was known to be embedded in the family genes; it was one of the reasons Cameron had installed the gymnasium and pool. That hadn't prevented him developing a potbelly, but otherwise he was generally fit and healthy. He didn't smoke and rarely drank spirits. The only occasion Meriel had seen him drunk was that ghastly Christmas the year before.

She felt ashamed of holding this death-wish over her husband. Keeping a diary was one thing, but picturing him having a heart attack was different – that was something she actually, literally wanted to happen.

She imagined various scenarios. Finding him dead in bed one morning, or slumped behind the wheel of his car in the drive, or floating in the bath.

She knew it was wrong of her, but she couldn't help it. It wasn't that she was frightened of Cameron – he had never struck her – but he was just such an odious person to be married to. The very antithesis of a man like . . .

Well, a man like Seb.

Meriel slowly sipped her gin and wondered exactly what was happening to her. She'd been thinking about the young reporter before she'd even set eyes on him, hadn't she? Entirely because of some silly office gossip. Then, when she'd realised she was finally going to see him in the flesh, she'd gone into the bathroom to get herself all prettified. Why? What exactly did she think was going to happen?

But actually something *had* happened, hadn't it? Seb had, in the nicest possible way, come on to her in the car park. And she'd encouraged him. Oh yes, she'd most certainly encouraged him. Indeed she was the one who'd made their date for next week.

She'd been thinking about him on and off ever since.

Meriel stretched out her long legs in the hot sunshine. They were good legs, one of her most attractive features. They looked their best in heels, which was why she'd slipped on a pair earlier. If she was honest she'd been slightly disappointed that Seb could only see her from the waist up when she was sitting behind her studio desk. She'd been glad when he joined her in the lift, and then walked with her outside. She couldn't help noticing him covertly admiring her figure, and failing to disguise it. He was sweet.

She found herself thinking about their age difference. Meriel reckoned it was around three years. Nothing, really. A fraction of the gap between her and Cameron; her husband was over a quarter of a century older than her. He'd be sixty in a few months. The difference hadn't bothered her at first; when she married him he was a still vigorous-looking man in his late forties. She'd lost her father to cancer several years before and, looking back, she was in no doubt now that she had been craving a paternal substitute.

She'd met Cameron at a glittering charity ball in London's Dorchester Hotel. Meriel was working as features writer for a women's magazine and was covering the event for them. She found herself seated next to Cameron and he'd been a charming dinner companion, talking very little about himself but asking her what seemed to be genuinely interested questions about her background and emerging career.

When he led the bidding at the charity auction that followed dinner, she realised just how wealthy he was. He paid thousands for a diamond ring donated by a minor member of royalty and, to her utter astonishment and against all her protests, insisted on presenting it to her.

'I was dreading this evening, quite frankly,' he confided. 'But sharing it with such a beautiful woman transformed my expectations. I'm afraid there *is* a condition attached to this little gift, though; you must agree to have dinner with me tomorrow. I won't take no for an answer.'

And so the courtship had begun. Meriel had been won over by Cameron's old-fashioned charm and attentiveness ('I feel like I'm going out with Cary Grant,' she told a friend) and, if she was honest with herself, she couldn't help but be attracted by the security the rich Scotsman represented.

When the same friend teased her – 'It's obvious, Mel. You're looking for a sugar daddy' – she hadn't troubled to deny it.

'What if I am? Lots of women have a bit of a thing for the older man. I'm not ashamed of it. Cameron makes me feel safe and secure and, yes, his money is part of that. I'm wouldn't say I'm *in love* with him, exactly – but I definitely love him. If he asks me to marry him, I'll say yes.'

He had, and she did.

But it gradually became clear to Meriel that if she had been looking for a sugar daddy, Cameron had been hunting for a trophy wife. Now he'd acquired one his inner character, so well hidden from her to begin with, had slowly emerged into view. His delight in tormenting and humiliating her was now so fully formed that she wondered whether, even as he assiduously wooed her, he had been fantasising about the time he would harrow and persecute her.

She vividly remembered one of the early warning signs. She'd been sitting at her dressing table, making herself up prior to joining Cameron at a large business supper, when he approached her from behind in his dinner suit and placed his hands lightly on her bare shoulders. He stared at her in the mirror for several long seconds before she laughed, a little nervously.

'What is it, Cameron? Why are you looking at me like that?'

He squeezed her a little harder. 'I was just thinking ... you're so beautiful ... Sometimes I want to hurt you.'

She couldn't say he hadn't warned her.

Ten years on, Cameron was not ageing well. There was that potbelly, which she hated, and it seemed his hair was becoming sparser by the week. But worst of all was the way his face had changed. 'Character will out,' her mother used to say, and Cameron's was now written plainly across his features. His mouth was habitually turned down in a sardonic twist, and his eyes seemed to have become sunken and narrowed in a kind of permanently suspicious, hostile stare.

She had come to realise, early in the marriage, that he had few friends. His business contacts gave him a spurious cloak of sociability – Cameron brokered many a deal on the golf course – but there was no warmth between him and his fellow man. Two Christmases ago Lake District FM had serialised a reading of Dickens's *A Christmas Carol* and Meriel, listening to the opening chapter as she drove home from the studios, found herself muttering aloud: 'My God, I've married bloody Ebenezer Scrooge.'

But she wasn't thinking about her husband now. She was thinking about Seb. As she did so she began to realise that when she told her agent that she had lost any interest in sex, she'd been deceiving herself as well as him.

Because she *was* thinking about it. She was imagining Seb holding her in his arms, kissing her, that dirty-blond fringe brushing against her forehead. She pictured herself running her fingers through his hair, and pressing herself against him as she kissed him back.

She closed her eyes and squirmed slightly. She hadn't felt like this in years. What was happening to her?

Suddenly she opened her eyes again and sat upright. This had to stop. Now. An affair with a work colleague? It was a ridiculous, stupid idea. If they got caught out – and *everyone* got caught out, didn't they, in the end; how often had she told her listeners and readers that? – the scandal would be huge. Meriel

Kidd, the happily married agony aunt, screwing a young – make that *younger* – radio reporter.

It didn't bear thinking about.

She couldn't stop thinking about it.

CHAPTER ELEVEN

The Romans called them the dog-days, those weeks from early July to mid-August when the so-called dog star Sirius rises and sets almost as one with the sun. The ancients believed that earthly dogs could be driven mad by the intense heat. Perhaps they were, on the Mediterranean's sultry southern shores.

But not in Britain. Not, at least, until this year. August remained a furnace of heat and searing light and even after Sirius had begun to slowly draw apart from his fiery master, the maddening, sweltering fever burned on with no respite.

In the Lakes, the Kirkstone Pass was closed to traffic. This normally only happened in winter when a heavy fall of snow blocked its passage. Now, the road surface itself was melting; sticky black tar that sucked at tyres and brought cars to a straining, squelching stop, trapping them like bluebottles on flypaper.

Reservoir levels were steadily falling because of heat evaporation, zero rainfall, and the daily draining away of what remained of the rains of winter and spring. Homes and factories were fast guzzling the vast rocky basins dry.

Talk turned to hosepipe bans, water-rationing and standpipes in the streets. The cabinet discussed creating a new government position: Minister for Drought.

In the Lakes, the unthinkable was being discussed.

'Yes, that's right, sir. A complete ban on swimming. In the lot of them – no exceptions.'

The county's environment chief looked around the table. Heads were shaking doubtfully from side to side. He pressed on.

'Obviously Windermere, Derwent Water, Ullswater, Bassenthwaite – but all the smaller ones too. From midnight tomorrow until further notice.'

The chief constable grunted. 'That'd take us to bloody Halloween, the way things are going. Absolutely no sign of a change in the weather, according to the Met Office boys. A massive belt of high pressure from here down to the Azores and halfway up to Iceland. It's just not moving.'

He drummed his fingers quietly on the file in front of him before continuing.

'I'm sorry, Terry' – he looked directly at the council

man – 'but my boys couldn't possibly police the ban you're proposing. I just don't have enough boots on the ground. And anyway, I simply can't see how we'd enforce it. Are we banning paddling in the shallows, too? If so, what d'you define as shallows? How far out can folk go? Can they swim if they stay in their depth? And what if they need to go in after their dogs?'

The environment officer shrugged. 'I was just answering the question we're all trying to square away, Chief Constable – how to guarantee no more drownings. I'm simply telling you that an outright swimming ban's the only way.'

'And I'm explaining why it's unenforceable. We're having a heatwave, for God's sake. It's human instinct to want to cool off in the water.' The police chief sighed. 'Anyone else have any ideas?'

'More boat patrols.' It was the region's head of tourism. 'The RNLI have said they can spare us some men and inflatables. And I'm sure we could rustle up a few retired folk with boats of their own. A sort of Dad's Navy.'

There was a general laugh. 'Good idea,' nodded the chief constable. 'No shortage of Captain Mainwarings around these parts, that's for sure. Anyone else?'

The chief press officer for Cumbria raised her hand. 'We've just got the *Carlisle Evening News* to agree to put a warning against swimming on every edition's front page. All the weeklies are doing the same. Lake District FM have started broadcasting alerts after every news bulletin, and the poster campaign rolls out across the national park from tomorrow.' She shrugged. 'I honestly don't think there's much more any of us can do.'

The policeman nodded. 'I agree. Obviously my men have stepped up foot patrols along the shorelines, offering advice to people who look like they're going into the water. It seems to be meeting with a generally positive response.' He looked down the table towards the coroner. 'Timothy? What's your verdict? Sorry, no pun intended.'

Timothy Young smiled. 'Not to worry, it's not the first time.' He nodded towards the PR woman. 'I agree with Janet. It's hard to see what else we can realistically do. I must tell you all that I think there *will* be further fatalities but with any luck the frequency will continue to fall, albeit slowly. It's pretty much the best we can hope for.'

The chief constable gathered up his papers, a signal that the meeting was at an end.

'Well, let's hope you're right.' The rest of the room stood to leave.

'In the meantime, may I suggest that we all say our prayers at bedtime and ask the Good Lord to conjure up a cold front for us, straight in from the

Arctic? Old-fashioned divine intervention would be awfully welcome, wouldn't it?' He turned to his secretary.

'I told you we should've invited the bishop.'

CHAPTER TWELVE

The post-programme lunch date had not materialised. Meriel went down with a strep throat on Tuesday. Two days later she had developed a mild fever and, much more inconveniently, almost completely lost her voice. Her show had to be presented by a stand-in, the programme's producer, Glenda Pile. Glenda was a nice enough woman but Seb, peering at her through the studio glass, was disinclined to ask her out for a drink. She was twice Meriel's age and approximately three times her weight.

He was idly wondering whether to buy Meriel a get-well-soon card on his way home when the station manager stuck his head into the newsroom.

Peter Cox was a genial ex-Radio 4 news producer who'd grabbed the chance to exchange foggy, smoggy London for the intoxicating beauty of the Lakes and a new career (and double the salary) in commercial radio. Former BBC colleagues from the capital who visited him and his ex-model wife marvelled at their stunning Georgian mansion, River House, perched on the banks of the River Eden.

'Cost us half what our place in Chiswick went for,' Cox never tired of telling them. 'We swapped five bedrooms for nine, and a shitty little garden for six acres of parkland with the occasional herd of deer wandering through. Must have been mad to stick around in London for so long.'

Now he brandished a fistful of invitations printed on cream-coloured cartridge paper.

'It's Sandra's and my annual summer garden party on Saturday,' he announced, walking from desk to desk and handing out the cards as he went. 'I was checking the guest list this morning and realised I'd clean forgot to ask you newshounds. Dreadfully sorry for the lapse. Do come if you can. At least it won't be a bloody washout like last year. Champers and sunscreen on the lawn, guaranteed.'

He paused directly in front of Seb.

'Ah, Sebastian. Sandra will be most disappointed if you don't grace us with your presence. She says she's fallen in love with your voice.' He winked. 'Obviously, I just want her to see what an ugly bugger you actually are.'

*

In the pub after they'd finished their shift, Seb drained his beer and nodded to the senior newsman.

'Another?'

Merryman shook his head.

'Nah. I have to be at a barbeque with the kids in half an hour. Now then, remember I'm off tomorrow and you're acting news editor. First time. Still OK with that?'

Seb nodded. 'Of course. I'll try not to screw up.'

'Balls to that; I'm not worried. You've found your feet.' Merryman finished the last of his own beer. 'You coming to Peter's garden party the day after?' he asked, wiping his mouth with the back of his hand. 'It's quite a place, I can tell you. Front cover of *Country Life*, that sort of thing.'

Seb shrugged. 'Oh, I don't know … I quite like Peter but there's more than a whiff of BBC bullshit still hanging around the bloke. I reckon a party at his country estate might be pretty heavy going.' He rose to leave.

'Your decision, old boy.' The news editor got up, scooping car keys. He shot Seb a sly glance as he did so. 'You realise that, assuming she's thrown off that bug of hers, Meriel Kidd will be there?'

Seb stared at him innocently.

'Why would that interest me?'

Merryman laughed.

'Oh, do me a favour.'

*

The morning of the station manager's garden party began unpromisingly; the sky was masked by an unbroken grey haze and there was a definite coolness in the air. Was this the day the heatwave was finally destined to break?

It was not. By eleven the gloom had been burned away and strong August sunshine was once again beating down on River House's vast lawn, one of the few that remained green that summer, thanks to sophisticated and expensive sprinkler systems.

The grass sloped down to the river where a twenty-foot twin-engined motor launch was tied up at a private jetty. Two wooden rowing boats alongside it gently rocked and bumped against each other in the sluggish current.

River House looked as if it might have once been on a visit to the Lakes from its home in the Cotswolds, and had decided to stay. The building was uncharacteristic of the area. It had been built in the late 1700s from blocks of honey-coloured limestone, brought up by wagon from distant Gloucestershire quarries.

The original owners had planted twin lines of elms along the long drive that led to the house from the Penrith road. Today, those same trees looked exhausted by the endless heat, branches drooping slightly, their parched leaves whispering unhappily to each other whenever a sudden gust of hot air disturbed them.

By one o'clock more than thirty cars had turned into the shady avenue, re-emerging into the brilliant sunshine of River House's gravel forecourt where two attendants were supervising parking. When Seb arrived he was one of the last guests to do so and there was almost no room left. He was told to leave his open-topped Triumph on the grass, tucked down one side of the house. He couldn't help wondering if they'd have assigned him the spot whatever time he'd arrived: his had to be the crappiest-looking car there. It definitely lowered the tone.

As he climbed out of the driver's battered bucket seat and peered around him, Seb had to admit that Merryman had a point. This place was classy, all right. It reminded him of a country house hotel near Stow-on-the-Wold he'd taken Sarah to last year for a long weekend together.

He sighed. He still missed her.

River House's double front doors had been thrown wide open under what he guessed was probably a Corinthian arch, and Seb made his way into the cool semi-darkness inside. Once his eyes had adjusted he could see that the windows in the high-ceilinged entrance hall were fitted with ancient but elegant wooden shutters, all of them tightly closed against the sunlight. The effect was almost continental. 'More like siesta time than party time,' he muttered to himself. 'Where the hell is everyone?'

The place seemed deserted. Perhaps he should go back outside and walk all the way around the house to what he supposed would be the garden at the rear. But as he was about to retrace his steps, a door on his left opened suddenly and he heard the sound of a toilet flushing.

Bob Merryman stepped into the hall, fiddling with his belt. He glanced across at Seb.

'Loo,' he said unnecessarily, jerking a thumb back over his shoulder. 'For God's sake, don't use the temporary one our hosts have rigged up out there in the garden. It's a bloody shipping container – no windows, hotter than Hades and, trust me, you don't even want to know about the smell.' He finished with his belt and pointed across the hall.

'Come on, it's that way. What kept you?'

Seb clicked his tongue as he followed Merryman through another door and down a long panelled corridor.

'I got a phone call at home just after breakfast. A police contact over in Ambleside. I stood him a few drinks when I was down there covering the last drowning – you know, that one in Rydal Water, the nurse – and he repaid the favour. Said he wasn't sure, but he'd heard rumours of another one over in Keswick, well, Derwent Water, early this morning. I called it in but, as you know, we've only got one bloke in the newsroom today on weekend cover – everyone else is here – so I thought I'd better check it out myself.'

Merryman glanced back at him as they entered what seemed to be a pantry towards the rear of the house.

'Blimey. And on your day off, too. Devotion above and beyond, young Seb. I'll memo you an official hero-gram on Monday. False alarm, I assume, otherwise you wouldn't be here.'

'Yup. It was someone's bloody dog, would you believe. An old Labrador that'd gone in after a duck or something. The tale must've got tangled in the telling. Still, it's only about twenty miles from Keswick to here so no real harm done. What've I missed?'

They rounded a corner into a wide conservatory, and suddenly the whole of the rear of the house opened up before them. A series of French windows were thrown open onto a wide, paved terrace, with gardens and the shining river beyond.

A big marquee had been set up in the middle of the lawn, and clusters of white-painted wrought-iron tables and chairs were dotted around it. Some were shaded under parasols but others had been left unprotected, presumably for the benefit of sun-worshippers.

Seb stared at the guests as they drifted from table to table, sipping what looked to be a choice of either Pimm's or champagne. Some of the older men were in brightly striped boating blazers and all the women wore summer frocks and sandals. Seb smiled and turned to his boss.

'I thought when I arrived just now that this place felt more continental than Cumbrian. Not any more, I don't. That's a perfect snapshot of England in summertime, isn't it? I'm glad I came. Looks like everyone's here.'

Merryman fingered his collar a little uneasily.

'Well . . . up to a point, Seb. Sorry to disappoint, but it seems I was wrong about Meriel.'

'What d'you mean?'

'She's a no-show, I'm afraid. Still, probably for the best, right? I've been thinking that I shouldn't really keep pulling your chain about her. You don't want to get involved with a woman like her.'

Seb, struggling to conceal his disappointment, affected indifference.

'Who said that I do? Want to get involved, that is? For Christ's sake, Bob, I've only spoken to her once. And what do you mean, "a woman like her"?'

Merryman appeared faintly irritated.

'Come on, chum, don't play the innocent with me. You know exactly what I mean. Meriel's a married woman. A happily married woman.'

As a despondent Seb moved out onto the lawn to join the party, Meriel was driving hard towards River

House. She knew the way – she and Cameron had been there at least twice for dinner with Peter and Sandra – but today, for the first time, she was on her own.

She'd just had another god-awful row with Cameron. God-awful. Her insides were churning and her heart was beating so hard she wondered whether she should pull over for a few minutes to give herself time to calm down. She couldn't arrive at the party like this. Her hands were trembling so much from rage and revulsion that she'd probably spill her drink all over herself or, worse, someone else.

In the end she found a layby just outside the pretty village of Lazonby, less than two miles from River House, and stopped there.

She switched off the engine of her Mercedes and listened to the ticking of the engine block as it began to cool. She took slow, deep breaths and looked around her. Yellow cornfields stretched away from both sides of the road. In the distance, she could see a bright red combine harvester threshing its way methodically through the tall stems of corn, throwing up a huge cloud of dust. The machine was too far away for her to hear. Apart from the ticking and clicking of the car's engine, all was silence.

Suddenly a bird, not much bigger than a sparrow, landed on her car's iconic bonnet emblem and stared intently at her through the windscreen, cocking its head rapidly from side to side as it did so. It didn't seem at all afraid. It was probably a male; she must be on its territory. There was likely to be a nest in the hedge next to the car.

Meriel knew a surprising amount about birds. Her late father had been a keen amateur ornithologist and he had taught her a lot. She was pretty sure this was a yellowhammer, with its bright yellow and chestnut plumage, and its typical lack of shyness around humans.

Then, when it began to sing, she was certain, and she smiled. It was such a sweet, funny little song. She could hear her father imitating it for her now.

'Little-bit-of-bread-and-no-cheeeeeeeeeese! Little-bit-of-bread-and-no-cheeeeeeeeeese!'

Suddenly, without warning, Meriel was overwhelmed by tears. She crossed her arms over the steering wheel and sank her forehead onto them, swamped with helpless sobs that juddered through her entire body. She didn't really know what she was weeping for. Her father? Herself? Shock at what had just happened; this whole horrible, horrible mess she'd got herself into?

She surrendered to the moment and, somewhere at the back of her mind, vaguely hoped that no one would pass by to witness her distress. But no one did.

It was just her and the yellowhammer.

*

Meriel had been aware of Cameron's growing sexual jealousy for some time but until now he'd managed to veil it, probably because he feared that to reveal it would put him in a weak, even supplicatory, position. He had, after all, absolutely no rational grounds to doubt his wife's fidelity.

But, that morning, the simmering cauldron of his covetous, malign mistrust had at last boiled over.

It had been ugly and frightening and she worried that it was a deeply disquieting sign of things to come.

They'd intended to go to the Cox's summer party together. Cameron had told Meriel he was 'rather looking forward to it, as long as I don't have to talk to anyone from your joke of a programme'.

Meriel knew that her husband's principal motive for going was to buttonhole Lake District FM's commercial manager. Cameron wanted to discuss some kind of cut-rate advertising deal for his businesses, not just on the local station but right across the network. Plus he'd be doing a bit of brown-nosing with Peter Cox. There'd been talk of the station manager presiding over an advertising hook-up between the radio station and the local ITV company, and perhaps even roping in the regional press outlets too. Cameron could never see a pending deal without wanting to stick a finger in the pie.

But when she'd come downstairs ready for the party, he'd exploded.

'We're not going with you fucking dressed like that. Go back up and put something halfway decent on. Jesus, Meriel, you look like a pimp's whore and I'm no pimp. Change. Now.'

She'd been genuinely at a loss.

'What are you talking about, Cameron? It's just a summer dress! I've worn it before! You said you liked it. You said—'

'Liar. I've never seen that thing before and if I had I'd have carried it in tongs to the nearest dustbin. Which I will most certainly do when you've taken it off.'

'I'm not going to take it off! It's fine! It's just a lace dress with—'

'Lace? *Lace?* I can see more flesh through the holes in that thing than if you were wearing a fisherman's net. And those shoes! What do they call things like that? Brothel heels, that's it. You look disgusting. You're going to change them, too.'

Meriel, whose voice had only started to return the day before, didn't want to risk losing it again by shouting, but she was struggling to keep her temper.

'Cameron,' she said huskily, 'these heels are three-and-a-half inches. Four at most. I've worn higher. What on earth's come over you? I think you've gone mad. You're behaving like a total ... oh, don't make me say it.'

But the next part had been the worst; the very worst, all the more so for being so utterly unexpected. He'd stepped quickly towards her, only stopping when they were a few inches apart from each other. She thought he was going to scream more abuse at her, but she was wrong.

He tossed his head back, hawked deep in his throat, snapped forward again and spat at her, full in the face.

She was so shocked that for a few moments she was rigid, unable to move.

'I'll tell you what's come over me, my darling,' he hissed. 'The realisation that my wife's a tart and a faithless one at that. You might not have shared *my* bed for months but I'll bet you've been in someone else's. God knows what you get up to when I'm not here.'

He reached forward, grabbed the sleeve of her dress and pulled it towards him to wipe his mouth. 'It's all this is fit for.'

Meriel had run blindly from him then, snatching up her handbag and keys from the hall table on her way outside to her car. She could hear him shouting behind her, but couldn't make out what he was saying. Then she was in the Mercedes and driving away. She thought she saw him in her rear-view mirror, gesticulating from the front door, but then she was on to the main road and heading towards Keswick.

As soon as she reached the town she drove to the Skiddaw Hotel in the market square, and walked straight into the ladies' room.

She needed to sponge the sleeve of her dress, wash her face, and reapply her make-up.

Her hands were trembling, but she managed it.

They'd be steadier later.

When she wrote the next entry in her diary.

CHAPTER THIRTEEN

The parking attendants at River House somehow managed to find the space for Meriel's Mercedes SL convertible that had been unavailable for Seb's Spitfire.

She'd had to wait for almost twenty minutes after she stopped crying before she felt ready to drive on to the party. She hardly ever smoked but she found a half-empty pack of cigarettes in the glove box and smoked two of them, one after the other. Listening to the radio helped calm her nerves too.

Then, just as she was about to pull out of the layby, she'd caught sight of her reflection in the rear-view mirror and realised her face was streaked and smeared with mascara.

It had taken another fifteen minutes to completely redo her make-up, for the second time that afternoon. By the time she eventually reached River House she was half-expecting to see the first guests leaving, but the gravel apron was still crammed with cars. She couldn't help looking to see if Seb's funny little two-seater was among them, but there was no sign of it and Meriel felt an unmistakable pang of disappointment.

She and Cameron had been to last summer's party here – how strange to recall that they were still sharing a bed then; now the very idea was unthinkable – so Meriel knew not to bother picking her way through the house. She walked around the side path that led directly to the garden. As she drew closer to it she could hear the sound of voices and laughter, and she had to stop for a moment to gather herself.

You're fine, Meriel told herself firmly. You're completely fine. Yes, you're married to an out-and-out shit but so are lots of women. You'll find a way, one day, to escape. Surely. There has to be an answer to this, whatever your sodding agent says.

Surely.

Seb saw her before she saw him. He'd been on the point of leaving, Meriel was the only reason he'd bothered coming in the first place and if she wasn't here, then he might as well go home.

He caught his breath. There she was, talking to their hostess at the entrance to the marquee. She must have only just arrived. He swallowed.

She was wearing a stunning off-the-shoulder cream

lace dress, cinched in at the waist with a narrow silver belt. The hem was trimmed with tassels that gently swayed just above her knees. The effect was distinctly 1920s flapper. On her feet she wore backless summer sandals that looked to Seb to be trimmed with satin – cream, to match the dress.

Seb thought she was the loveliest creature he had ever set eyes on.

He wasn't usually shy with women but now he found himself hesitating before going over to her. It wasn't just her extraordinary beauty that dazzled him. There was something else, an elusive feeling he couldn't quite bring into focus. He was conscious of standing on the threshold of something; an instinct – no, a *certainty* – that in the simple act of crossing the lawn, he would in fact be crossing the Rubicon and committing himself irrevocably to some unknown future. The sense that he was exactly, perfectly balanced on a point of no return was so strong that he felt almost paralysed.

And then Meriel turned, and saw him, and smiled, and put her head slightly to one side, as if to say: '*There you are.*'

And he swiftly crossed the soft lawn, and stood by her side, and he was with her.

CHAPTER FOURTEEN

He'd discovered the secluded seventeenth-century inn purely by accident – his accident. The old inn was tucked away in the sleepy village of Faugh, six or seven miles further down the Eden Valley from River House. The place had recently cropped up in a local news bulletin for some reason and he had blithely pronounced it 'Faw'.

It joined the long list of Seb's mispronounced Cumbrian place-names. Colleagues gleefully listed every one of his howlers on the newsroom noticeboard, along with the frosty letters of complaint from locals that invariably followed each gaffe.

Gradually he learned where the pitfalls lay. The village of Torpenhow was inexplicably pronounced *trappena*; Aspatria was *spattry* and Brougham *broom*. As for Rogersceugh, a tiny hamlet perched close to where Hadrian's Wall marched into the sea on

Solway's coast, the place was double booby-trapped for an unwary newsreader. It was *rogerscuff* to the plain-spoken; *rogerscew* if you were posh.

Faugh had turned out to be *faff*, and when the news editor had finished hauling him over the coals for that particular solecism ('Why the *fuck* don't you just *ask* someone before you go into studio, Seb? I'm going to start fining you a fiver a time if this goes on much longer') Merryman had calmed down, adding: 'There's a good pub there, too – the String of Horses. Great food, cosy rooms ... very romantic. You should take that girlfriend of yours for the night, next time she's up here. Oh sorry, I keep forgetting. She's dumped you, hasn't she?'

Now, as the sun began to settle in a cloudless sky towards the fells that lined the western horizon, Meriel's and Seb's convertibles were winding their separate ways towards Faugh along country lanes that closely shadowed the course of the Eden.

He'd left River House a few minutes before her; there was no point in arousing needless suspicions.

Although, actually, the hell with that, Seb thought defensively as he took a final sharp right towards the pub, now barely a few hundred yards away. Suspicions about *what*, exactly? As far as the world was concerned he and Meriel were just going for a drink together, weren't they? And perhaps some supper. They were colleagues, after all. This was 1976; modern times.

They weren't in some angst-ridden scene straight out of *Brief Encounter*.

What was more, he reminded himself, they'd planned to have lunch together earlier that week, hadn't they? It would have been in a pub that was a favourite with station staff. All completely open and above board. Going for drink with Meriel ... sinking a couple of beers with Bob Merryman after work ... where was the difference?

He groaned aloud. It was no good. This was total horseshit, and he knew it. He shook his head at his own meretriciousness as he swerved into the String of Horses car park and pulled on the handbrake.

Seb ran both hands through his hair.

The difference was bloody obvious: he wasn't falling hopelessly in love with Bob Merryman; he was going down, and going down hard, for Meriel Kidd.

An image of taking her to bed suddenly flashed vividly into his mind. The thought alone was practically enough to stop his heart.

He stepped out of his car and stood for a moment in the warm early-evening sunshine, forcing himself to take a couple of slow, deep breaths. He closed his eyes; he was almost dizzy with expectation and excitement. After a few moments he opened them again and stared at the three-hundred-year-old building in front of him.

Seb began walking towards its ancient oak door,

framed by blue wisteria that clustered in long, tumbling drapes on either side.

He was going to see about a room for the night.

Five miles behind him, Meriel was conducting her own inner conversation.

It had begun almost as soon as she slipped away from the party, discreetly following a little while behind Seb. She drove between the same hedgerows that occasionally parted to offer glimpses of the gleaming river below.

Unlike Seb, Meriel made no attempt to deceive herself.

'What are you *doing*?' she muttered for the third or fourth time. 'What *do* you think you're doing, Meriel Kidd?'

She beat a rapid tattoo with her fingers on the steering wheel before answering her own question.

'I'll bloody well tell you. Playing with fire, that's what.'

She could not remember feeling so conflicted and confused.

And aroused.

Twice she stamped on the Mercedes' brakes and skidded to an abrupt halt in the middle of the road. She *must* turn around. *Now*. This was complete madness.

But both times, instead of making a three-point turn and heading back the way she'd come, she somehow found herself driving on towards her assignation. She felt her willpower evaporating as swiftly as that morning's mist had done.

She *must* give herself some space to think.

Meriel spotted an open gate up ahead on her left, with a farm track leading into the field behind it. She braked hard again and swung her car through the narrow gap, pulling up just inside.

Old-fashioned hayricks and bales dotted the meadow that lay in front of her, with dozens of rooks clustering on the yellow stooks and feeding among the stubble below.

Her father had loved rooks; Meriel remembered him telling her they were probably the most intelligent of British birds.

So here's Daddy again, she thought as she switched off the engine. Twice in one day. Maybe he's trying to get through to me, tell me what to do.

She smiled ruefully to herself and once more spoke aloud. 'Don't kid yourself, Meriel – you're on your own. You'll have to work this one out for yourself.'

She settled back in her seat and, as accurately and calmly as she could, replayed her conversation at the party with Seb.

When she'd caught sight of him, staring at her with the strangest look on his face, a warm thrill had at once flooded her entire body. She couldn't help wondering

113

if the radiance might be in some way visible to others. She felt suffused in soft, golden light.

Then he was walking quickly towards her, and the sensation faded just a little.

He reached her side and they stared at each other for a moment. Then both of them spoke at the same time, in the same words.

'But I thought you weren't here!'

They laughed together, and Seb – unselfconsciously, unthinkingly – leaned in to kiss Meriel's cheek. It was only the second time they'd made physical contact; the first was when he had shaken her hand outside the radio station nine days before. She experienced the same quiver that she had then, but managed to disguise it by quickly returning the kiss.

'Seb ... hello. What a lovely surprise. I didn't see your car when I arrived just now. I thought ... well ...'

'I got here late,' Seb explained. 'I was on a story. A wild-goose chase as things turned out. When I arrived the parking goons made me stick my car round the side. I reckon the reason was that they didn't want a heap of junk spoiling the motor show out there. I counted at least three Porsches.'

He hesitated before asking her: 'Have you come with your husband?'

It was almost imperceptible, but he noticed her flinch.

'No. Cameron decided ... not to come. He said he

had some contracts to go over. Something about a deadline on Monday. I came on my own.'

He tried not to look pleased.

'Right. And you got here late, like me.'

'Yes. I had to stop in Keswick for ... for a while. Then I pulled over along the way to look at the views and I lost track of time. I'd forgotten how beautiful the Eden Valley is. No wonder they named it after Paradise.'

He laughed, and they considered each other in silence. The moments lengthened.

'Well, this is very odd,' he said at last, smiling at her.

'What is?'

'Standing here together not talking but feeling ... well, totally OK with it. This is only the second time we've seen each other but it seems I've known you for ... well, I don't know how long. Ages. For ever. It's weird, I don't feel I have to make any effort to make conversation with you. Sorry, does that sound mad?'

Meriel shook her head. 'Not at all. I know exactly what you mean. I'm feeling it, too. Perhaps we knew each other in a previous existence.'

'Oh please, don't tell me you believe in any of that rubbish.'

She laughed. 'No, not really. It's just that earlier today I found myself thinking of my late father. When I stopped to look at Paradise, as it were. It left me feeling a bit thoughtful, that's all.'

'Mmm.' Seb looked around them. 'Over there,' he said suddenly, nodding towards the river. 'There's a table come free – that one by the jetty, a bit apart from all the others. Why don't we sit down and get to know each other properly?'

'I'd like that.'

Seb elaborately offered her his arm, bowing theatrically from the waist as she took it. Meriel dropped a mock curtsey in return, the tassels on her dress bobbing and swaying in sympathy.

'So very formal, Mr Richmond.'

'So incredibly desirable, Miss Kidd.' Seb's smile was instantly replaced by a look of anguish and he pressed his free hand to his forehead.

'Christ, I'm *really* sorry, Meriel. That was completely out of order. I should never have said it; I don't know what I was thinking. I just—'

She squeezed his arm reassuringly against her side and smiled up at him.

'Don't be silly. It was a lovely thing to say. In fact, you're rather lovely yourself.'

There had been few pauses in their conversation after that, Meriel reflected now as she stared, unseeing, at the rooks foraging in the field in front of her. Seb had brought them a couple of glasses of champagne and they'd spent the next hour telling each other the stories of their lives. They were so obviously engrossed

116

in each other that the other guests instinctively left them alone, and neither Seb nor Meriel noticed that the party was winding down around them, and that they were among the last there.

The more they talked, the more she liked him. Oh, never mind *liked* him: she was falling for him, she knew that. It wasn't just that he was ridiculously attractive, he struck her as being wise ahead of his years. Seb's days on newspapers had given him an insight into how the world worked, she decided, without making him cynical. He was funny and well informed and interesting and charming.

He was totally irresistible.

And, she was about to discover, formidably direct.

'So, now I know all about your doctor father and English teacher mother,' he said eventually. '*You* know about my journo dad and happy-to-be-at-home mum. We've swapped our best school stories, and how you got started on magazines, and me with the local rag.

'I've told you about my girlfriends and you've told me about your boyfriends. But you know what, Meriel?'

She suddenly knew what was coming. Damn. *Damn.*

'You've barely said a word about your husband. I know he's a guy called Cameron, I know he's a hot-shot businessman. You've told me that much, although I knew it already from the articles I've read about you, which also, by the way, never fail to inform me what a perfect marriage you have.'

'We do.'

'Bullshit.'

Meriel stood up.

'I think I should go.'

'Really? *I* think you should stay.'

'You can't talk about my marriage like that. You don't know a thing about it.'

Seb had not taken his eyes from hers.

'Meriel, listen to me. I may be a cack-handed, green-as-grass, bumbling broadcaster, but I'm a bloody good reporter. *Bloody* good. I have a nose for a story, always have had. I can read people. I can *see* them.'

'Oh really? That's quite a gift. What do you see now?'

'I see a lot of pain and confusion. I see a beautiful young woman whose marriage to a much older man is anything *but* perfect. You can hardly bring yourself to speak his name, for Christ's sake. And just look at the way you're behaving right this second, Meriel. If you loved the guy you'd be laughing in my face, quoting me a dozen examples of wedded bliss to prove how wrong I am. Instead, you've disconnected, pulled the plug, threatened to leave.'

She stared blankly down at him. 'I *am* leaving.'

'I wish you wouldn't, Meriel ... Please sit down again. Please.'

'Why? What's the point? Even if you're right, what possible difference could you make to anything?'

Seb looked around them. There was no one near.

He reached out and touched her fingertips with his own. She shivered.

'All the difference in the world. Because this is a classic *coup de foudre*, can't you see that? A bolt of lightning. We've both been struck. When I saw you earlier, and you turned and saw me, it happened. You know it did. Both our lives changed this afternoon.'

Her eyes widened and, after a long moment, she sank back down into her chair, still staring at him. Finally she dropped her eyes. It was a surrender.

'All right. All right, Seb. So what are we going to do about it? Just what exactly are we going to do?'

'We're going to start by getting out of here. Come on.'

Meriel started the engine and reversed back out into the lane. If she turned left, she'd be back at Cathedral Crag in no more than forty-five minutes. If she turned right, she'd be with Seb in less than five.

She'd already made her decision.

CHAPTER FIFTEEN

As things turned out, they didn't trouble themselves with supper.

Seb was sitting in the bar nursing a half of bitter when he heard the door that led to the pub's beer garden open behind him. He knew straight away that it was her; the sudden change in the barman's expression told him that. The guy looked stunned, like he'd just been whacked over the head and was seeing stars.

Seb turned around and looked at her. She was backlit by the setting sun. The tassels of her lace dress rippled in the evening breeze, casting long, fluttering shadows across the flagstoned floor towards him.

'Hello, Meriel.'

'Hello, Seb.'

'You took your time.' He said it with a smile, sliding off the bar stool and reaching for the little tray which held the gin and tonic he'd ordered for her half an hour before. He put his beer next to it. 'Shall we take these outside?'

'If you like.'

The barman looked crestfallen.

There were only two other people in the little garden, a couple in their mid-thirties. They were deep in conversation and didn't even glance in their direction.

Seb set down the tray onto a wooden picnic table and touched Meriel's elbow as she was about to sit down.

'No; wait . . . come round here.'

He led her to the far side of a gnarled apple tree that grew close beside a weather-worn, mellowed old brick wall. Now they were completely hidden from view.

He slipped both arms around her and pulled her firmly to him. She rested one hand on his shoulder and then, just as she had imagined that afternoon when she was sitting daydreaming in the sun, she slid the other around the back of his neck and pushed her fingers into his hair.

My God, thought Meriel. It's happening. It's actually happening.

They gazed steadily at each other for several moments. Seb lifted one hand and softly stroked her cheek. At last he spoke.

'I'd started to think you'd changed your mind.'

'I nearly did.'

'What happened?'

She gave a tiny shrug. 'I'm not sure. I think ... I think I've decided to put my faith in you.'

He traced a finger around her mouth. 'Meriel, I promise you won't be sorry.'

She laughed softly.

'I might be, if you don't hurry up and kiss me.'

After that there'd really been nothing else to do but go to the room. Seb had secured the inn's sole four-poster bedroom. Meriel was delighted when she saw the old-style velvet drapes hanging on all four sides of the bed.

'We can pull them closed around us while we ... when we ... it'll be like being in our own enclosed, separate world! Oh, I *love* this place, Seb. How clever of you to think of it.'

He turned from locking the door behind them, laughing as he crossed the room to wrap her in his arms again.

She began laughing too. 'What's funny? Tell me!'

'You. When you make up your mind, you make up your mind, don't you? You look happier and more relaxed than I've seen you all day. And even more beautiful, if that's possible. Now please stop laughing, Miss Kidd. I want to kiss you properly.'

'What, you mean outside just now wasn't kissing me properly?'

He pushed her gently backwards onto the bed.

'Ask me that question again an hour from now.'

Meriel shuddered and arched her back again. They had been making love for longer than she had ever thought was possible. As she subsided once more, the back of one hand pressed to her mouth and the fingers of the other tightly gripping Seb's hair as it brushed her belly, she felt him finally relax. After a few moments he moved back up the bed to lie, trembling slightly, full-length beside her. Gradually their breathing slowed and he turned her face towards him.

'You're absolutely beautiful.' He kissed her and then fell back again, passing one hand across his eyes before staring up at the ceiling.

'Jesus, Meriel, that was ... I don't know ... like nothing I've ever experienced. You're incredible.'

She turned her head to look at him. 'It was a first for me too, Seb.'

'What? Honestly?' He propped himself up on one elbow and began to lightly stroke her thigh with his fingers. 'A woman as gorgeous as you? I find that very hard to believe.' He leaned forward and nuzzled her throat, adding indistinctly: 'You must have had heaps of paramours, beautiful Meriel.'

She smiled and slowly rubbed the back of his neck.

'No. Honestly. I was so young when I married, remember. Yes, I'd had plenty of boyfriends before then but both I and they were pretty inexperienced. As for Cameron ... oh God, I don't even want to think about it.'

'Don't, then ... just a minute.'

He slid out of bed and padded over to the mini-fridge that hummed quietly in the corner.

'Let's see what we have in here ... aha!'

He pulled out two miniatures of gin and a bottle of tonic water, and waved them triumphantly over his shoulder at her. 'Success!'

Meriel sat up, laughing. 'Well done, lovely man.'

'And for my next trick ...' Seb lifted the lid of the little plastic ice bucket that sat on top of the fridge.

'*Voila!* We have ice, too ... not much of it, though. Now, where's the bottle opener?'

A few moments later he'd mixed their drinks and was sliding back on his knees onto the bed beside her, a crystal tumbler in either hand.

'Here's yours. Bet you never thought you'd be finishing the day drinking G&T stark naked in bed with someone you'd only kissed for the first time that afternoon. I certainly didn't. Sorry, there's no lemon. Raise your glass, please, my darling.'

She did so. 'That's the first time you've called me that. I like it. Very much. What are we drinking to?'

'Us, of course. You and me.'

She clinked her tumbler against his.

'To us.'

CHAPTER SIXTEEN

Cameron looked despondently out at the lake through the picture window of the lounge. It was getting dark and he suspected his wife would not be returning home until late tonight, and possibly not until tomorrow.

He had already attempted, three times, to write a conciliatory note to her, to be left on her pillow for when she eventually came back. They all lay crumpled at the bottom of his waste basket.

He left the sofa and walked over to his desk, flicking on the green reading lamp as he sat in the big wheeled leather chair. One more try. One more attempt to get it right before he gave up and went to bed.

His solitary bed.

Cameron had enough intelligence and insight to know he'd behaved badly – very badly – earlier. Meriel hadn't looked remotely ill-dressed when she came downstairs. She'd looked fabulous, as always. But the mere thought of other men at that blasted party thinking the same had pushed him over the edge into a jealous rage.

Why? What was wrong with him? Was it because he was acutely aware that he was losing – no, had *lost* – his own looks? Perhaps he should never have pursued and married a woman so much younger than himself. It had always been likely to end in tears, he could see that now. Inevitable that one day a stunning woman like Meriel would want . . .

Vivid images of her with another man – a *younger* man – suddenly swamped his imagination again and he trembled. Obviously he shouldn't have accused her of fooling around, not without evidence, but he found it impossible to dismiss the idea that she was seeing someone else. Sometimes she got back quite late from the radio station, and he himself had been spending more and more time away recently, closing the Edinburgh deal. Meriel was so extraordinarily desirable, any man in his right mind would covet her.

Evidence. It wasn't as if he hadn't looked for it. By God, he'd gone through her bedroom with a fine-tooth comb, many times, when she was safely out of the house. But he'd found nothing; not so much as a phone number scrawled on the back of an envelope or an ambiguous note from one of her colleagues.

There *had* to be something. He felt the old famil-iar flames of suspicion and certainty flicker and rise within him. He couldn't help himself. He simply had to search again.

He peered out through the window at the drive. There was no sign of her. Not even a flare of headlights from the main road below.

Cameron pushed the writing pad away from him and carefully returned his engraved fountain pen to its holder. Then he crossed the rectory's hall, and stood at the foot of the stairs.

This time – *this* time – he was sure he'd find what he was looking for. And then it would be Meriel who would be the one on her knees, begging for forgiveness.

He caught his breath.

Begging him.

CHAPTER SEVENTEEN

Meriel looked at her watch. It was quarter past eleven. She'd have to be going soon. She had no idea what she was going to tell Cameron – he would almost certainly be waiting up for her. But she realised she didn't much care what he thought any more, not after this morning. Ghastly though it had been, she was beginning to realise that it had actually liberated her.

She glanced down at the sleeping man beside her. They'd made love again. It had been wonderful, and different from the first time, quieter, slower. They had paused frequently to kiss and whisper to each other. Seb had said the sweetest things. After his climax he had rested his head on her shoulder and taken her hand, and the next thing she knew he'd fallen asleep.

As Meriel reached down and stroked his hair, prior to waking him, she suddenly understood the profound sensation of relief that had been spreading through her for the last hour. At first she thought it was simply the sheer physical release that lovemaking with Seb had triggered. A great lake of sexual tension and frustration, deepening and spreading for years, had been comprehensively drained, as if the dam holding it back had been suddenly and decisively breached.

But there was something else, too. Something that went much deeper than this quiet, purring, sexual satisfaction.

She felt rescued. Delivered. Redeemed, even. The future was suddenly alive with hope again.

Which made no sense, really. All the repercussions of leaving Cameron, the publicity that would result from divorcing him, still hovered malignly in the wings. She would almost certainly lose her career; her agent was probably right about that. But at this moment, lying in bed with her man, her saviour, she couldn't summon up the will to care much any more. And anyway, maybe something would miraculously happen to prove David Weir's prophecy (and her own) false.

'Penny for them.'

Meriel jumped slightly; he was awake, looking curiously up at her through lazy, half-closed eyes.

'Oh, hello. You were sleeping.' She hesitated. 'Actually I was thinking about ... don't take this the wrong way ... I was thinking about Cameron. And what's going to happen.'

132

Seb sat up beside her, stretching.

'Yeah, I thought so. You looked miles away. Are you OK?'

'Mmm ... I think so. Look, Seb, can I ask you something?'

'Anything.'

'Well ... how exactly did you know ... that is, why were you so *certain*, that I've been so unhappy for all this time? With Cameron, I mean.'

'I told you. The way you virtually excised him from your life story this afternoon. And you actually winced at the mere mention of his name when I asked if he'd come with you. I think you thought you'd hidden it, but it was obvious. You looked as if I'd pressed on a bruise.'

She sighed. 'I'm normally rather better at pretending. I was very off balance today.'

Seb took her hand. 'Why? What happened? Wouldn't you like to tell me about it?'

And suddenly, she decided that she would. About all of it – the entire, doomed voyage of a marriage to Cameron.

'It might take me a while.'

'We've got all night.'

Meriel realised that they had. What possible difference did it make what time she got home now? There was going to be a dreadful row in any event. Why hurry back to it?

133

She made up her mind. 'In that case, I think I'll have another drink first. You might find you could do with one too, by the time I'm finished.'

'Wow. That *does* sound heavy. Hold on, I'll see what's left.' Seb rolled out of bed and went to the little fridge. 'There's a couple of Scotch miniatures,' he called. 'The ice is all gone but the meltwater's still pretty cold. Will that do us?'

'I think whisky would be just the thing, actually.'

When he was back in bed with her, she turned to face him. 'Sure you really want to hear this?'

He kissed her. 'Meriel, you were always going to tell me about it. Now's as good a time as any. In fact, I'd say it's the perfect time. Whatever it is you've been bottling up all these years, the sooner you let it out the better. Just as long as you're sure, my darling.'

'I am. I've put my faith in you.'

'And I've put mine in you. It's a nice feeling, isn't it?'

She smiled at him. 'Actually, it is. Trusting someone, I mean.'

'So where do you want to begin?'

She sipped her drink and considered a moment before answering him.

'At a charity auction.'

'He spat in your *face*?'

Meriel nodded, miserably.

She was exhausted. She'd told him everything.

Everything, that is, except for the part about her secret diary. Lying cradled in Seb's arms, she could scarcely believe she'd written it. It seemed absurd now – a weird, bizarre lapse in sanity. Good God, recently she'd even given it a title: *The Night Book*.

Mad, mad, mad. The moment she returned to Cathedral Crag, she was going to burn it. A first step. The first of many.

Seb was frowning with disgust. 'What a vile man. You can't go back there.'

She shook her head. 'I have to, Seb. Cameron and I must have it out. I have no idea what I'm going to tell him about where I've been tonight, but that doesn't matter, I'll come up with something.

'The main thing is, I think I've decided what I'm going to do. I'm going to insist on some kind of trial separation. That way we can hopefully keep it all low-key, to begin with at least. There's no point running headlong into the whole publicity thing I was telling you about. I want to put that off as long as possible. I'm dreading it.'

Seb snorted. 'And there's another vile man – your prick of an agent. He should be coming up with ideas of how to handle the fallout when you and Cameron separate, not exploiting your anxieties and making them worse. He just doesn't want his precious boat rocked, the selfish bastard.'

'What do you mean?'

'Meriel, this, this, oh, what's his name, *Dick* Weir, *Dan* Weir?'

'David Weir.'

'Hmm, right first time, then. This dick's got it all *completely* wrong – and so have you.'

Seb took both of Meriel's hands in his own.

'Look. People won't hold you in contempt for trying to keep a shockingly bad marriage together, for God's sake. Most will respect you for it. They'll sympathise and some will identify. So what if you did your level best to put a brave face on things? It never lessened the value of your advice, did it? Just think how many of your listeners and readers have told you how you've changed their lives immeasurably, for the better.'

Meriel began to speak but he shook his head impatiently.

'Wait. I'm not finished. I sneaked a look at some of the fan letters on your office wall when you were off sick. The ones from women you've helped. They adore you and they'll forever be grateful to you, can't you see that? I wouldn't be surprised if they formed a "she helped us, now it's our turn to help her" Meriel Kidd support group! I'm not joking.'

She stared at him.

'I never thought of it like that before.'

'That's because you've had to deal with this entirely on your own. Well, apart from your poisonous agent's so-called advice. You've got everything wildly out of proportion. I feel *so sorry* for you. What a frightening time you must have had of it.'

He saw tears beginning to form in her eyes and drew her closer.

'Well, it's all coming to an end. You've got me and you're going to get a new life. It's started already. There's no going back now.'

She hugged him tightly. 'I can't believe how much better you're making me feel. I've been so unhappy and afraid.'

He kissed the top of her head. 'It's exactly as I told you yesterday – our lives have changed. It *is* yesterday now, by the way; we've been talking for hours. I think it's actually beginning to get light out there.'

'Then it really is time I got up.' Meriel sat up, dabbing her eyes with a corner of the sheet. 'I'm going to take a quick shower and go straight home to talk to Cameron. The sooner I get started, the better.'

She looked at Seb, her face flushed with determination. 'I've got a lot to do.'

She would start by destroying *The Night Book*.

CHAPTER EIGHTEEN

He'd almost given up. He'd gone through every single one of her cupboards and drawers. He'd taken all her handbags out of their wardrobe and opened every compartment in each of them. He'd even slipped his hands deep inside her shoes and boots, in case there was something secreted in them.

He was in her en-suite bathroom now, where he had just finished rifling through the used towels she'd thrown in the wicker laundry basket. He looked *under* the basket, and even felt inside the cotton lining of its lid.

There was nothing. Nothing to suggest that she was seeing someone else, or flirting with someone else, or even thinking about doing either.

His eyes fell on a large blue and white china jug sitting in a matching bowl on her washstand. He'd never thought to look in there before, and his pulse quickened with expectation. He went over and peered into it, before lifting it out to see if anything was concealed underneath. He checked the bottom of the bowl, too.

Nothing.

Cameron sighed. His hands felt damp and sticky – his palms were perspiring freely – and he rinsed them under the hot tap in the wash basin. He looked around for a towel, but the heated rail was empty. Meriel must have forgotten to replace the ones she'd dropped in the basket.

He went back out onto the landing and found the airing cupboard that served the part of the house his wife had been using since Christmas. He supposed he ought to have searched in here too, but somehow he didn't think she'd hide anything outside her own bedroom or bathroom. Anyway, he couldn't explore every bloody nook and cranny in the rambling rectory; he'd be at it for weeks.

The airing cupboard had a sliding door on railings. Cameron rolled it open. The fresh towels were piled immediately at the front of the shelf, but when he took a couple from the top of the heap he saw there were some more shoved all the way towards the back. They looked old and thin and had a fairly revolting orange and purple pattern, nothing like the fluffy white towels he and Meriel used. They must have been there for years. Someone should have chucked them out a long time ago.

He reached further inside to retrieve them.

As soon as his fingers touched them, he could feel that they had been carefully wrapped around something.

Something flat and hard.

Cameron froze.

He knew, with cold certainty, that he had just found what he was looking for.

CHAPTER NINETEEN

Meriel had no clear idea what to expect when she finally reached Cathedral Crag and pulled up next to her husband's car. Cameron's vintage Bentley was still parked in exactly the same position as it had been when she fled the house yesterday. That meant he had not been out and her apprehension grew. He must have been sitting in the house all alone, stewing over the row they'd had and then, surely, wondering where she'd spent the night. God knows what state he'd be in by now.

She glanced at her watch. Just past eight. She'd been gone for almost twenty hours.

Mentally, she braced herself. This was going to be rough.

Cameron heard the distant thud of his wife's car door slamming and, a few moments later, the sound of her key in the door. He was sitting in the little breakfast room that overlooked the lake. Croissants sat squat on a hotplate on the sideboard, and he'd poured out two glasses of orange juice the moment he heard the Mercedes' tyres scrunching on the gravel outside.

Coffee was ready in an electrically heated pot. He'd placed Meriel's favourite Sunday paper to one side of her place setting.

He'd been here, ready and waiting, for over an hour. He would have sat there all morning if necessary.

He reviewed his plan one last time. It was important to behave as calmly as possible; maintain the element of surprise. He'd contrived everything down to the last detail: wherever she'd been, whatever she'd done, was supremely irrelevant to him now. To his surprise, he found he genuinely didn't care.

Not now. Not after what he'd discovered, and the power it had given him.

For the time being, this was going to be a Sunday just like any other.

Until the moment was exactly right.

Then he'd move faster than a striking cobra.

'Cameron?'

'In here.'

Meriel hung her handbag by its strap from the bottom banister before taking a deep breath and walking across the hall to the breakfast room.

She was acutely conscious of being in the same clothes she had worn to the party the day before, and that her hair was still damp and tangled from the shower (the room at the String of Horses had boasted no hairdryer). But she lifted her chin and crossed the threshold. She was ready for almost anything.

But not for what happened next.

As soon as she entered the room, Cameron rose to his feet and tossed the newspaper he'd been pretending to read to the floor.

'Don't say anything, Meriel. Please let me speak first.' He raised one palm almost pleadingly as she opened her mouth. 'No, please, Meriel, really ... there's something I must say to you right away.'

She studied him warily before nodding. 'All right.'

'Thank you.' He picked up the coffee pot and filled the china cup opposite his own. 'Here. Come sit down and have some of this. Let me get you a croissant.'

Meriel didn't move.

'Just say what it is you want to say to me.'

'Of course. I'm a little nervous, that's all ... well ... Here's the thing, Meriel ... I ...'

He gestured helplessly towards her. 'The thing is ... I'm sorry. I'm *so* sorry, Meriel. For spitting at you like that. For saying the things I did. You were right: I must have been mad. I don't know what came over me. I'm thoroughly ashamed of myself and I can promise you, here and now, nothing like it will *ever* happen again.'

145

She stared at him. It was years since Cameron had apologised to her. For anything. This was the last thing she'd been expecting. Didn't he want to know where she'd been all night?

As if reading her thoughts, he spoke again, quickly.

'I'm not surprised you stayed away last night. I expect you went to some hotel or other, but I have no right to know anything you don't want to tell me. I put myself beyond the pale yesterday.'

Meriel breathed a little easier. 'Yes. I stayed at a hotel on the other side of Penrith. After going to the party, that is.' She hesitated. 'Cameron . . .'

'Yes?'

'I think things have gone rather beyond apologies, don't you? You and I need to talk. About everything. About us. What we should do next.'

He nodded at once. 'I've been thinking the same thing. Look, let's get out of the house, shall we? After you've had some breakfast, I mean, and got yourself straight. Changed, and all that.' He offered her a crooked smile.

'Sundays are still one of our better days, aren't they, Meriel? Out on the boat together? Why don't we do that now? There's a farm food market in Keswick today – I can go and get us something nice for a picnic lunch out on the water. We'll take some champagne, and we'll talk. Sort things out. Decide what's for the best. Yes?'

He saw her hesitate, and quietly played his best card.

'It's all right, Meriel. Really. I know exactly what you think of me, and I think we are agreed – we can't go on like this. I quite see that. No more arguing. Just a quiet afternoon on the lake, sorting things out like civilised grown-ups. I believe we can manage that, don't you?'

She nodded, at last. Perhaps this was going to be easier than she'd thought.

'Yes, Cameron. I do. I think we can manage that.'

'Good. You get some coffee and croissants inside you. I'll go and sniff us out some lunch.'

A few minutes later, the moment she was sure Cameron's Bentley had swept out of the drive and turned towards Keswick, she was in the hall, dialling Seb's number.

'He's up to something.'

'I don't know, Seb … He seems to have had an extraordinary change of heart. Some sort of epiphany.'

'Did he actually mention separating? Divorce?'

Meriel shook her head. 'No. Not exactly. But something's happened. It's very odd. He doesn't seem in the remotest bit curious about where I … what I … well, you know, what might have happened last night. He just seems resigned to the fact that the marriage is over. Perhaps he's had some kind of long, dark night of the soul.'

Seb was silent.

'Anyway,' Meriel went on, 'it should make what I have to say to him a lot easier. And he's right – for some reason we communicate better out there on the boat. We always have done. Seb? Say something.'

She heard him sigh before his voice crackled into her ear again. 'Of course, Meriel. I'm sure you're right. But be on your guard. I mean, this time yesterday the man was spitting in your face. You've been gone all night and now he wants to take you on a picnic. Something's not hanging right. What time do you think you'll be back from the lake?'

She thought for a moment. 'Around four, probably. Why?'

'Call me. Make some excuse or other. Say you need petrol or something. Just get to a phone box to let me know you're all right.'

'Of course I'll be all right. Cameron would never do anything to hurt me – not physically. Not now. Honestly, Seb, he's full of contrition.'

'He's full of something, all right. I tell you, Meriel, he's up to no good. I can smell it. Make sure you call me.'

'I know exactly what you think of me.'

Cameron's words echoed in her mind as Meriel changed into denim shorts and a pale-blue cheesecloth shirt. She pulled her hair back into a ponytail and looked thoughtfully at her reflection in the bedroom mirror.

It had been an odd thing for him to say. For some months now she had managed to avoid telling her husband exactly how much she loathed him. She had found a way to disengage from him when he was being at his most repulsive. It helped that they now routinely slept in separate parts of the house.

Meriel frowned. The perfume she liked to wear during the day wasn't on the little shelf on her dressing table; she was certain she'd left it there yesterday. Now it was in a quite different position on the main glass top beneath. The realisation crystallised a sense of disquiet that had been steadily growing from the moment she'd gone upstairs.

She went back and reopened the wardrobe where she kept her casual clothes, including the shirt and shorts she was wearing now.

Yes. It had *definitely* been disturbed. Now that she looked closely she could see that one of the breast pockets of a cotton blouse was turned almost inside out. On the floor beneath, her boots and shoes were in slight disarray, no longer in quite the neat pairings she invariably left them in.

Cameron had been going through her things. There could be no other explanation. His jealous rage had swept him into this room, desperate to find proof to substantiate his mad fantasies.

Not quite so mad now, though, she thought wryly to herself. As things had turned out, there'd been a predictive element to his suspicions.

She closed the wardrobe again. It was unsettling to picture Cameron in here, rooting among her most intimate possessions. Thank God she didn't keep the diary in here.

'*I know exactly what you think of me.*'

She froze.

She ran back out onto the landing and down the passage leading to the airing cupboard. She yanked the door open and felt the first ripples of reassurance at the sight of the pile of fluffy new towels stacked along the front of the main shelf.

She pushed them to one side. Yes, the ancient multi-coloured ones were there, neatly squared away right at the back of the cupboard. She reached out for them.

Oh, the relief. The *relief*! They were still wrapped tightly around her diary, just as she always left them.

With trembling fingers, Meriel slipped the leather-bound book from its ugly shroud and drew it out into the sunlight that streamed through the full-length window at the end of the passage.

She realised it was the first time she could remember looking at the diary in natural light. It was a thing of the night, something she only confided in during the dead hours between sunset and sunrise.

She couldn't bear to open it now and read the

detailed, twisted revenges she had composed over the years. Even the title she had recently inscribed in gold marker pen on both the cover and spine seemed, in the glorious Sunday sunshine, as close to insane as a sane person could get. She grimaced. *The Night Book* indeed. Preposterous.

Meriel glanced at her watch. It would be at least another hour before Cameron returned from Keswick. She had time enough.

Less than five minutes later she was in the rectory's vegetable patch, methodically ripping sheet after sheet from the diary and dropping them into the freshly lit garden brazier. The pages flared and burned brightly, helped by an occasional splash of paraffin oil she'd found in a little bottle in the shed nearby.

No one would ever read them now. It would be as if the diary had never been. From this moment, it existed only in Meriel's memory.

And that, she reflected as the last pages were blackened by the flames, was sealed as securely as the mummy's tomb. A secret known to her, and her alone.

As she walked back towards the house, she shuddered slightly.

Thank God Cameron had never found the bloody thing.

CHAPTER TWENTY

Cameron's boat was moored at Glenridding, Ullswater's most southerly point. As he and Meriel drove the short distance from Cathedral Crag, Lake District FM informed them that today was expected to be the hottest August Sunday in the Lakes on record.

'Yup, it's certainly one for the logbook,' Cameron called to Meriel from the cabin as she followed him across the little gangplank and onto the deck. 'Look at this – the thermometer's nudging ninety-five already.' He tapped the barometer mounted next to it. 'And the pressure's crazy-high, too. I bet old Ulfr never saw a day like this.'

Ulfr was the Viking chieftain thought to have bestowed his name on the lake a thousand years ago, although Meriel sided with local historians who argued that because *ulfr* was also Norse for wolf, the true etymology of Ullswater was Wolf Lake. Perhaps a pack of the animals had once hunted beneath the frowning peak of Helvellyn that dominated the valley. The theory was a brisk antidote to Wordsworth's sentimental poem 'Daffodils', inspired by the sight of the flowers growing on Ullswater's shoreline as the poet walked to Grasmere on a blustery day, eight centuries after the Norsemen had sheathed their swords and drifted away.

Cameron was continuing to be extraordinarily punctilious. He had insisted on making up their picnic when he returned from Keswick ('No, no, *I* can do it. You go and read the Sundays in the garden') and once they were on the boat, he fussed with cushions and bottles and ice ('I'm not casting off until I'm sure you're nice and comfortable, Mer') and made sure to place sunscreen at her elbow ('We don't want you burning, do we?').

It was all extremely out of character and very unsettling, but she could hardly protest. Perhaps he really was ashamed of his behaviour the previous day, and was trying to make amends. But at the same time he'd made it clear that he'd come to the same conclusion as her: they'd reached a watershed in their marriage, and probably a terminal one.

So what exactly was he up to? Why all this unctuous, caring behaviour? Were Seb's instincts correct? Was Cameron playing some kind of calculated game with her?

'I know exactly what you think of me.'

Why did those words sound so loaded? They seemed to her to be pregnant with meaning.

She decided she was being paranoid.

Sleeping with another man could do that to a woman's conscience.

The boat moved smoothly away from the jetty, its powerful outboard purring on low revs quietly behind her. She could hear Cameron humming a tune as he steered them well away from one of the five passenger steamers that plied the lake every day.

A sudden sense of fatalism tinged with determination overtook Meriel. *Screw* it. If Cameron was trying to pull off some kind of double-bluff, she'd find out what it was in due course. But it wouldn't change a thing. She was going to insist on a trial separation starting the very next day, come what may. She'd move out; rent a cottage somewhere in the fells. Seb could discreetly join her there and they'd start to really get to know each other. She felt her heart lift at the prospect.

Meanwhile she'd go down to Manchester or London and see a lawyer, get some proper advice, not the crummy self-seeking guff her agent had spouted.

The boat began to pick up speed and Meriel stopped worrying. *Qué será será* and all that. She was still feeling extraordinarily physically relaxed after her night with Seb. She peeled her blouse off and swapped her bra for the bikini top she'd stuffed into her shoulder bag before leaving Cathedral Crag. She stretched out on the padded deck lounger and closed her eyes, gratefully surrendering to the warm breeze that was blowing through her hair.

This was the day everything was going to change. She was going to go with the flow, and to hell with Cameron's pathetic little *jeu de jour*.

Cameron eyed his half-naked wife stealthily from the cabin as he steered the boat towards the centre of the lake. Increasingly, theirs had become a voyeuristic relationship – albeit an entirely one-sided one. Meriel didn't have the slightest idea. She was completely unaware that, three or four nights a week, her husband crept from his room in the small hours and crouched in her bedroom doorway, watching her as she slept.

And Meriel slept naked, this steamy, stifling summer, her bedsheets kicked to the foot of the bed. Cameron only made these nocturnal visits when Meriel's bedside lamp was off. He used a small, low-powered pocket torch to illuminate her body, using one hand to shield the dim light from her sleeping face. Even so, she had half-woken once or twice – but he always melted away and was back in his own room before she was properly conscious.

But most nights he gazed his fill at her breasts, her

genitals, her legs, before bringing himself to a silent, juddering climax.

She was *his*.

There had to be a way of reclaiming what rightfully belonged to him.

Last night, he'd found it.

'Do you want anything else? There's plenty more of this cold chicken.'

Meriel shook her head.

'I'm fine. Cameron ...'

'Yes?'

'Can we talk now? About us? About the future?'

He nodded. 'Yes, of course. That's why we're here, isn't it? Just let me get this.'

He walked to the rear of the boat and pulled the idling outboard's kill-cord. The throaty, burbling engine died at once and a peaceful silence settled over the boat, broken only by the plish-plash of tiny waves breaking around the base of the hull.

He moved back towards her and sank down on the bench-seat opposite.

'There. Just you and me and ...' he pointed up and across the water – 'Helvellyn. An apt spot, eh, for negotiating one of life's peaks? One of its watersheds? So ... do you want to go first, Meriel, or shall I?'

'I'd like to, please.'

Meriel could feel her shoulders beginning to burn in

the sun, but she was even more uncomfortable with the way Cameron was staring at her breasts. As casually as she could she reached for a towel and wrapped it around herself like a cloak.

'It's like this, Cameron,' she began. 'We're locked into a horrible, never-ending war, aren't we? I don't know how it's happened, but you've ended up despising me and I ... well ... I ...'

'Oh, spare your breath, my dear.'

She stared at him. He was smiling. Dammit, he looked almost *happy*.

This wasn't right. This wasn't right at all.

'All right. I'll get straight to the point then. I think we should have a trial separation. Time apart, to reflect. You need to decide what you want from a wife, and I need to think about you, too. I need—'

'To *think*? I know exactly what you think of me, Meriel, and so do you, evidently. What on earth is there for you to think about?'

If anything, the smile had broadened.

'Why do you keep saying that?

'Saying what?'

'That you know exactly what I think of you. I don't see how. We haven't spoken properly for months.'

Cameron sighed, and reached behind him into the cool-box.

'True. But communication isn't always about the spoken word. There are so many other forms it can take. You of all people must know that. You're always lecturing folk on improving their communication skills, after all.'

He dragged the dripping bottle from the ice. 'More champagne? Actually, I think you may be about to need it.'

A cold presentiment began to creep over her. Outwardly she affected calm.

'Oh all right, Cameron. It's as I thought; you're playing some kind of weird game with me. Well, I've told you what I want. A separation. Unless you have something sensible to say I'd like to go back to the house now, please. I have packing to do and arrangements to make.'

She stood up. 'I'm going into the cabin to get dressed.'

He shook his head and motioned her to sit down again.

'Not yet you're not. Not until you've heard what I have to say.' All pretence of humility and kindness was falling from him now like a cast-off cape. 'Fair's fair. I listened to you. Now it's your turn.' His eyes glittered with cold triumph as she reluctantly sank back onto the cushions.

'You have some packing to do, do you? Well, indeed you have. Not that you'll be going very far. Just a few yards, actually. You're going to pack your things and return with them to the marital bedroom. For good.'

'Cameron, you obviously haven't heard a word I've said. *I'm leaving you.*'

'Saying something doesn't make it so, Meriel.'

He examined his fingernails before continuing.

'I want you to pay me your fullest attention. You *are* going to return to my bed. Tonight. And from then on you will make yourself available to me at any time of my choosing, as a good wife should. In fact, that is what you are going to become, Meriel. A good wife.'

She stared at him. 'You've gone completely mad. Seriously, Cameron, I mean it. I think you must be having some kind of breakdown.'

He laughed. '*Me*, mad? That's a good one, dearest. Pots and kettles come to mind. Just give me a moment to recollect ... oh, yes ...'

He stood, putting his hands behind his back, like a child about to recite a poem. 'I think this is how it goes.

'*A fountain of blood explodes from the scimitar-shaped, gaping incision I have just made. This is incredibly funny. I wasn't prepared for that.*'

He smiled at her. 'Did I get it right? I think so ... My goodness, Meriel, you've gone quite pale. You look as though you might faint.'

He poured more champagne into his glass and squinted at her through the golden liquid.

'Yes, I found it, Meriel. I found your grotesque,

depraved ramblings, all those throat-slitting, castrating, poisoning, strangling, butchering fantasies. The brief sentences I just quoted don't even begin to do it justice, do they? But it was quite a revelation. I had no idea how much you relished the whole business of pain.'

He delicately sipped his glass. 'As do I, Meriel. In fact, your book has given me some interesting ideas. I'd like to try some of them out on you. We could start this evening. What do you say?'

She was trembling. 'I won't be there this evening, Cameron. As soon as we get back I'm packing a case and getting out. Tomorrow I'm going to see a lawyer. It's over. What on earth makes you think I'd agree to join in your sordid, depraved games?'

'Well, perhaps it's the glimpse you've given me into your sordid, depraved imagination, my dear. But not only that. Have you considered what sort of reaction you'd get from your devoted followers if they could read your delightful musings? The entry where you remove my genitalia with a carving knife would certainly have many rushing to the nearest lavatory to throw up.'

He sighed, almost regretfully.

'If this gets out you're finished. No unhappily married woman looking for advice is going to want to contact a phone-in hosted by a psychopath, or write to her. What'll your counsel be? "Kill him"?

"Disembowel him"? "Pour boiling water on his face"?'

'It's not going to get out, Cameron. Ever. I've burned it. All of it. I wish you hadn't found it, but it's ashes now, thank God. You can't threaten me with my own foolishness.'

He made a little *moue*. 'Oh Meriel, you disappoint me. What sort of nincompoop do you take me for? I was up until after two in the morning downstairs in the study, photocopying every page. In fact, I've made multiple copies, and hidden them where you'll never find them.'

She tried and failed to keep her voice steady.

'I see. And what exactly do you intend to do with them?'

He drained his glass and stood it next to the ice bucket.

'Absolutely nothing. Unless you're very silly indeed and give me no choice. In which case I'll see my own lawyer and instruct him to file for divorce on the grounds of your unreasonable behaviour. We'll use your diary as our principal plank of evidence. I can't think of many husbands who'd be happy to live with a wife who writes down detailed fantasies about how she's going to castrate and murder him. My God, do you know how many ways you kill me in that book? I'm stabbed, poisoned, suffocated, drowned in the bath – *very* original use of a shower curtain, by the way – and I invariably die writhing in unspeakable torment. Meriel Kidd, agony aunt? More like agony enthusiast.'

She managed to stand up again. 'I'll counter-sue. I'll tell the world what a controlling swine you are. How you—'

Cameron burst out laughing. 'Based on precisely what evidence, my sweet? You've spent the last eleven years telling anyone who'd listen what a wonderful husband I am. The press cuttings are inches thick with glowing testimonials to my uxorious nature. You can't simply take all of it back now that it suits you.

'And remember – I'll have the diary. Two pages of that alone will guarantee ours is the divorce of the decade. I'll come across as poor Mr Rochester, married to the mad woman in the attic. Your career and reputation will never recover. Think about it.'

He walked over to the chromed ladder that dropped down into the water below, and began stripping to his boxer shorts.

'Look, Meriel! Here's that dreadful potbelly that so revolts you. Better get used to it; you'll be seeing a lot more of it from now on, right up close and in your face, too.'

He gave a throaty, comfortable chuckle. 'In fact, I think we can guarantee it, don't you?'

She was struggling to fight back tears. 'You unbelievable bastard. What exactly is it you want?'

'Good God! *Now* who's not been listening? I told you! I want your body, my dear, nothing more, nothing less. Given to me unconditionally, unequivocally, unhesitatingly. And I want us to have some adventures, too. We can explore the possibilities of pain together – remember me telling you that time how I wanted to hurt you? Well, now you're going to let me. Your diary has given me the right.'

She tried to sound defiant. 'The right? No, Cameron. I have the right – the right to refuse you.'

'By all means do so. But then your devoted followers would, in turn, have the right to know just how sick and twisted is the mind of their redeemer. Be very careful about quoting your so-called rights to me, Meriel; everyone has rights, you know. At this juncture you need to be exceptionally cautious about exercising yours.'

As usual before swimming, he slipped the gold Rolex from his wrist and placed it carefully on the deck, before climbing down the silver rungs towards the surface of the lake.

'Have a good think about your options, Meriel, while I take a swim. Really, as equations go, this one couldn't be simpler. Do as I suggest, and you keep your good name, your extremely financially advantageous marriage and your career.'

He slid into the warm water with a satisfied sigh before turning onto his back and calling, a little louder: 'Deny me and you lose all three.'

He grinned up at her before pushing away from the side of the boat and back-stroking slowly out into the lake.

'Aw, c'mon, Mer. It's only sex with a *soupçon* of suffering. Who knows? You might even come to enjoy it.'

CHAPTER TWENTY-ONE

Meriel stared out unseeing at the sunlit lake, smoking furiously.

She had finally managed to fasten the buttons on her top, in spite of trembling fingers, and crossed the cabin to a cupboard where she hoped she'd find some cigarettes.

Sure enough, there was almost a full packet lying on the floor of the locker next to a damp book of matches inscribed 'Pheasant, Bassenthwaite Lake'.

After several attempts she eventually managed to light a cigarette and went back out on deck. She had to calm down and think this mess through.

No doubt that Cameron had discovered her diary. No doubt at all. That quote had been word-perfect. And his summary of the various chapters (including the one involving shower curtains) ... Well, he'd obviously read every *fucking* page, hadn't he?

So why go to the trouble of replacing the book exactly as he'd found it, only to confront her with the fact of it barely hours later?

She sighed. It was obvious. So that she wouldn't see what was coming. He'd enjoyed his *coup de théâtre* on the boat just now. Controlling Cameron strikes again, Meriel thought bleakly. Nothing new there, eh?

So what now?

One thing was immediately plain to her. There was no question of staying at Cathedral Crag, not for one night, not even for one hour. The mere thought of surrendering herself to one of Cameron's sadistic games made her feel physically sick. In fact, she was having difficulty holding down what little she'd managed to eat for lunch.

Meriel forced herself to take long, deep breaths until her nausea subsided. Suddenly she didn't want her cigarette and she tossed it overboard. It fell, hissing, into the water.

She would leave Cameron, just as she had planned. But that would involve calling his bluff. Would he really take her vile scribblings to a lawyer? See them used against her in a horribly public divorce?

She looked out at her husband as he paddled in slow circles around the boat. He caught her glance and lifted one dripping arm out of the water in an ironic wave.

God, she wouldn't put it past him, the shit. Cameron

was accustomed to winning, and he wasn't too fussy about how he did it. It was one of the reasons he had no real friends: he had a reputation for sacrificing anyone in a business deal in order to come out on top. Why would he behave any differently with her? He was indomitable. He'd obviously gone to a great deal of time and trouble to find a diary that he couldn't possibly have known even existed.

Winner's instinct, again.

Meriel ground her teeth. *Christ*. If only she'd destroyed the bloody thing sooner. Even a *day* sooner.

Too late for 'if only' now. She forced herself to sketch out the likely coming chain of events.

One: she'd leave Cameron. Two: he'd divorce her, citing the diary. Three – and 'three' was the biggie – there'd be a sensation: screaming front-page headlines, personal profiles in the features sections, weeks of lurid speculation and comment pretty much everywhere.

It would be a freak show. But was Cameron right? Would it swamp and sink her career?

She simply didn't know. At one level, she wasn't even sure she cared.

But she cared about Seb. What about him? What would *he* make of the diaries, never mind the sick carnival triggered by their publication? Would he even want to be with someone capable of harbouring such sick fantasies? Let alone a person who painstakingly wrote them down in such grisly detail?

'Oh God, what have I done?' Meriel whispered to herself, rocking slowly back and forth on her haunches. 'What am I going to *do*?'

Cameron's voice cut through her thoughts and she started. He had paddled close to the boat and was treading water only a yard or so away from her.

'I said, what time is it? Didn't you hear me? Why are you talking to yourself like that?'

She looked at him with loathing.

'If you wore your watch you'd know what time it is. You've got a fucking Rolex, for Christ's sake. They're waterproof for hundreds of feet. Why do you always take it off before you swim? It's stupid.'

'Yeah, so's realising the damn thing's slipped off your wrist and gone straight to the bottom. I'm not risking that. Just tell me the bloody time, will you?'

'Bloody well tell it to yourself, Cameron.' She reached down to sweep up his watch from the deck.

As Meriel bent her head, a door in her inner universe silently swung open.

Her breath caught in her throat. She could see into an alternative reality. It shimmered on the other side of the threshold that had suddenly materialised directly before her.

She knew exactly what she had to do to cross over and enter it: it was so clear; so obvious.

And it was completely up to her. Only she had the power to decide whether to stay, or go.

But either way, it had to be now.

Right now.

She looked at the watch dangling from her fingers. Its delicate second hand seemed to her to be motionless, as if time had, for an incredible moment, reached a frozen full stop. Infinitely slowly, she switched her gaze to her husband in the water below. He seemed caught in the same freeze-frame, his expression freakishly preserved in one of petulance and exasperation.

All Meriel's senses were singing to her now. She knew, without having to move her head, that there were no other boats near. Theirs was drifting on the blind side of the headland that hid them from the villages of Glenridding and Patterdale. Her back was to the main road that ran along the lake's northern edge so that Cameron, bobbing on the far side of the boat, would be perfectly invisible to anyone walking or driving along the shore.

A voice whispered inside her head.

'Now or never, Meriel. One shot.'

'Father?' She spoke his name aloud.

'One shot, my darling.'

'Father?!'

Then everything was juddering back into motion, like a train suddenly jolting away from the platform.

Meriel could feel the moment slipping away.

NOW. Do it NOW.

She flexed her arm.

'Here. Catch, Cameron.'

Meriel tossed the Rolex into the air towards her husband. The timepiece moved in a glittering arc, winking and flashing in the sunlight as it ascended and then descended.

Cameron bellowed with rage.

'What the *fuck* are you doing?! That's a five-thousand-pound watch, you stupid bitch! You – oh, *Christ*!'

The Rolex had splashed into the water a couple of feet ahead of him. It briefly flashed greenish-gold, then began to sink.

'Oops. Missed, sorry. Quick, Cameron, you can still get it.'

'I don't *fucking* believe this! *Shit!*'

Cameron arced his body into the air before snapping his head and arms forwards and down, plunging under the surface. A moment later, Meriel could see the white soles of his feet kicking hard, and then he had disappeared entirely.

The boat rocked slightly in his boiling, descending wake, and then settled again.

Meriel looked around her. The only other vessel she could see was one of the passenger steamers, on its way back from Pooley Bridge. It was easily a mile away. She dismissed it from her mind and turned back to the water below her. There was no sign that anyone had been swimming there moments before.

She was finding it difficult to breathe. God knows what he was experiencing. How long had he been under now? Fifteen seconds? Twenty? She chewed at the knuckle of a forefinger. It must be at least twenty.

Thirty, now. Still no sign of him.

And then, suddenly, there he was. Movement, far below. A vague brown-green swirl at first, quickly resolving into the head and shoulders of a man, rising swiftly through the water. Meriel instinctively took a step back.

Cameron broke surface, threshing wildly. He wasn't swimming: this was a convulsive, reflex series of completely unco-ordinated movements. He looked to Meriel as if he was having a fit.

'Cameron? *Cameron?* Can you hear me? What's wrong?'

His eyes were tightly shut and she could see a ghastly greenish-white froth bubbling from his mouth and nostrils.

'Hold on! I'll get the lifebelt!'

It was on the other side of the deck, next to the little ladder from which he'd climbed down into the water.

Meriel ran across, yanked the ring from its snap-fastenings and turned around, breathing hard.

And remained exactly where she was.

She couldn't see Cameron from here, but dear Christ she could hear him. He'd started making a bizarre honking noise; he sounded like one of Ullswater's geese when they flew south for the winter. Presently it faded to a rasping gurgle and, almost exactly one minute after he'd dived down after his watch, he fell completely silent.

Meriel didn't move. One hand gripped the guard-rail behind her, the other held the lifebelt. She stood motionless while she tried as calmly as she could to count another sixty seconds. Then, very slowly, she crossed back to the other side of the boat, and looked down at the water.

He was completely still. Face down, head haloed by the greenish foam that had boiled and erupted from his lungs.

His legs floated wide apart and his arms and shoulders were hunched forward in an oddly obscene, crab-like pose.

Cameron Bruton was very dead.

His wife calmly considered him a while longer.

Then she leaned out over the railing, and carefully tossed the lifebelt into the water to land beside him.

CHAPTER TWENTY-TWO

Seb had been uneasy ever since his phone conversation with Meriel that morning.

An experienced reporter, he had learned over the years that if something didn't seem quite right, it usually wasn't. One of his favourite movie lines was from Hitchcock's *Psycho*, when private investigator Milton Arbogast tells the killer, Norman Bates: 'See, if something doesn't gel, it isn't aspic ... and this ain't gellin'.'

Cameron's reaction to Meriel's return after a night's unexplained absence wasn't, as Arbogast might have said, 'gellin'.' It was most odd, to say the least. No histrionics, no interrogation of any kind. Just a suggestion that the two of them go out on their boat for a picnic.

Seb didn't like it. It bore all the hallmarks of a manipulative personality, and Cameron Bruton was certainly possessed of one of those. Some of Meriel's stories about him last night had almost defied belief.

So what was the man up to now? Could Meriel be in danger out there on the lake?

On balance, Seb decided not, although he had to struggle hard against the impulse to jump in his Spitfire and race down to Ullswater. There was no point in that, of course. There would be boats of all descriptions out on the water this beautiful Sunday afternoon. He didn't even know what Cameron's was called, let alone looked like.

No, best to stay here by the phone and wait for Meriel's next call.

Seb had prepared himself for a lengthy wait. He'd gone out and bought most of the Sunday papers, and his own picnic of bread, ham and wine. Now he sat in a tatty garden chair on the tiny rear terrace of his rented ground-floor flat in Carlisle's Warwick Road, soaking up the afternoon sunshine in shorts and T-shirt and waiting for the phone in the communal entrance hall behind him to ring. Sometimes the girl who rented the flat above his came downstairs to make a call, and Seb had to resist the urge to go and tell her to keep it brief. What if Meriel was trying to get through?

By seven o'clock the sun was losing its strength and half an hour later it had dipped behind a cluster of horse-chestnut trees that grew in the much larger garden backing on to his.

The great heat remained, but at least the days were beginning to get a little shorter.

Seb went inside. His disquiet was growing. She *must* be home by now. Surely she could have made an excuse to get away for a few minutes and ring him from a call box? Or if not, just use the house phone and talk in simple code to him so Cameron wouldn't suspect anything. Pretend she was talking to her producer, or something. Say she was looking forward to next week's show, and she'd be in tomorrow to talk about it. At least then he'd know she was all right.

When the phone rang at last it was almost nine o'clock and getting dark. Seb reached the receiver halfway through the second ring.

'Meriel?'

There was a faint buzzing on the line before a hesitant voice replied: 'Er ... no. Chris in the newsroom, actually. Is that you, Seb?'

Seb silently cursed himself.

'Yeah ... sorry, Chris, I'm expecting a call from ... from my cousin Muriel in London. What's up? Shouldn't you be home this time on a Sunday? No more bulletins now until the breakfast show, surely?'

'Yup, but it's all hands to the pumps tonight, mate. I was just packing up after the eight o'clock bully when I got a call from our stringer down in Keswick. There's been another of these drownings – this afternoon, on Ullswater. No false alarm this time; the cops have just confirmed it. Merryman wants you to ring him at home right away.'

Seb's bowels turned to liquid, but he managed to keep his voice steady. 'Ullswater? Is there any ID on the victim, Chris?'

'Not a lot, other than it's a bloke, just like the last one there. That retired engineer.'

Seb sagged against the wall in relief. 'Not a woman, then? You're quite sure about that?'

His colleague sounded nettled. 'I just bloody told you – it's a bloke, Seb. As in man – you know, fella, geezer, chap, proud possessor of one X and one Y chromosome. Male of the species, just like you and me. Clear?'

Seb smiled faintly. 'Sorry, Chris, I downed the best part of a bottle of wine sitting in the sun this afternoon. I'm a bit muzzy. Anything else? You know, like age or profession?'

'Nope, nowt else yet. They're not even saying exactly how it played out, other than it was a drowning. But there's a press conference first thing at Glenridding, close to where it happened. That's what Bob wants to talk to you about. I reckon it's gonna be an early night for you tonight, mate.'

'I'm on it.'

Seb felt a little calmer as he went to bed after speaking with Merryman.

Meriel's failure to call him, he decided, was almost certainly explained by this new drowning. The police would have taken witness statements from anyone who'd been out on the water, and there were probably checkpoints on the road that bordered the lake, in case some passing motorist had seen something. Meriel might have been delayed for hours. By the time she got home it would simply have been too late to make a plausible excuse to leave the house again.

Seb set his alarm for four-thirty and snapped out the bedside light. He was going to rendezvous with Jess at the radio car in Glenridding in time to broadcast live into the first bulletin of the day at six. Details of the death would probably still be sketchy and he'd have to pad his report out with background stuff on the earlier drownings, and do much the same on the seven o'clock bulletin, too.

But the police press conference was scheduled for eight o'clock right down by the water's edge and he'd have a lot more to sink his teeth into there. With any luck the cops would produce some witnesses for interviews.

His news editor told him that once again the network was going to take his report live.

'This is your story, mate,' Merryman had finished, wrapping up their conversation. 'I don't want anyone else fronting it. The listeners associate you with it and they trust you to get it right and get it first. The way things are going either you or the station are going to pick up an award for the coverage. Maybe both. Now get some sleep – you've got a busy day ahead of you. I'm hitting the hay myself. We'll talk first thing via the radio car.'

But it was a long time before Seb was able to drift off.

He wasn't thinking about the story.

He was thinking about Meriel.

Partly about what might have transpired between her and Cameron on the boat today.

But mostly, he was thinking about making love to her.

Over and over again.

As Seb was falling asleep, an exhausted Meriel was being courteously shown into the back of the squad car that would chauffeur her home to Cathedral Crag.

The officers who had interviewed her at Keswick police station throughout the late afternoon and into the evening had been gentle and forbearing, but even so she was utterly drained. Perhaps she should have accepted their kindly meant suggestions that she call her solicitor; have a lawyer present to metaphorically hold her hand and help bear the load of their polite but insistent questioning.

But Meriel had instinctively felt that asking for a legal representative to sit with her might convey the wrong message, make her look defensive, or worse, somehow guilty of something.

In any case, her account of what had happened could hardly be more straightforward. She knew that if she stuck to it, refused to embellish or alter it in any way, there was nothing for her to fear. The brutal facts were simple enough.

Cameron had gone for a swim.

Cameron had vanished.

Cameron had reappeared.

Cameron had been in the grip of some sort of seizure.

Cameron had been unable to grasp the lifebelt she had thrown him.

Cameron had stopped moving.

The rest of it – her repeated screams for help (even now, she was still quite hoarse), the eventual response from a passing tourist hire boat, the arrival of the police launch – all were events that others would bear witness to and corroborate.

But as to the drowning itself, that was testimony she and she alone could give. There was no one to contradict or correct her. Certainly not Cameron. He was lying naked on a refrigerated slab in the county mortuary thirty miles away, awaiting the scalpels and clamps and gently sucking drains of a postmortem examination the following day.

Meriel had steadfastly resisted the temptation to extemporise. She kept her answers short and to the point and repetitive. Neither did she make any attempt to feign emotion; there was no need. She was genuinely in shock.

No, she didn't know why her husband had gone beneath the surface of the lake. No, it wasn't something he usually did. No, she had no idea whether it was deliberate or involuntary; she'd been reading the Sunday papers on deck and hadn't been looking at him at that precise moment. She could only say that one second he was there, and the next he wasn't. No, she couldn't estimate precisely how long he was underwater for, but it couldn't have been for more than two minutes at the very most.

No, she'd never learned to swim. She'd always been extremely apprehensive of going into water. That was why she'd thrown her husband the lifebelt rather than make her way over to him with it and help him put it on. She would feel guilty about this for the rest of her life.

Yes, she would be willing to formally identify his body next morning before the postmortem took place.

Yes, she would very much appreciate being driven home now. Her husband's car was still parked where they'd both left it by the lake. Yes, she would be extremely grateful if another officer drove it back to Cathedral Fell. She had the keys here in her bag.

No, she didn't need a doctor and no, there was no one she wanted them to call to come and be with her. She would manage by herself tonight.

Yes, she would be dressed and ready to be driven to Kendal at nine o'clock tomorrow morning.

No, she *really* didn't need a doctor. But they had all been very kind.

She just wanted to go home.

Meriel decided not to mention that she needed to find some papers there that belonged to her husband.

Her late husband.

CHAPTER TWENTY-THREE

She changed her mind about looking for the photocopies even before the car reached Cathedral Crag. There was no great urgency; she was the only person who knew of their existence, after all. There'd be plenty of time to find them later. Anyway, she needed a clear head to think of all the obscure places Cameron might have chosen to secrete them. Right now she was so emotionally expended she could barely remember her own name.

Once the red tail-lights of the departing police Rover saloon had disappeared down the drive, Meriel walked straight into the study and poured herself an enormous Scotch from the decanter on the oak sideboard. She didn't normally drink spirits this late in the day but there was a time for everything and this was a moment for whisky.

She tentatively touched the liquid with the tip of her

tongue, and grimaced. As she'd suspected, the Scotch was lukewarm. When *would* this bloody heatwave break?

She checked herself. Without the heatwave and its consequences, she might have found herself in Cameron's bed tonight, enduring God knows what humiliations.

She went into the kitchen to get ice from their American fridge.

Their American fridge?

Her American fridge.

This house and everything in it belonged to her now.

Meriel thoughtfully made her way back into the study, ice cubes gently clinking from side to side in the heavy crystal tumbler. She sank down in one of the armchairs that looked out across the lake. A quarter-moon was rising above the fells opposite, its faint silver light silently skipping and dancing across Derwent Water's gently rising and falling undulations. It was as if the lake was asleep.

Two mountains separated her from Ullswater, High Seat and then the giant, Helvellyn, which brooded above the lake in which her husband had perished that very afternoon.

It had been a horrible death. Horrible. Meriel took a couple of swallows from her glass and closed her eyes. Then, for the first time since it happened, she forced herself to consider exactly what Cameron must have gone through, emotionally and physically.

Undiluted rage, of course, at the very beginning. Undoubtedly one of Cameron's last emotions on earth had been blind fury with her for tossing his precious watch into the water.

Had he realised she had deliberately thrown it a fraction beyond his reach? Meriel didn't think so. He hadn't had time to reflect on anything as subtle as that. He'd just been desperate to retrieve the thing, perhaps egged on by her *'Quick, Cameron, you can still get it!'* and down he'd gone. Anyway, the question of whether he'd suspected anything was immaterial now, wasn't it? He was lying demi-frozen in some mortician's fridge. Cameron wouldn't be sharing any thoughts with anyone about anything, ever again.

So, what next in her husband's aquatic *danse macabre*? Considering how vigorously she'd seen him kicking downwards, it could only have been two or three seconds before his head and neck and shoulders, and then the rest of him, plunged into the icy water that lay just beneath the freakishly warm mantle above.

The shock must have been overwhelming and, judging by all that ghastly foam she'd seen coming from his mouth and nostrils when he eventually surfaced, Cameron must have immediately and deeply inhaled; a reflex gasp.

Would that have rendered him unconscious? Probably not straight away. The sensation of sucking ice-cold liquid into his lungs must have been excruciating. Cameron had remained underwater and beyond sight for many more seconds. God knows what torments he had suffered during that time.

Perhaps, Meriel thought, such extreme and desperate corners of the human zoo were better kept beyond witness.

She took a deep swallow from the tumbler and threw her head back.

Well, there. She'd done her best to face up to the reality of Cameron's last moments. She hadn't tried to fool herself by minimising his agony. Indeed, she accepted that what she had put him through was probably more dreadful than anything she or anyone else could possibly imagine.

And it *was* she who'd put him through it. She was completely responsible. She'd made it all happen. She'd set a snare and encouraged him to throw the noose around his own neck.

Then she'd calmly stood back and let him die.

But she didn't feel a shred of guilt or remorse about any of it, did she? Not a crumb of compassion. No empathy, no regret. Meriel had to admit it to herself: her conscience was entirely undisturbed.

She suddenly sat up and addressed the shimmering lake opposite.

'Perhaps I'm a psychopath.'

She swirled the thought around her half-empty glass,

considering the question for a few more moments. Then she stood up.

'All right, then. Let's go and see, shall we?'

She crossed the passage that led into the library – it had been a library back in the rector's day and still housed some of his original books – and found her weighty new-edition *English Dictionary and Thesaurus*.

Meriel ran a forefinger down the margin of the page that was helpfully headed '*psycho*'.

'Psychometry, psychomotor,' she muttered. 'Here we are. *Psychopath*.

A person with a personality disorder characterised by a tendency to commit antisocial and sometimes violent acts without feeling guilt.

Meriel was thoughtful. This was interesting. She hadn't been actually *violent*, had she? She'd only chucked his stupid watch into the water. Lots of people in bad relationships did crazy things like that.

And none of what she'd done could be described as a *tendency*, could it? Nothing like it had ever happened before in her life. As for antisocial ... well, society was hardly worse off for a vile, cruel man's passing, was it?

That part of the definition regarding absence of guilt was spot-on, obviously. She was bang to rights there. But only in relation to Cameron's death. She was perfectly capable of experiencing guilt about lots of other things, wasn't she? She had morals. She wasn't some sort of unfeeling, killer robot.

On impulse, she searched the pages until she found the exposition of 'killer'.

Person or animal that kills, habitually.

Habitually? Meriel snorted. Not guilty.

She flipped forward again, this time to 'murder'.

Unlawful premeditated intended killing of one human being by another.

Not guilty again. There was absolutely nothing premeditated about what had happened on the lake this afternoon. As far as intent went, all she'd intended when the boat left the jetty was to ask Cameron for a trial separation.

So ... what exactly *had* taken place between her and Cameron out there on the water? Could it even be defined in a single word?

Perhaps. A suspicion of what that word might be had been slowly forming in the back of Meriel's mind.

She turned the dictionary's pages again. She knew what she was looking for.

There it was; three syllables.

Manslaughter.

The definition beneath perfectly summarised what she'd done that day.

The unlawful killing of one human being by another, without malice aforethought.

She drained off what was left of her whisky in one steady swallow.

'Without malice aforethought.' Meriel spoke the words aloud.

Definitely manslaughter, then.

She reckoned she could live with that.

Especially if no one ever found out.

CHAPTER TWENTY-FOUR

It was a little before quarter to eight when Seb dialled Bob Merryman's personal hotline. The news editor not only had his own extension, but a completely separate landline too, dedicated to his exclusive use. Lake District FM's accountants had grumbled at the expense, but Merryman had insisted on it when he'd been poached to join the station.

'I'm fucked if I'll fight for switchboard space with my reporters during a breaking story,' he said bluntly during discussions over his contract. 'It's part of my package. No line, no deal. Non-negotiable.'

Today, he'd come in especially early to co-ordinate coverage of the latest Lakeland drowning. It was going to be a big story and not just locally. There was a general sense that a tipping point had been reached. Two deaths in Ullswater in a week. Eleven in the Lake District inside two months. There were rumours that a special government inquiry was about to be announced.

The news editor was on his third coffee and his fourth cigarette when his personal phone rang. He didn't rush to answer, giving himself time to take a gulp and then a drag before picking up.

'Merryman.'

'Bob, it's Seb. I'm calling from the Glenridding Hotel. The press conference starts in fifteen minutes.'

'I know. Morning, Seb. Good holding work on the six and seven o'clock headlines; you managed to make some half-decent bricks without straw. But I'm assuming we'll definitely get victim ID and a lot more background during the conference. Network's been nagging me.'

'Yeah, I thought they would. That's why I'm calling you, so you can tell them yes, it's definitely worth their while taking us live. But listen, Bob, that isn't the only reason I phoned. There's something *bloody* funny going on down here.'

Merryman took a quick draw on his cigarette. 'Meaning?'

'I don't know yet – not exactly. But it's something specifically to do with the identity of the guy that drowned yesterday. About ten minutes ago the police press officer buttonholed me. I know him – we were on the same journalism course at college. He said he wanted to do me a favour. As an old mate. Took me aside from the rest of the pack and told me I should be prepared for a twist in the tale.'

'Uh? What sort of twist?'

'He wouldn't elaborate. Said he couldn't pre-empt the Chief Constable's statement at eight.'

The news editor stared at the receiver.

'What the fuck's he talking about?'

'That's exactly what I was going to ask you,' Seb replied. 'Have you heard anything?'

'Of course I haven't! I would have tipped you off straight away if I had.'

'So what did he mean?'

Merryman rubbed his chin, considering.

'I've no idea,' he said at last. 'Anything else?'

'Yeah, actually. The cops have set up a little trestle table for us to put our mics on; already three or four of them are sitting behind it ready for the press conference. And they all keep shooting me these weird looks.'

The news editor finished his cigarette and dropped the stub into his half-empty cup of coffee.

'Well, forewarned is forearmed,' he said at last. 'I'd better tip off the network. Meanwhile if I hear anything between now and eight o'clock I'll tell Jess over the radio car link so he can pass it to you in your earphones. You're fully rigged for outside broadcast, right? The network might want to do a live two-way with you right off the back of your piece.'

'Yup. Locked and loaded. Well ... this'll be an

interesting one. I wish I knew what was coming. I'll do my best, Bob.'

'You'll do great. I'll talk to you straight after transmission. Hey . . . I wonder exactly what we'll be saying to each other about this then, eh?'

'Christ knows. But I'm starting to get the damnedest feeling.'

'. . . *take you now to the shores of Ullswater in the Lake District, and our reporter Seb Richmond. Seb?*'

Seb was extremely tense. This was only his third live network broadcast, and it was going to be the trickiest by far.

The first, at the start of this month, had been mostly pre-recorded, consisting largely of edited sound bites from the press conference that Jess had helped him lash together. All he'd really had to do was link from one clip to the next with short pieces of scripted commentary.

The second had been even simpler: a straightforward ad-libbed conversation with the programme host.

But this was turning into a sodding minefield. The chief constable, who was chairing the press call, had only just sat down and had yet to begin speaking. Seb would have to 'fill' until he did, and then judge when to come in quietly with his own commentary, all the while trying to keep one ear open to what the policeman was continuing to say in case he needed to cut straight back to it.

Then there was the press officer's warning of a 'twist in the tale'. Whatever that was, he'd have to deal with it on the hoof.

Yup. A sodding minefield.

Seb licked his lips and settled himself into the plastic chair he had been allocated in the front row of the outdoor press call. The media had been assembled on a sun-browned patch of grass that stretched straight down to the lake itself, as if the lawn was reaching out to it, desperate to drink. Parched mountain tops encircled them and even this early in the day, the sun was already hot.

Here goes nothing, Seb thought grimly as he heard his simultaneous cue from Carlisle and London.

'Thank you. You find me on the sunlit banks of one of the most beautiful stretches of water in Lakeland, as police are poised to reveal the identity of the latest victim in this summer's unprecedented litany of drownings. The question many here are asking this morning is . . .'

Meriel felt strangely light-headed as she stepped from the shower.

She had managed to get to sleep sometime after one, but she had snapped awake again less than two hours later, and from then until dawn she had been unable to stop herself endlessly replaying events of the previous day.

She scarcely thought about Seb. Their night together, their plans, seemed utterly eclipsed and irrelevant now, even surreal. She had enough insight to know that was probably the consequence of shock, but there was nothing she could do about it. Her mind was flooded with insistent, crystal-clear images from yesterday.

A glittering timepiece twisting and spinning lazily through space.

Sparkling droplets fanning up and out as the Rolex splashed into the water and vanished.

Kicking white feet fading from view.

Froth and foam, thrashing limbs, terrible, animal cries.

The stillness of death.

Meriel shook water from her hair as she reached for a towel. She looked up at the brass ship's clock, jauntily mounted above the lintel of the bathroom door. Eight o'clock. The police would be here in an hour to take her to the mortuary.

She moved back into the bedroom and switched on her bedside radio. It was her habit to listen to the breakfast show's main news as she dressed.

Seb's voice filled the room.

CHAPTER TWENTY-FIVE

Seb wasn't sure how much longer he could fill before he started to repeat himself. Others must have been having the same thought because he heard Jess's voice suddenly crackle in his earphones.

'Network says if the conference doesn't start in thirty seconds, hand back to studio.'

Unwittingly, Seb nodded as he continued to talk into his lip mic. He felt a little embarrassed by lip mics; they were more usually associated with sheepskin-jacketed football commentators.

'*So there it is. A grim record, in this summer of broken records. Eleven drownings, averaging almost two a week. Perhaps an absolute ban on going into the water is indeed now on the cards here in Lakeland – just a moment. I think we're about to begin. Yes, the Chief Constable, Tom Harris, is ready to make his statement.*'

There was a small portable mixing desk in front of Seb. He quickly closed the fader controlling his own mic and opened the one connected to the chief constable's. The policeman had already begun speaking.

'... *to you all for coming this morning. Let me immediately confirm the identity of the latest drowning victim here in the lakes. Yesterday, the body of Mr Cameron Bruton was recovered from Ullswater, at a point approximately a mile to the north of where we are currently ...*'

Seb jolted back in his seat as if he'd been shot. His eyes widened and his mouth fell open. He almost dropped the microphone. Meriel's husband! *Holy Christ!* The picnic on the boat. Her plan to tell him she wanted a separation. What in the name of God had happened out there yesterday?

He had to force himself to focus on what the policeman was saying now.

'... *will of course be known to many as one of the UK's leading entrepreneurs. He was also a prominent local figure, living as he did above the neighbouring lake of Derwent Water.*

'*The exact circumstances of Mr Bruton's death are still under investigation but at this point all the indications suggest accidental drowning. He and his wife, the broadcaster Meriel Kidd, were on board their motor launch – a regular Sunday outing for the couple, I understand – and had hove-to so Mr Bruton could enjoy a swim around the vessel. Again, this was his custom. His wife states that her husband suddenly vanished beneath the surface of the lake and when he reappeared he was in a state of great distress. She attempted to throw him a lifebelt but he was unable to respond and, shortly after, he ceased breathing. A passing hire boat offered assistance, but the occupants were unable to revive Mr Bruton. Neither were the officers who arrived by police launch shortly afterwards.*

'Mr Bruton was declared dead by a local GP, who happened to be sailing nearby, at 3.17 p.m. yesterday, Sunday. A postmortem will be performed later today in Kendal after formal identification by his widow.

'That concludes my statement, ladies and gentlemen. I shall now be happy to take questions.'

Seb's mind was reeling. He felt as though he had been struck violently in the face, but his was the first hand in the air. The chief constable nodded towards him. *'Yes, there on the front row.'*

Seb stood up unsteadily. *'Seb Richmond, Lake District FM. Mr Harris, can you tell us—'*

Jess's calm voice immediately came through his earphones. *'Open your fader, Seb. We can't hear you.'*

Shit. He slid the control downwards and began again.

'I'm sorry about that ... Seb Richmond, Lake District FM. Mr Harris, can you tell us any more

about Miss Kidd? As you may know, she's a regular broadcaster on the radio network that I represent. This news will come as a considerable shock to her listeners, and indeed her colleagues . . . as it has to me. Did she enter the water herself during the incident? Is she . . .' he hesitated. *'Is she all right?'*

The policeman nodded, although he looked curiously at his questioner.

'Mrs Bruton was obviously deeply traumatised by witnessing her husband's death, but she has demonstrated remarkable composure in the hours since. She was able to make a detailed statement to my officers before returning home last night.' He glanced at his watch. *'She is due in Kendal in a little over an hour to make, as I say, formal identification.*

'Concerning the sad events of yesterday, I am advised that Mrs Bruton did not at any stage enter the water. As I understand it, she is unable to swim. She did manage to throw one of the boat's lifebelts to her husband, as I believe I have said, but unfortunately he was unable to avail himself of it.'

Seb would have asked another question but other hands were waving in the air. The chief constable pointed to his right. *'Yes, Carlisle Evening News. Morning, Harry.'*

'Morning, sir. As you know there has been extensive publicity about the risks of swimming in the lakes during this unprecedented heatwave, and in particular

the specific danger of going beneath the surface. Is there any suggestion as to why Mr Bruton should have done just that – gone under, that is – and if it contributed to his death? And – I'm sorry, just one more, please – shouldn't the authorities now impose a complete ban on swimming while these uniquely treacherous conditions persist?'

The policeman shook his head.

'It's a "no" to the first part of your question, Harry. We have absolutely no evidence at all to suggest why Mr Bruton should have swum below the surface of the lake. Indeed we don't even know if it was a conscious action or an involuntary one. Mrs Bruton has only been able to tell us that one moment her husband appeared to be swimming perfectly normally, and the next he had disappeared from view.

'As to the precise cause or causes of death, we may know more after today's postmortem. Meanwhile a decision on banning all swimming in the national park is under continuous review. Next question, please.'

The following query was procedural, concerned with the postmortem, and Seb knew this was the moment he should fade the chief constable down and deliver some commentary of his own. But he was entirely incapable of it. He couldn't think of a single thing to say. All he could think about was Meriel, what she must have gone through yesterday and what she was about to go through today in the morgue.

Jess's voice again in his earphones.

'Come on, Seb, give us some bloody colour. The network's going ape.'

With a tremendous effort he closed the policeman's mic and boosted his own. For a moment he genuinely thought he wouldn't be able to speak, but, haltingly at first, words began to flow.

'So ... ah ... for those of you who are just joining us, the, ah, shock news here on Ullswater is that yesterday's drowning victim has just been revealed as, ah, one of this country's most successful businessmen, Cameron Bruton. His wife, Meriel Kidd, well known to many in her role as radio and newspaper agony aunt, was with him. But during what have just been described as profoundly traumatic scenes, it seems she was unable to save her husband.'

He came to a complete full stop again. But before it became obvious to anyone that he had dried, Seb was relieved to hear the confident voice of the programme host fill his earphones.

'So this is very much a breaking story and one that's turning out to be something of a high-profile tragedy, isn't it, Seb? Perhaps even a celebrity one. As you say, Cameron Bruton was no stranger to the business columns of the newspapers and his glamorous wife has a fast-growing public profile, with all the attendant media interest. Is Meriel Kidd expected to make some kind of public statement to her fans later today?'

Seb thought it a prurient question and he felt his anger quicken.

'*I simply don't know the answer to that, Graham, I'm afraid. I should imagine her first priority will be to get the extremely stressful business of formal identification over with. I very much doubt she sees this in the terms you've just described – as some sort of celebrity-driven story. She's just lost a husband, and in deeply shocking circumstances.*'

Seb swallowed, and couldn't help adding: '*This is a personal tragedy, Graham, not a showbiz sensation.*'

He could immediately tell by the presenter's acid response that he'd piqued him.

'*Yes, well, of course we must keep in mind that Miss Kidd is a colleague of yours. This must be quite a difficult story for you to cover, on a personal level.*'

Seb gathered himself to reply but before he could speak Jess's voice murmured in his ears.

'Careful.'

Seb slowly exhaled and managed to bring his emotions back under control.

'*Yes,*' he replied, in a dangerously quiet tone. '*I suppose it is.*'

Satisfied that he'd re-established dominance, the host moved swiftly to wrap the item.

'*Seb Richmond, reporting for us from the shores of Ullswater in the Lake District, thank you.*'

Jess cut the link before Seb could say anything else.

In the radio car five minutes later, the engineer poured them both coffee from a steaming Thermos.

'You almost lost it there, matey,' he said, handing Seb his mug. 'I thought your career might be over before it'd begun.'

Seb took the drink in hands that were slightly shaking.

'Yeah, well ... with a shallow bastard like that ... anyway, thanks for giving me a jog, Jess. Appreciated. Although I reckon the listeners would have quite enjoyed hearing me losing it and calling that little git a tosser.'

Jess sipped his own coffee. 'Never mind, Sebastian. They heard you *think* it.'

CHAPTER TWENTY-SIX

She heard the entire broadcast as she sat naked and motionless on the end of her bed.

It was one of the most surreal experiences of her life. Seb Richmond – her lover, the man who just over twenty-four hours earlier she had decided she was going to leave Cameron for – was asking questions about her at a national police press conference. A press conference about her dead husband. The whole country was listening.

Meriel wondered if others had noticed the concern in his voice when he asked the chief constable: 'Is she all right?' She thought Seb's anxiety was palpable.

She had gone cold when another reporter began asking questions as to exactly why Cameron had dipped beneath the surface of the lake, but she forced herself to remain calm. She must always be absolutely resolute about this: *she simply didn't know*. He was there, and then he wasn't there. That was all she could say. She must never, ever embellish or deviate one degree from her account.

Now, an hour later, Meriel had no idea that as the police car chauffeured her through Ambleside on their way from Cathedral Crag to Kendal, Seb was some five miles in front of her, negotiating Windermere's holiday traffic. He'd be in the county town at least fifteen minutes before her, parked up outside the pathology lab that doubled as a mortuary.

As Seb left the bustling lakeside town behind him, he reflected that this was probably the most unsettling day of his life, and certainly the most challenging of his career. He was still in mild shock after learning that Cameron Bruton was the drowned man. Now he'd been sent to interview his widow. The last time he'd seen her they'd been in bed together.

It was all taking quite a lot of adjustment.

Seb was certain of his feelings for Meriel, and, as far as he could tell, she felt the same about him.

But now her husband was dead.

He tried to think. When Meriel had secretly phoned him yesterday morning from Cathedral Crag she'd sounded calm and determined. Optimistic, even, that Cameron might be receptive to the suggestion of a trial separation. So what on earth had happened just a few hours later out on the water? Had there been some sort of argument? A struggle, even?

Seb hadn't bought Meriel's description of a newly contrite and conciliatory Cameron. He'd never met the bastard but from everything she'd told him about the man, he sounded about as capable of remorse as a rattlesnake.

Bruton had, patently, been up to something. But what? And why, whatever it was, had it ended in his drowning? Could it really have been a random accident, as the police were obviously inclined to think?

He sucked his teeth as he took a left turn towards Kendal.

Accident, my Aunt Fanny. Seb didn't believe in coincidences. If Cameron Bruton's death really was down to misadventure, on the very afternoon his wife was planning on leaving him, then everything Seb knew about the way the world worked was wrong.

Which brought him back to precisely where he'd started.

What the *fuck* had gone on out there on the lake?

His news editor had been cool with him earlier and theirs had quickly deteriorated into an uncharacteristically ill-tempered exchange.

'Not exactly your finest hour, Richmond,' Merryman observed crisply down the phone. 'You were doing OK until the Brutons entered the picture, and then you went to bloody pieces. The network's not impressed and, frankly, neither am I.'

Seb never took his beatings lying down.

'Then you can all piss off, actually,' he'd snapped back. 'It was a real shock when I heard who'd drowned. Of course I was thrown off balance. Anyone would've been. I—'

'Why? If Meriel Kidd was the latest floating corpse I'd understand. A colleague, the girl you've got the hots for, all of that. Fine. But her husband? You didn't even know him. Face it – it was a *bloody* good story, it fell plumb into your lap and you dropped the ball.'

'Crap. I was first in with a question, wasn't I?'

Merryman snorted. 'Yeah, and you sounded like a fucking teenage girl with a crush. "Ooh, ooh, is she all right?" That won't win any Pulitzer Prizes. Graham Elms, the *extremely* capable news anchor you were so snotty to, tried to help you get back on track with his question about the whole celebrity angle and you threw it right back in his face.'

'And I was right to! He was being a—'

'*He was being a good journalist!* Of *course* this is a celebrity story! You've got a beautiful, famous brunette and her millionaire husband – make that her *dead* millionaire husband. Where's your fucking news sense, Seb? Did you leave it by the river at Peter Cox's party on Saturday? Oh, and on that point, what was going on there between you and Meriel? When I left, the two of you were completely wrapped up in your own little world. Everything looked very cosy to me, down there by the water.'

Seb had been expecting this and had his answer ready.

'Nothing was going on, other than a little harmless flirting. Anyway, we left soon after you did. Separately, as a matter of fact.'

Merryman snorted again. 'That old trick. Well, it's none of my business. But my advice to you is to be extremely careful over the next few days and weeks. The press are going to cast Meriel Kidd as the tragic, ravishing widow. Just make sure they don't cast you as the ravisher. That won't play well for either of you, trust me.'

Seb was silent. Merryman let the warning hang in the air for a few moments before he continued.

'Right. I make it just gone eight-thirty. I'm going to give you a chance to get back on the horse you so spectacularly fell from half an hour ago – not that the network will thank me, so don't bloody well let me down again. Get yourself from Glenridding to Kendal – take the Kirkstone Pass, they've sorted all that melted tar out now – and find the mortuary. Meriel should arrive there at around ten. See if you can persuade her to say a few words on tape.'

Seb was appalled.

'*What?* You have to be joking! She's going there to

identify her husband's dead body, Bob! Jesus, I can't doorstep the woman at a time like that!'

Merryman sighed.

'You'll be doing her a favour, you idiot. The world and his wife are going to be there with microphones and flashing cameras and flapping notebooks. It'll be a total scrum. So if she talks to anyone, it's going to be you. Which means you have the opportunity to protect her – get her away from the baying rabble and give her a bit of privacy.

'Explain to her that if she says something on the record to you, we can tell the rest of the media it's a shut-out; an exclusive. But we'll *also* tell them that they can have it half an hour before we broadcast it. On condition, of course, that they leave her alone.

'Come on, Seb, you know this makes sense. You'll be helping her.'

CHAPTER TWENTY-SEVEN

Seb knew that most postmortems were usually carried out by a consultant pathologist in the local hospital, so when he got to Kendal he followed the signs to the Westmorland General. It was down towards the south of the old market town, across the River Kent.

Seb knew he'd made the right call as he approached the building; he could see a gaggle of men and one or two women hanging around the entrance.

Reporters. You could spot them a mile off.

He parked his Triumph around a corner and walked back to the loitering press pack.

'Morning, all. She here yet?'

They looked at him without interest. Eventually someone replied.

'No. Who are you?' It was one of the women, a red-head in a tank-top and Bowie-style stack heels.

'Seb Richmond. Lake District FM.' He patted the portable tape recorder hanging from his shoulder.

There was a faint titter and the redhead smirked at him.

'Well, well, how about that? We were just talking about you, Sebby. You were the big sulk on the breakfast show this morning, weren't you? Mr "Oh, please, I don't do tacky celebrity stories". So why are you here now, Sebby, slumming it with the likes of us?'

Another titter, louder this time.

Seb smiled at them.

'I'm not. As in, slumming it. I'm here for an exclusive. So be nice, and I might just toss you a bone.'

Without waiting for their reaction he pushed past them and through the swing doors that opened into the hospital reception area.

Once inside and hidden from their hostile stares, his shoulders sagged.

What the hell was he going to do now?

'Can I help you, sir? If you're press, I'm afraid you'll have to wait outside.'

Seb turned around. One of two women sitting behind the hospital's reception desk was addressing him. This one was middle-aged and tightly permed and she was staring with undisguised suspicion.

Seb thought on his feet.

'I'm not exactly press, no.' He fished inside his wallet for his radio station identity card and showed it to her.

'My name's Seb Richmond, Lake District FM. I've been sent down here to personally assist my colleague, Meriel Kidd. She'll be here shortly to identify the body of her late husband, Cameron Bruton. Mr Bruton drowned yester—'

The woman nodded, her expression beginning to soften a little. 'Yes, we're expecting her. I heard you on the wireless this morning, Mr Richmond. I thought you sounded rather upset, if you don't mind me saying so.'

'Well ... it came as something of a shock. None of us at the station had any idea until that moment. That's why they've sent me straight on here from the news conference, to see if there's anything we can do to help.'

Yeah, to help ourselves to a scoop, he thought cynically to himself. Although, if he was honest, the prospect of seeing Meriel again under any circumstances was lifting his heart.

The receptionist was smiling at him. 'Of course, I quite understand. Now, let me see. My colleague here will be escorting your friend and the police to the ... well, the room where the identification will take place. Obviously that comes first. Then I can bring her to you. Come this way, please. I'm sure you'll both appreciate some privacy.'

A few moments later Seb found himself in what he supposed was a consulting room. It was furnished with a plain wooden table, chairs placed on either side and a small green sofa in the corner.

He sat down to wait.

Outside, Meriel stepped from the police car to a cacophony of shouts and a blizzard of flashing cameras.

'Miss Kidd! Mrs Bruton! Can you tell us anything about what happened yesterday? How are you feeling now? Will you be making some kind of statement? Miss Kidd!'

One of the two policemen with her took her by the elbow and guided her firmly through the throng while his colleague spoke above the clamour.

'Come on now, boys, let us through! Miss Kidd has nothing to say at the moment. She has some very difficult business to get through here, you all know that. Come on now. That'll do. Let the lady pass.'

Reluctantly the scrum parted and Meriel and her minders pushed their way through the hospital doors and into the hall behind.

'Sorry about that, Mrs Bruton,' the officer said to her. 'We'll see if we can find a back way out of here so you don't have to go through that again. Must be very distressing for you at a time like this.'

Meriel looked gratefully at him. 'Thank you, I would appreciate that. They're just doing their job, I suppose.'

'Hmm. Not much of a job if you ask me. Bloody

vultures . . . I *do* beg your pardon, ma'am – forgive my language.'

'Not at all.' Meriel looked around her. 'Where do we go now?'

The receptionist who had spoken to Seb joined them.

'Mrs Bruton, I'm very sorry for your loss. We all are. A terrible business. We'll make this as easy as possible for you.' She beckoned her younger colleague over.

'This is Bridget. She's going to take you to where your husband is. Afterwards, you can have a nice cup of tea with your colleague. I've put him in a private room so you can both have some privacy.'

Meriel looked blankly at the woman.

'My colleague? I'm sorry, I don't know what you mean.'

The receptionist smiled kindly at her. 'He told us that your radio station sent him down here to see if there's anything they can do for you at this time.'

Meriel nodded her understanding. 'Ah, I see. That's very thoughtful of them. Did this person give you his name?'

'Oh yes. Richmond. Seb Richmond. I assume you know him?'

Cameron looked a damn sight better this morning than the last time she'd seen him, Meriel thought to herself.

An attendant had gently folded back the white cotton sheet covering her late husband's face. It was pale – 'deathly pale' she found herself thinking – but serene. The expression of agony that had been imprinted on it in death yesterday was gone now, thankfully. As was the revolting green foam that had covered his mouth, chin and throat.

Someone had combed his hair, not in the side parting that he wore in life, but straight back from the brow. She had to resist the temptation to reach into her handbag for a brush and do it properly. Perhaps she owed Cameron at least that.

'Well, Mrs Bruton?' The policeman's voice behind her was soft, almost tender.

She nodded.

'Yes. That's my husband. Or it was. Cameron Bruton.'

'Thank you, madam. Would you like a few minutes alone with him?'

Meriel couldn't think of anything she'd like less.

'No, thank you, that won't be necessary.' She stepped towards the body and stretched out her hand so that her fingertips lightly touched the forehead.

It felt very, very cold.

Meriel cleared her throat.

'Goodbye, Cameron.'

She withdrew her hand, fighting against the impulse to wipe her fingers on the sleeve of her blouse.

She turned to the officer.

'I'd like to leave now, please.'

She couldn't wait to see Seb.

He'd just finished checking his recording equipment when the door opened and there she was, a uniformed policeman at her back.

'Hello, Meriel.'

'Hello, Seb.'

She turned to the officer. 'I'll be fine now. I'll see you in reception in a few minutes.'

The man nodded and closed the door behind Meriel as she entered the room.

A moment later Seb had taken her in his arms. She clung to him, burying her head between his neck and shoulder. They stood like that for a long time.

At last he spoke.

'Jesus Christ, Meriel . . . what an incredibly *horrible* thing to have happened. Are you all right? Sorry, what a stupid question . . . What I mean is—'

She stopped his lips with her fingers, the same fingers she had placed on Cameron's brow. Seb's mouth felt extraordinarily warm by comparison, and his breath moistened her fingertips.

'I'm fine, Seb. Pretty much still in shock, but basically I'm fine, honestly. I'm not going to pretend to be the grieving widow, certainly not with you. You know how I felt about Cameron. I hated him. I still do. The fact that he's dead doesn't change that one bit.'

Seb took her by the hand.

'Come and sit down over here. Look, they've brought us some tea. Would you like some?'

'I'd kill for it.' Perhaps I already have, Meriel reflected.

How much was she going to tell him? She needed time to think.

When he'd finished pouring the tea, Seb put his hand on her knee.

'What happened? Can you talk about it?'

Meriel came to a decision. She simply *must* buy herself some time.

'Well ... a little. I don't think I'm ready to go through it all again just yet. The police went over and over and over it with me yesterday. I realise they had to, obviously, but I'm drained. You'll need to give me a few days to recover my balance.'

He reached for her hand and brought it up to his lips, kissing her fingers one by one.

'Of course, of course ... Look, I know something of what you went through. I was at the police press conference this morning. I—'

'I know. I was listening. Just the sound of your voice brought me some comfort, some sanity. But you sounded very shocked. Did you honestly have no idea who it was who had drowned?'

'No. When they said your husband's name I almost fell off my chair. It never crossed my mind it would be him.'

Seb paused. 'Don't answer this if you don't want to, Meriel, but ... did what happened yesterday have anything at all to do with ... well, *us*? You know ... your decision to leave him?'

Meriel was beginning to realise that Seb had an uncanny knack of cutting straight to the heart of things.

She hesitated, before saying: 'I *will* tell you everything about what happened yesterday, I promise, although, as I say, I need some time. But yes, I did tell Cameron that I was going to leave him. I said I wanted to leave that very evening.'

'What did he say?'

She chose her words with care. 'Well ... he wasn't happy about it. He ... he told me he'd make any divorce extremely difficult, and very public. Threatened me, I suppose. Then he went for his swim. He told me to think it over. I told him to go to hell. Something of a prophecy, you might say.'

Seb stared at her. 'Did you tell the police any of this? That you'd had a row?'

She shook her head. 'No.'

She drank some of her tea.

'It was the most terrible thing I've ever seen, Seb. So sudden, too. One second he was paddling around the boat, giving me nasty little sarcastic waves, the next he'd just vanished. I have no idea why. He never normally went below the surface; he didn't like getting water in his ears, he said.

'And then suddenly he was back again, all ... all ... oh God, Seb, it was dreadful. I threw him a lifebelt but he was ... he was ...'

Seb moved closer to her on the sofa and gently cupped her face in his hands.

'Shhh, now. Don't say any more. You've been through enough. Including just now, for God's sake, here at the hospital.'

Meriel shook her head. 'That was all right, actually. I was quite surprised. I've never seen a dead body before. I was expecting it to be ghastly, but it felt almost ... *normal*. But it's strange, even though I saw him die, right there in front of me, I can't quite believe he's gone. All morning while I was getting ready at the house I kept wondering if it was all some kind of weird dream, and that he would suddenly come back in through the front door. Seeing him lying there just now was a bit like waking up to reality. I'm actually glad I agreed to come and identify the body. It feels like a full stop.'

Suddenly she stared at him.

'Talking of reality ... why are you *really* here, Seb? *Did* the station send you, to offer me support, as that woman said?'

He pushed his hair back from his forehead with both hands before answering her.

'Up to a point. Which is another way of saying "not exactly". It's a bit more self-serving than that, I'm afraid.'

Seb told her about his conversation with Bob Merryman.

When he had finished, Meriel calmly drank what was left of her tea.

'That's the business you're in, I suppose,' she said at last, putting the cup down. 'At least it means you could be here and we could see each other. Don't feel guilty about it. But what do you think I should do?'

'What, in terms of making some sort of statement for broadcast?'

'Yes. I'll do whatever you think is best.'

Seb nodded. 'In that case, I'll be straight with you. Make a statement. The office can transcribe it and release it to the press – on the understanding that you're left strictly alone from then on. No door-stepping you at Cathedral Crag, nothing like that. We'll broadcast an edited version so that the one we give the papers has extra exclusive material to keep them quiet. It should get them off your back, for now at least.'

He touched her cheek. 'I'm sorry. It's shabby stuff, Meriel, I know, but I'm afraid it's just the way these things work.'

To his surprise, she kissed him.

'Thank you. For being straight with me. Anyway, if I have to say something I'd rather it was to you than anyone else.'

He sighed. 'Yeah, bloody Bob bloody Merryman said as much, damn him. It makes me feel so cynical, though, Meriel. All I want to do is scoop you up and take care of you.'

She smiled at him. 'There's time enough for that ... although we'll have to be careful for a while, won't we?'

He nodded. 'We will. Bob had something to say about that, too.'

She looked startled.

'What? But he can't possibly know that we—'

Seb interrupted her. 'Don't worry; he doesn't *know* anything. No one does. But Bob's nobody's fool. He clocked us getting to know each other at River House on Saturday. I told him nothing happened and that we left separately, but he just said something about "that old trick" and warned me off. Said if the press finds out we'll both be sorry. I'm afraid he has a point.'

'You're not saying we can't see each other! I couldn't bear that!'

'Of course not. It's simply as you said – we'll have to be careful, at least for the time being. We'll work something out, I promise.'

He gathered her into his arms again, and kissed her comprehensively.

'I'm yours forever, beautiful Meriel. Never doubt it.'

Meriel's statement went down well generally, with both press and public. It was brief and dignified. She did not go into detail about what had happened on the lake, but spoke of her shock and her difficulty in coming to terms with her husband's sudden death.

At Seb's suggestion she raised the question of an outright swimming ban in the Lake District until the heatwave ended, pointing out that such a measure would have probably saved Cameron's life.

She paid tribute to her husband's career and business success, his dynamism and his dedication to their eleven-year marriage.

But she couldn't bring herself to say that she loved him.

CHAPTER TWENTY-EIGHT

Muriel and Seb had managed to see each other several times since the drowning. Sometimes she would come to his flat in Warwick Road, always after dark but wearing enormous Sophia Loren-style sunglasses all the same, which she jammed onto her nose as soon as she'd parked her Mercedes in a nearby side-street.

They usually watched late-night television together, cuddled up on the sofa after Seb had cooked them supper in his little kitchen, before going to bed. Their lovemaking, they both agreed (in a kind of astonished mutual gratitude), just got better and better.

If he was due on the breakfast show production team, Meriel would leave the flat with him in the late-August pre-dawn, and drive straight back to her house above Derwent Water.

On the evenings Seb was on the late shift, putting the following morning's programme together, he usually finished soon after midnight. His car would be pulling into the drive of Cathedral Crag before one in the morning.

Neither of them felt any guilt about sleeping together at Warwick Road, but both experienced a certain awkwardness at first about sharing a bed in Cathedral Crag. Especially Seb.

'I know this is going to sound weird, but somehow I feel as if I'm being disrespectful,' he told her after the first time they had made love in her bedroom. 'I know you never slept with Cameron in here but we *are* under his roof, aren't we? And his funeral doesn't even take place until next week. I feel like . . . well, I feel like he's *watching* us, almost, here in his house. It's spooky.'

'I know what you mean,' Meriel told him. 'It's almost as if his spirit is still here, isn't it? I feel it too. I've heard people say that when someone dies, it takes a while for their presence to fade from the fabric of the place they once lived in. But I'm damned if I'll feel guilty because, well look, Seb, we *have* to see each other, don't we? And I can't keep coming to Warwick Road, it's too risky. We're lucky no one in the flats above yours has spotted me before now, arriving or leaving.

'It's much more private here – Cathedral Crag is completely secluded and I'm the only one in the house. But listen; I'll make you a promise. As *soon* as the funeral's over and the will's been sorted out, I'll put this place on the market. So this is only for the time being. But yes, you're right – Cameron was *never* in here.'

Apart from when he was searching through my bloody things, she thought to herself.

Her own searches – for the photocopies of her diary – had proved fruitless. Meriel was certain she'd gone through every drawer and cupboard in the place. She'd looked under table-tops and chairs, indeed any surface that might have something craftily taped to its underside. She had shaken open book after book and looked inside every vase and pot in the place, but she had drawn a comprehensive blank.

There were two safes in the house, one in the master bedroom where Cameron had, of late, slept alone, and the other in a small attic room. Both were hidden behind sliding wooden panels and both were opened by stout steel keys. Meriel knew where they were kept; inside an innocent, dusty china vase that stood on a little table in one of the smaller spare bedrooms.

But the safes didn't contain anything beyond the obvious – some UK currency, French francs and US dollars; hers and Cameron's passports, a few documents relating to investments, and a copy of the joint will they had drawn up early on in their marriage. The original was now with lawyers and they had told

Meriel that she would be granted probate shortly. She stood to inherit everything.

She was surprised that Cameron had made no attempts to control her from beyond the grave, in the form of a will that bristled with restrictive codicils and conditions. Perhaps he would have eventually got around to that, in time – when he was older, or if he had become terminally ill. But he hadn't expected to die any time soon. The will was unaltered.

The day of the funeral arrived and Meriel felt nothing but an enormous sense of relief. She just wanted the thing over and done with.

She'd deliberately kept it a low-key affair. Both Cameron's parents were dead and he had no siblings, so the only mourners had been Meriel herself and a handful of her husband's business associates. After the briefest possible ceremony at the county crematorium, Cameron had been consigned to the flames. A few press photographers had hung around the crematorium gates, but all the cars had swept past them at speed and Meriel made sure her own limousine had blacked-out windows. None of the pictures had made any of the morning papers.

Much later that same day, Meriel slipped into Seb's flat. She had her own key now and she let herself in.

After they wordlessly embraced, she kicked her shoes off and sank down with him on the sofa, gratefully sipping the enormous brandy he handed to her.

'Christ, I need this. What a day.'

'How did it go?'

She closed her eyes. 'You know, I used to think I'd married Ebenezer Scrooge. But now I reckon he was more like Jacob Marley.'

'What do you mean?'

'Well ... there was no one today to mourn Cameron, just as Dickens wrote that there was no one to mourn Marley. Oh, a few of Cameron's commercial contacts showed up but I'm sure they were only there to do a bit of business ... again, exactly as Scrooge did at Marley's funeral.

'I, of course, the unloved and unloving wife, was there to go through the motions ... but that was it. Honestly, Seb, it was so *sad*. What a horrible way for a person to end up – utterly alone. Spiritually, I mean. Not a soul in the world who gives a damn about you. I almost felt sorry for him. In fact, I'd rather not talk about it any more, if you don't mind. It's too depressing.'

Next morning Meriel made another exhaustive search of Cathedral Crag for the hidden photocopies. Again, she drew a blank. She knew they had to be somewhere in the house, but she'd completely run out of ideas. She could only hope inspiration would strike her at some point. If she ended up selling Cathedral Crag before finding them, she'd simply have to trust that they would remain hidden indefinitely. Anyway, there was nothing more that she could do, and she told herself she had more pressing concerns.

Such as the inquest.

Dr Timothy Young arrived in his little office behind the courtroom before nine that morning; earlier than usual for him on the day of an inquest. He didn't want any surprises unfolding in front of a massed media today. Not in his courtroom; not if he could help it.

He wanted to go over the case notes one more time before opening the hearing into Cameron Bruton's sudden death. This inquest was going to be crammed with newspaper, radio and television reporters. The previous evening John, his clerk, had installed a temporary row of plastic chairs in front of the venerable polished oak press bench.

Now the coroner carefully sifted through the various witness statements, until he came to the wife's account of what had happened on the day of the drowning.

He carefully read through the neatly typed paragraphs. This must be the third or fourth time he'd done so, he reflected. So what *was* it? What was niggling him, nagging at the edges of his consciousness like a restless question mark?

He shook his head. However hard he tried, he just couldn't put his finger on it. The woman's statement seemed clear and logical enough. There were no gaps or contradictions that he could see.

And yet ... and yet ... a lifetime's experience in medicine and then the law was whispering to him, telling him something was out of joint. But what?

The coroner sighed and pushed the documents away. Perhaps whatever it was that troubled him would somehow crystallise later, when the widow – he noticed she had signed her witness statement in her maiden name of Kidd, and dammit, *that* was somehow odd, too – presented her evidence from the witness box.

Meanwhile, if he was honest with himself, he had to admit that there was another itch he wanted to scratch and it was nothing whatsoever to do with the facts of this case. He had a thoroughly unprofessional impulse to simply set eyes on this woman. By all accounts she was a beauty.

His thoughts were interrupted by the sound of his clerk tapping on the door.

'Come in.'

John Armstrong entered carrying a small tray with two mugs of steaming coffee and a little silver jug of hot milk.

'Just time for a bevvy, sir, before we start. You said you wanted to open proceedings at nine-thirty sharp.'

The coroner nodded. 'Yes, I know that's a bit ahead of our normal start time but I'd like to wrap this case up by close of play today, John. I think there's a risk of it turning into something of a media circus and I'd really rather it didn't carry over into another day, in this case Tuesday – it's the bank holiday weekend tomorrow let's not forget.'

His clerk gave a short laugh. 'You're right about it being a circus, sir. It's packed to the rafters already. Most of Fleet Street's finest are here, squabbling over who sits where. I've had to intervene twice now to restore order.'

He added milk and sugar to their coffees. 'Mind you, it's even worse out there on the pavement – I've never seen so many photographers, and there must be at least three TV camera crews. I had to order them all back from the entrance. They're a bolshie lot and I was obliged to get quite salty with them, as my old man would've said, before they'd shift.'

Dr Young grinned. He didn't think even the most hard-boiled news reporter would be impervious to the salty quality of Armstrong's tongue.

'What about the witnesses?' he asked, stirring his coffee. 'All present and correct?'

'Yes sir, all here, safe and sound. The couple who were on the tourist boat, the police officers on the launch, and that GP who happened to be passing and who pronounced the gentleman dead. The widow too – she's just arrived. My word, I must say that Miss Kidd's quite a looker, if you'll pardon my saying so. No wonder we've got so many press photographers here. They're like bees round a honeypot. She looks more like a film star than an agony aunt.'

The coroner nodded, sipping his coffee.

'Yes. So I've been told.'

Seb had managed to grab one of the chairs that now formed the temporary front row of the press bench. It was insufferably hot in here; outside the sun continued to burn unblinkingly from a cloudless sky. The little dais where the witnesses would sit had been provided with a small electric fan and a jug of iced water, as had the coroner's raised desk. The rest of them were simply going to have to sweat it out.

Seb had been with Meriel at Cathedral Crag the night before. She had been awake for most of it, full of anxiety about today's hearing. She had told him almost everything that had happened that fatal day on Ullswater – all except the part about the Rolex, and her calculated delay in throwing Cameron the lifebelt.

Seb had done his best to soothe her.

'Of *course* you're in a state,' he'd told her at around five o'clock that morning after she'd woken him yet again, sliding her arms around his body and clinging to him for comfort. 'You're about to relive the whole ghastly thing in front of a roomful of strangers.

'But remember – *I'll* be there too, reporting for the network. When you're describing it all, just imagine you're speaking to me, me and no one else. I'll only be a few feet away from you – it's a really small courtroom. And inquests aren't like big trials or anything, honestly – I've covered loads of them. Coroners are usually incredibly kind and thoughtful, and do their best to get people like you through it. You mustn't worry. You'll be fine, I promise. Just say what happened, and it'll all be over and everything will be truly behind you – inquest, funeral, the lot of it. Then we can start building our lives together.'

She had hugged him even closer.

'You always make me feel so much better. I adore you, Seb.'

To their slight surprise, they had made love.

The pathologist today was the same diffident young man who had given testimony earlier in the summer, at the inquest into the Buttermere drowning. If anything he was more nervous and hesitant than he had been then, unsettled now by the large media presence in court.

His summary was virtually identical to the one he had previously delivered from the same witness box.

'. . . my conclusion is that Mr Bruton suffered death due to cardiac arrest caused by the inhalation of water.'

'In other words, he drowned,' Dr Young prompted him, exactly as he had done a few weeks before.

The pathologist closed his eyes in self-reproach.

'Er . . . sorry, sir. Yes, I mean to say, he drowned.'

'Thank you, Dr Bullen. You may stand down. Clerk of the court will call the next witness, please.'

236

Armstrong shuffled the papers in front of him and stood up.

'Call Mrs Meriel Bruton.'

A few moments later Meriel walked into the court-room. She was dressed in a fitted black jacket and a matching knee-length pencil skirt. The cuffs and collar of a cream silk blouse were at her wrists and throat, and she was in black patent court shoes. Her make-up was minimal and her dark hair was pulled back in a ponytail.

She looked sensational.

The watching press pack stirred and whispered to each other.

Seb managed to catch Meriel's eye as she stepped into the witness box, and he gave her a nod of encouragement. She smiled faintly at him, and then turned to face the clerk of the court.

'You are Meriel Bruton, also known as Meriel Kidd, widow of the deceased?' Armstrong asked her.

Meriel nodded. 'Yes, I am.'

'The coroner here would like to ask you some questions. You may sit down if you wish.'

Meriel gave a quick shake of her head.

'Thank you ... I'd prefer to stand.'

Dr Young leaned forward, trying not to be dazzled by the young woman in front of him. She was certainly, as his clerk had told him, 'a looker', even though the extraordinary heat in the cramped, stuffy courtroom was already beginning to fray Meriel at the edges. The collar of her blouse was curling inwards and her forehead was beginning to shine a little as perspiration broke through the powder she had applied only minutes earlier.

'Good morning, Miss Kidd, and thank you very much for being here today. I do appreciate how difficult this must be for you and I assure you I won't detain you for any longer than is necessary.'

Meriel smiled gratefully at the coroner. 'Thank you, sir. I appreciate that.'

He couldn't help smiling back at her. God, she was quite adorable.

'Very well ... We have already heard testimony from Mr and Mrs Briggs, the couple in the boat who came to your assistance on the afternoon in question, and from the police officers who arrived shortly afterwards. We have also heard from the pathologist, who confirms the cause of your late husband's death as drowning.

'What I would like to do now, Miss Kidd, is firstly to go through the events immediately prior to that tragic event. Would you begin by telling us what you were both doing out on Ullswater that Sunday afternoon?'

Meriel paused a moment to collect her thoughts before replying.

'Well ... we'd decided to have lunch on our motorboat, a kind of picnic. Cold chicken, that sort of thing. My husband had prepared it himself. We often spent our Sundays like that, out on the lake, especially during this incredible summer. We usually took the Sunday papers with us and browsed through them.'

The coroner nodded. 'We've heard that a small amount of alcohol was found in the deceased's blood. Can you tell us how much your husband had had to drink?'

'Only about half a glass of wine – white wine. Cameron wasn't a big drinker.'

The coroner nodded again.

'I'd like you to tell me what transpired on the boat in the minutes before Mr Bruton went for his fateful swim. What did the two of you talk about? What were you doing?'

Meriel glanced involuntarily across at Seb. She had told him as much as she dared about her conversation on the boat with her husband. Seb was the only person other than her who knew that Cameron had promised her a very messy, public divorce if she left him.

But Seb didn't know that the warning had been backed up by a threat to produce her diary as grounds for divorce. Seb had no idea *The Night Book* even existed.

Meriel turned back to the coroner and, trying to keep her voice as calm as she could, she told her first calculated lie.

'It was just an afternoon out on the lake, much like any other. I remember that we chatted about how hot it was again ... Cameron read a few things aloud to me from the *Sunday Times*' business pages ... there was nothing at all out of the ordinary.'

'How soon after eating did your husband enter the water?'

'Quite soon. About fifteen minutes or so. But he'd only had a small piece of chicken and some salad. I don't think either of us was concerned about him getting cramp or anything like that. And of course the water was very warm, at least on the surface.'

'Hmm.' Dr Young looked thoughtful. 'Was your husband aware of the recent spate of drownings in our region's lakes?'

'Yes.'

'Was he aware that experts are of the opinion that these drownings are often occurring when swimmers go beneath the surface and encounter the near-freezing layer of water below?'

'Yes.'

'And were you aware of this too?'

'Yes.'

'So were neither of you concerned that your husband might stray into the extremely cold conditions just beneath him, and get into difficulties?'

Meriel shook her head. 'No ... you see, Cameron didn't like going underwater. He hated getting it in his ears. I don't think I ever once saw him really having to dry his hair after swimming in the lake.'

'I see. So do you have any theory as to why Mr Bruton went so completely beneath the surface on this occasion that he disappeared from sight for ...' the coroner consulted his notes '... approximately half a minute?'

Meriel lied again.

'Absolutely none, no. As I told the police, one moment he was there, swimming around and speaking to me, the next he had vanished.'

Timothy Young frowned. 'Speaking to you? Just a moment, please, Miss Kidd.' He perched a pair of reading glasses on his nose and carefully examined the documents on the desk in front of him.

'Ah yes, here we are.' The coroner slid a sheet of paper from the file.

'This is your witness statement to the police. You told them, as you just told me, that you saw your husband swimming around the vessel before he vanished. But I can find no mention here of him speaking to you.'

He removed his glasses and looked quizzically at her.

'Could you explain why that discrepancy might be, please?'

Meriel hesitated. 'Well ... no, not really. I mean, I thought I had told the police that.'

'No, it seems that you did not.' The coroner carefully

placed the page back in the file. 'Well, perhaps you can tell me about it now. What exactly did your husband say to you while he was in the water?'

'Well . . . not a great deal. He waved to me, I remember . . . and then . . . let me think . . . he might have asked me the time.'

The coroner looked calmly at Meriel.

'Might have done?'

Meriel almost bit her tongue. Why had she strayed into this? She should *never* have mentioned Cameron calling up to her from the water.

She swallowed. 'Well, yes, he did. Ask me the time, that is. I'm sorry, I'm finding this all very stressful.'

Dr Young inclined his head sympathetically towards her. 'Of course. I quite understand, Miss Kidd. Just take your time. Now . . . why would your husband need to ask you the time? Was he not wearing a watch on this particular occasion?'

Shit. The watch was the last thing she wanted to talk about. Despite the electric fan, Meriel felt herself begin to perspire even more. And it was nothing to do with the cloying, oppressive heat.

'Well . . . you see . . . he always took it off before swimming.'

'Why? Wasn't it waterproof?'

God, this was getting worse.

'Oh yes, yes, it was . . . it was a Rolex. But it was very expensive, and I think he was just nervous about

242

it slipping from his wrist, so he used to leave it on deck.'

'I see. So you referred to this watch in order to tell him what time it was, did you?'

'Yes, I, er, think so.'

'You *think* so, Miss Kidd?

'No ... I mean, yes. Yes, I did.'

Shiiit!

Timothy Young poured himself a little iced water before asking his next question.

'Why did he want to know the time?'

'I don't know.'

'Did you have any subsequent conversation with your husband?'

Meriel began to feel marginally less alarmed. They were moving away from dangerous territory now.

'No. In fact it wasn't long after that I noticed he'd disappeared.'

The coroner nodded. 'So ... you told him the time, he carried on swimming ... and then he disappeared.'

'Yes.'

'Very well.' Dr Young looked at his own watch. 'I think we might adjourn here for ten minutes. Thank you, for the moment, Miss Kidd.'

'That was all a bit funny, and not as in funny ha-ha, either, don'tcha think?'

The *Sun* journalist sucked at his cigarette. The press

corps were congregated outside on the steps of the building, smoking and sipping coffees fetched from a snack bar around the corner.

'I mean,' he went on, 'she almost sounded like she was hiding something, I thought.'

There were scattered nods around him, and a faint chorus of agreement.

Seb didn't know what to think. Meriel had never mentioned Cameron asking her the time to him. Why not? And the *Sun* guy was right – she had looked ... well, *shifty* when the coroner had pressed her on the matter. Again, why?

Then there was the business of Cameron's Rolex. Earlier that week at Cathedral Crag, Seb and Meriel had had quite a long conversation about what she should do with her late husband's personal effects. She'd put them carefully away in a mirrored box, and fetched it to show him. There were gold and platinum bracelets, diamond cufflinks, bespoke fountain pens ... but no Rolex.

She'd never even mentioned a Rolex.

Why not?

And where was it now?

'Court's reconvening, ladies and gents.' It was the coroner's clerk, gruffly calling to them from the entrance.

Seb trooped back in with the rest of them.

He was beginning to feel slightly sick.

*

Dr Timothy Young had learned that his clerk's considered opinion on a case was well worth consulting, and he had done this during the adjournment.

'Cards on the table, John – what do you think?'

John Armstrong pushed his spectacles back up onto the bridge of his nose. They kept sliding down it in the constant perspiration this infernal heat caused.

'I'm not sure, sir, to be honest,' he said after a few moments. 'Obviously she's holding back on something. Whether it's important or not is another matter. My instinct is that they had some kind of row.'

The coroner nodded. 'Yes, that's what I thought. Why is she so touchy about this business concerning the watch, though?'

His clerk shrugged. 'Who knows? Could be anything. Such as, it was a present from a mistress. Or carried an engraving from a former lover. Something like that. Forgive me for saying so, sir, but I reckon you may have missed a trick there.'

'Go on.'

Armstrong shrugged again.

'I think you should ask her where the watch is now, sir. Even ask to see it. We could get a car over to her house and back again before close of play.'

'You think the watch is in some way involved in the cause of death?'

'Dunno. Might be, although I can't see how. But

it's obviously a sore spot with her. You should press down on it.'

She was so taken aback by the question that for several seconds, Meriel was unable to speak.

'I'm sorry ... I don't quite understand,' she managed at last. 'You want to know the whereabouts of my husband's watch?'

Dr Young nodded, almost kindly – but inside he was beginning to vibrate with the quiet certainty that he was on to something. Good old John. A creature of rare instinct. Meriel Kidd's reaction to his query on the whereabouts of the Rolex was telling, to say the least. The game's afoot, Watson, he thought to himself. But he bided his time.

Standing stock-still in the witness box, Meriel worked to fight down the tide of panic that was rising within her. With an almost physical effort, she managed to bring her thoughts into focus.

No one knows anything. No one knows anything about what I did with the watch. Or with the lifebelt afterwards. I just have to stay calm and stop allowing myself to be thrown off balance like this. Get a bloody grip, Meriel.

STARTING RIGHT NOW.

'I don't know,' she said as slowly and deliberately as she could. 'I haven't seen it since my husband drowned. I may have lost it.'

246

The coroner – a man of considerable instinct himself – immediately felt his witness slipping away from him. It had happened before, sometimes, most often during his career at the criminal bar. Whatever it was Meriel Kidd was concealing, she had just thrown another thick blanket over it, and now she was stepping back, ready to face him down.

Damn. *Damn*.

'Lost it? Have you looked for it?'

'Yes. Without success, I'm afraid. I remember putting it into my handbag before I left the boat with the police. I must have put it somewhere when I got home that night. I was still in shock from seeing my husband lose his life right in front of me. Forgive me, sir, can I ask why you are pursuing me with these questions? My husband drowned. What has his watch got to do with anything?'

In a criminal court, Young reflected, the judge would instantly have rebuked the witness for bandying words with the prosecution. But this was not a criminal court, he was not counsel for the prosecution, and he was certainly not a judge.

He was going to have to let this go.

'That's quite all right, Miss Kidd. I am merely trying to establish all the facts.'

He pretended to shuffle the documents on the desk in front of him. After a few moments, he cleared his throat.

'Miss Kidd ... you told the police that when your husband eventually resurfaced, he was in a state of some distress.'

Meriel immediately knew the worst was over.

'Yes ... he was thrashing around and making terrible noises. I threw him the boat's lifebelt, but he was completely unaware that I'd done so. I think he was already unconscious.'

'Was there no possibility of you taking it to him, perhaps placing it around his shoulders?'

Meriel appeared stricken.

'No ... I've never been able to swim. I feel dreadful about that now, obviously. I suppose I could have used the lifebelt to support myself as I paddled over to him, but what then? If I'd given it to him, I would probably have drowned myself. There was nothing I could do. As I say, I feel absolutely awful about this. But the fact is, I can't swim.'

The coroner politely inclined his head towards her.

'Thank you, Miss Kidd. I have no further questions for you.'

Seb did.

But they'd have to wait.

CHAPTER TWENTY-NINE

'*Recording a verdict of death by misadventure, coroner Dr Timothy Young said he wanted to emphasise that during the current extreme weather conditions, it remains unsafe to swim in Cumbria's lakes. To underline his warning, he commented: "One wouldn't go swimming in a force-nine gale or a thunderstorm. People should be equally sensible of the hazards of doing so while this unprecedented heatwave continues."*

'*This is Seb Richmond reporting for Lake District FM and network news, live from Kendal Coroner's Court.*'

Seb lowered the microphone and pulled the earphones from his head. Jess, sitting on the other side of the radio car's transmitter, flicked several switches to off and gave him the thumbs-up.

'Nice one, Seb. Want a drink in the Shakespeare before we head back?'

Seb shook his head.

'No thanks, Jess. I've got to go and see someone.'

'That someone being Meriel Kidd, I take it.'

Seb stared at him. 'What do you mean?'

Jess snorted as he pushed the button to retract the radio mast above them.

'Do me a favour, sunshine. Where d'you think you work, for Christ's sake? A Trappist monastery? People talk. Everyone knows about you and Meriel.'

Seb gave it up.

'How?' he asked weakly.

Jess smiled at him.

'Well, for starters the licensee of the String of Horses is brother-in-law to one of the cleaners at the station. She told everyone who'd listen that you and Meriel spent the night at the pub. And believe me, everyone listened.

'Then there's the young couple who live opposite you in Warwick Road. She's Helen Briar's daughter – you know Helen, she runs accounts. They were coming home from dinner one evening and they saw Meriel slipping into your flat. Seemingly had her own key, they told Helen. Said they probably wouldn't have noticed her if she hadn't been wearing giant sunglasses after dark. Made her stand out a bit, apparently.'

Seb sighed deeply. 'Anything else?'

'Yup,' Jess replied cheerfully. 'Tony in advertising keeps a little sailboat on Derwent Water. He was driving past Meriel's house – what's it called? Cathedral something, right?'

'Cathedral Crag.'

'That's it. Anyway, Tony was tootling past there early last Saturday morning and whose Triumph Spitfire d'you suppose he saw turning out of the drive?'

Seb put his face into his hands.

'Shit. What's everyone saying about it?'

Jess looked surprised.

'What do you think? They're loving it. You work for a radio station, Sebby old chap. Everyone shags everyone else on a radio station. Except me. I'm too old and I'm happily married.'

Seb thought for a moment.

'Bob Merryman warned me that if Meriel and I were seeing each other and it got out, the press would have a field day with us. Well, with her mainly.'

Jess finished with the mast and began winding a long electric cable back into its housing above a wheel-arch.

'Well, you'd know more about that than me. I just drive the bus. But I wouldn't worry about that for a while. Our people might enjoy a good gossip among themselves, but we're family and what happens on the station stays on the station. No one's going to do the dirty. Apart from anything else, everyone's rather fond of both of you.'

He snapped the lid down over the coiled flex and turned back to Seb.

'It'll come out eventually, of course, but by then this Cameron guy will have been long buried ... well, at least for a month or two. And why shouldn't his widow seek a little comfort from one of her handsome colleagues? It's only natural. Anyway, this is 1976, not 1876. Having sex is allowed.'

He paused, and looked curiously at the younger man.

'What was all that business in your report just now about the dead guy's watch? I couldn't work it out.'

Seb shook his head. 'I honestly don't know. The coroner obviously seemed to think it might be important and ... well, I'm sure the papers will report that Meriel looked a bit thrown when he asked her about it.'

'Did she? You didn't mention that.'

'No, I didn't see the point. She was bound to be upset, Jess, she was telling the world how she watched her husband drown, for God's sake.'

Jess nodded sympathetically. 'Well, go on then, back to Cathedral what's-it-called, and do your arm-around-the-shoulder routine. A very pretty shoulder, I might add. I'll finish up here.'

'Thanks.' Seb paused. 'Jess ...'

'Yeah?'

'It's not what people might think, you know. Oh, we are seeing each other, there's obviously no point denying that ... but what I mean is ... This isn't just a casual fling, you know. When things settle down we're probably going to get married. I mean it.'

The engineer patted the reporter's shoulder.

'Well, all I can say is – you'll make a lovely couple.'

The police had offered Meriel a car to the inquest but she preferred to drive herself. Now, less than an hour after listening to Dr Young dispassionately giving his verdict, she turned into her driveway and brought the Mercedes to a crunching halt on the gravel. She glanced at the car clock. Almost six o'clock; time for the news.

A few minutes later she was listening to Seb's voice summarising the main evidence from the inquest. The part about the missing watch was only briefly mentioned, but she knew he was going to ask her about it later. He'd want to know why she hadn't mentioned her final conversation with Cameron, too. But, like the coroner, he'd probably be more curious about the missing Rolex.

The trouble now, Meriel reflected as she went through her front door, was that Seb would inevitably start to wonder if there were other things she hadn't told him. After all, he was a reporter. He was trained to follow a lead.

What was she to do? Make a clean breast of it? Tell him everything, starting with the reason she'd used the watch to lure Cameron to his death? In other words, tell him about *The Night Book*? And that Cameron had found it? She'd have to, wouldn't she, to explain her motive for drowning her husband.

Yes: drowning her husband. That's what she'd done. Let's not forget that, Meriel, shall we? You drowned him with a trick.

She shivered. She must be mad to even *think* about telling Seb the truth. What man could ever trust a woman who wrote such grotesque, violent fantasies about killing her husband? And then went on to do precisely that, and in cold blood, too?

She walked slowly into the lounge with its views across Derwent Water, and felt a ripple of unease as she stared out at the lake. Its placid surface was darkening now that the sun had sunk behind the mountains to the west, and Meriel felt almost haunted. Would she ever be able to look at any lake again without remembering what she'd done?

When she poured herself a Scotch from the drinks table, she noticed that her hands were shaking slightly.

She must pull herself together. Seb would be here soon.

She must have her story straight before then.

But as it turned out, Seb was circumspect. In fact, he had been lovely, Meriel thought as they finished their evening meal together. All he seemed concerned about was her state of mind after being questioned so persistently, albeit politely, in court earlier.

'I'm fine, honestly,' she told him. 'I *was* a bit thrown when he asked me why I hadn't mentioned to the police that Cameron had asked me for the time ... and then all that stuff about his bloody watch.'

But Seb hadn't taken the opening she'd given him, not straight away. He'd only replied that she'd probably simply forgotten. 'After all, they were interviewing you barely two or three hours after it happened. Your mind would have been all over the place. Anyway, who cares if he asked you the time? Or where the watch went?'

Meriel began to think that it was going to be all right after all.

But later, when they'd taken their drinks out onto the lawn and the warm dusk was falling, he'd asked her the question she'd been expecting.

'Meriel ... going back to that part about Cameron asking you the time ... As I said, it's easy to understand why you didn't think to mention it to the police that day.'

He turned from the lake to face her.

'But why not tell me about it? After all, you said how horrible he was to you, threatening you with a ghastly divorce – and I quite see why you chose not to share that with the coroner today. But why have you never told me about Cameron's last words? They were pretty mundane by comparison.'

Meriel shrugged, as casually as she could.

'Haven't I mentioned it to you? Are you sure? I honestly thought I had done. But it's hardly important, is it? I don't regard someone asking "what's the time?"

as a conversation, do you? If I haven't remembered it before now it's probably because it was so irrelevant. And completely overshadowed by the much nastier exchange we had before he got into the water.'

Careful, Meriel. Don't go on so much. Briefer is better.

Seb digested what she'd said, before saying: 'Fair enough. But what about the watch? You showed me all his personal valuables the other day, when you were wondering what to do with them. You never said anything about a Rolex, or that it was missing. I mean, come on, you don't buy a Rolex from Woolworth's, do you? It must have been worth a small fortune. Probably as much as everything in that box put together. I can't understand why you haven't said anything about it.'

Meriel contrived to look embarrassed, even slightly ashamed.

'Now *that* sin of omission I plead guilty to,' she said. She reached for his hand, and he took it.

'I *have* lost the damn thing and the reason I didn't tell you was because I just feel so stupid about it. You're right, it's worth a great deal of money and I can't believe I could have been so careless. I just didn't want to talk about it, that's all. I suppose I didn't want you thinking I'm some kind of . . . well, what my father would have called a flibbertigibbet.'

Despite himself, Seb laughed.

'A *what*?'

She smiled at him. 'Flibbertigibbet. I suppose what today we'd call an airhead. A silly female with no idea of the value of anything.'

Seb shook his head, still smiling. 'I could never think that about you. But listen, Meriel, you never have to keep secrets from me. Never. Certainly not something trivial like this, for heaven's sake. Everyone loses stuff. It's hardly surprising you mislaid that watch, after what had just happened.'

He squeezed her hand. 'Anyway, I'll help you find it. Might it still be on the boat?'

She shook her head. 'No. As I told the coroner, I remember dropping it into my handbag before I went to the police station. I must have put it somewhere here in the house when I got back, either that night or soon after. I just can't for the life of me remember where.'

He reached for her empty wine glass. 'Another?'

'Mmm . . . please.'

Seb rose to go inside.

'Well, not to worry – it'll turn up. I bet I find it. I'm a good finder. Whenever my mother lost something she'd set me on the scent of it. She still does – she calls me her bloodhound. Last Christmas she lost her engagement and wedding rings. Guess where I found them?'

Meriel shook her head.

'In the butter dish, *in* the actual butter. She'd used it to ease them off her fingers because they were making them itch. She'd totally forgotten the next day.'

Meriel knew there was no possibility of him or anyone else ever finding Cameron's Rolex. As far as she was aware, bloodhounds weren't much good under sixty feet of water.

Later, when they were in bed, he stroked her temple with the back of his forefinger.

'I know it's been a shitty day, but there's something else we need to talk about.'

She sat up and pushed her hair back. 'What is it?' She tried to keep the anxiety from her voice. What now?

'Jess – you know, the station engineer – took me to one side earlier. He told me ... well, he told me that just about everyone knows about us. On the station, that is. Seems they have for some time, almost from the start, in fact.'

She swallowed. 'How?'

Seb took her through Jess's account. When he'd finished, Meriel shrugged philosophically.

'I suppose there's nothing we can do about it, is there? Anyway, it isn't a crime.'

'No, but the papers might think it is. You know, the merry widow angle.'

She shrugged again.

'I'd already accepted that I was going to have to admit my marriage had failed, remember? I was going to leave Cameron and that story would have got out soon enough. So if and when the papers find out about us—'

'It'll be *when*, not if,' Seb interrupted.

'Fine. *When* they find out about us, I can truthfully tell them that I stuck by my husband right to the very end. That I kept up a cheerful front in public, despite everything having gone wrong. And now I've found happiness.'

Seb stared at her.

'You've come a long way from our night at the String of Horses, haven't you?'

She nodded. 'I have. Because of you. You stopped me being frightened that night, Seb. You showed me a way out of the living hell of my marriage. Now Cameron is dead and I'm free to do what I want. And I'm going to, just you watch me. I don't care what the papers say. I don't care what *anyone* says.'

Seb kissed her before turning to switch out his bedside light.

'Fine. But let's just not rub their faces in it, OK?'

An exhausted Meriel was asleep in a couple of minutes; Seb could hear her slow, steady breathing beside him.

But he lay awake for a long time.

He couldn't stop thinking about the missing watch.

And wondering why on earth she was lying about it.

CHAPTER THIRTY

Next morning was a Saturday. Seb was up early, not for work but to drive into Keswick and buy all the papers.

He parked in a corner of the medieval Market Place and carefully vetted first the tabloids and then the broadsheets.

Meriel's photo, showing her arriving at court in her black-and-cream outfit, was splashed all over the front pages. No surprise there, Seb thought – she looked stunning. Editors knew a circulation-booster when they saw one.

The *Sun* headline was: *PHONE-IN BEAUTY: 'I COULDN'T SAVE HIM.'* The *Mirror* chose: *AGONY AUNT'S AGONY AS HUBBIE DROWNED.* The *Mail* went with: *THE LOVELY WIDOW WEEPS* even though Meriel hadn't shed a tear. One or two of the stories on the inside pages briefly mentioned the matter of the missing watch, but the majority ignored it. It was a quirk in the case that most news editors had obviously decided led straight up a blind alley.

Seb tossed the papers onto the front passenger seat beside him and tried to focus. He didn't know it, but his thought processes were remarkably similar to the coroner's the previous day.

Something was out of joint, but he couldn't say what. Last night, Meriel had given a perfectly logical explanation for not mentioning the Rolex business to him and – just like Dr Young – Seb had felt he couldn't reasonably push the issue any further.

But that didn't mean it had gone away.

'What's the matter, Timothy? You're not yourself this morning. In fact, you haven't been since you came home from the inquest yesterday.'

Dr Young's wife was looking at her husband with concern.

He smiled at her across the breakfast table.

'I'm sorry, darling. I'm just a little preoccupied, I suppose.'

'With this Cameron Bruton inquest? But you decided it was a straightforward case of misadventure, didn't you?'

He nodded slowly. 'Well, yes ... up to a point. I

didn't really have any alternative, given the evidence. It's his widow I can't stop thinking about.'

Miriam Young rolled her eyes, stood up, and crossed to the little card table in the alcove by the bay window. Outside, less than a hundred yards below the house, Bassenthwaite rippled cheerfully in the bright morning sun.

She picked up the folded copy of the *Telegraph* and shook it open.

'I'm not surprised you can't stop thinking about her,' she said crisply, staring at the picture of Meriel on page one. 'Quite the dish, isn't she?'

Her husband laughed. 'Don't be silly, I didn't mean like that. Anyway, I'm at least twice her age.'

'Thanks. As am I.'

He rubbed his chin. 'Bugger. I'm not expressing myself too well this morning, am I?'

His wife laughed in turn. 'I'm teasing you, Tim. But seriously – what's the matter? You look like you did in your barrister days after you lost the Coultrose case. That was perjury, wasn't it? He got away with it, didn't he?'

The coroner nodded. 'Yes, it was. And he did.'

He left the table and went over to join his wife. Together they looked at Meriel's picture.

After a few moments, Dr Timothy Young gently tapped it with his fingernail.

'You're absolutely right, Miriam, as usual. That

woman reminds me of Jeremy Coultrose. She was lying to me, just as he did. I don't know why, and I don't really even know what about, either.'

He stared out, unseeing, at the lake.

'But she was definitely lying.'

CHAPTER THIRTY-ONE

Meriel woke up in the grip of something approaching total panic.

Her stomach was in knots and her pulse was racing. She had never felt anxiety like it. Her instinct was to take a double dose of the sleeping pills her GP had prescribed her after Cameron's death, burrow deep under the sheets and fall into a chemically induced semi-coma as soon as possible.

She was reaching for the pills in her bedside cabinet when the phone on top of it began to ring.

She stared at it for a few moments before reluctantly picking up the receiver.

'Hello ... Meriel Kidd.' She sounded OK. No hint of the agitation boiling inside. It must be the latent broadcaster in her, she decided, and she began to feel very slightly calmer.

'Meriel, it's Peter here, Peter Cox. How are you?'

She liked the station manager. She owed her break in radio to him and he'd been a kind and encouraging mentor to her ever since.

'Peter . . . honest answer? Terrible. I just woke up and I feel completely shattered. In bits. I've been fine up to now; ever since it happened, actually. I was fine all day yesterday. But today . . .' Meriel's voice trembled and broke. 'Today I can't . . . I just can't . . .'

Her voice gave out completely.

She heard her boss clear his throat before he spoke again.

'Now look here, Meriel . . . we all think you've been holding up extremely well. Incredibly strong. Yesterday must have been a ghastly ordeal, simply ghastly, and judging by this morning's papers you came through it with extraordinary dignity and courage. I'm sure what you're going through now is a reaction not just to the inquest but to everything, the whole lot of it, ever since . . . since . . . well, since what happened to Cameron.'

Meriel managed to recover something of her voice.

'Yes . . . It has been an unbelievable strain, Peter. I can't begin to tell you.'

'Of course. I just want you to know that you can take as much time as you need before you come back to work. Glenda can cover for you for as long as you like. And your loyal fans will wait for you. You should see your postbag, Meriel. You've had literally thousands of letters of sympathy and support. It's much the same with today's papers, as I said. Have you seen them yet?'

'No, Seb went ...'

There was a long silence.

It was the station manager who broke it.

'Meriel, it's OK. We all know about you and Seb. If he's helping you to cope during such a difficult time, well, that's all to the good, isn't it? Anyway, it's no one's business but yours.'

She felt a wave of gratitude wash over her.

'Peter, that means so much. And you must be wondering ... you must *all* be wondering ... about the way things were with Cameron and me. I—'

Her boss interrupted her.

'Meriel, that's no one else's business either.'

'But you must ... you must be thinking ...'

'All right. Given what's happened with you and Seb it's fairly obvious things can't have been exactly perfect between you and Cameron, and I'm very sorry about that. But all anyone wants is for you to be happy, Meriel – your colleagues, your friends and your listeners. So you mustn't worry. Take all the time you need to recover your balance. And I want you to feel you can ring me or come and see me at any time you like.'

She sensed he was bringing the conversation to a close.

'I will. Thank you, Peter. I feel better already after speaking with you.'

'Well, that's good. Bye, Meriel. Take care.'

But she was still feeling jarred and deeply unsettled. She dressed in T-shirt, jeans and walking boots, before going downstairs into the kitchen where she put the kettle on. She found a jotting pad and scribbled a note for Seb.

> S,
>
> Woke up feeling in bits. Delayed reaction, I think, now that it's all over. Have gone out for a walk on the fells. Don't worry about me – I'm fine, just need to clear my head.
>
> Peter (Cox) called, was lovely. Knows all about us – you were right about that. Tell you what he said later but v. reassuring and non-judgemental.
>
> See you later. I love you. M.

Five minutes later she had filled a Thermos with instant coffee and made herself a peanut-butter sandwich, wrapping it in tinfoil. Putting both into a small backpack, Meriel left the house by the kitchen door and joined the footpath that ran from east to west at the bottom of the garden.

She turned west, and almost at once the track began to rise.

For the first time since moving to Cathedral Crag,

she was going to climb the mountain that gave the house its name.

When she reached the top, there was something she knew she had to do. Something she had been instinctively avoiding since the very moment she had tossed Cameron's watch into the water, deliberately beyond his reach.

She was going to try and work out what sort of person would do a thing like that.

And she was dreading the answer.

CHAPTER THIRTY-TWO

For almost the first time that summer, Meriel actually felt cool. She was sitting on a rock, perched on the very top of the Derwent Fells. Up here the southern breeze was beautifully fresh; a wonderful contrast to the stale, almost fetid air of the valleys more than two thousand feet below.

As always when she climbed the fells, Meriel wondered why she didn't do so more often. On a day like this, under spotless skies and with the rarefied air allowing astonishingly clear views for dozens of miles, the senses were heightened, sharpened somehow. There was an almost primeval, instinctive awareness of what her father called *the bigger picture*.

She looked around her. From here, Derwent Water looked like a little blue puddle. Down there to her right was Borrowdale, and straight in front, six miles away to the east, brooded one of the highest mountains in England, Helvellyn.

Meriel shivered slightly, and not because of the breeze. She had witnessed one of her closest school friends die on Helvellyn, fifteen years earlier.

Beth Portman had inexplicably fallen from Striding Edge, the razorback ridge that approached the summit. There were twenty of them in the party, sixth-formers on a school-sponsored walking tour of the Lakes. Beth had been bringing up the rear of the group. The girls weren't roped together; although Striding Edge was described in their nearby youth hostel's guidebook as a 'soaring tightrope walk', it was deemed more dramatic than dangerous.

But Beth had joined the register of those who fell from it to their deaths – one person a year, on average – when she somehow missed her footing and tumbled in a grotesque and seemingly endless cartwheel down the vertiginous slope. She had come to rest five hundred feet below the others, her neck and back broken.

No one had seen how she went over; they were only aware that she had gone when she screamed, just once, as her hip slammed into the mountainside at the beginning of her long fall.

The other girls had spun around, but Meriel had been one of the few not to immediately turn away again in horror. Many clung sobbing to their nearest companion, unable to watch as Beth performed her whirling, descending gavotte.

'Death by misadventure' had been the coroner's verdict. Just like yesterday's on Cameron. A tragic accident. No one to blame.

And of course Beth Portman's death *had* been an accident. What else could it have been? It wasn't as if someone had pushed her.

But hang on, Meriel thought, staring at Helvellyn's peak. Just hang on a moment. It was *exactly* as if someone had pushed her, wasn't it? You just had to look at it from a different perspective. Suppose the girl walking in front of Beth had hated her, suppose she was psychotic? Suppose, when everyone else in the single file of hikers was looking ahead and concentrating on keeping their balance, Little Miss Psycho had turned around, placed her hands on Beth's shoulders and silently thrust the girl over the edge?

Nobody would have known or suspected a thing, would they? Not if the killer kept her head, and her mouth shut.

Meriel had no serious doubts that poor Beth died because she lost her footing, *but that wasn't the point*. There was a measurable possibility – however small – of a different, sinister explanation.

It must be a statistical certainty that a proportion of so-called accidental deaths were nothing of the kind. Someone engineered them and escaped the consequences.

Like Meriel.

She took strange comfort now in the thought that she was not alone. She couldn't be. Out there, in the wide world that stretched on all sides below, there *must* be people like her. Those who had managed to disguise a wilful killing as a capricious stroke of chance; a fateful, fatal mishap.

She supposed some were consumed by remorse, or suffered some kind of breakdown, but others would surely be quietly getting on with their lives.

Exactly as she intended.

Meriel reached into her bag for the coffee and sandwich. She hadn't planned to kill Cameron. She couldn't say it had never entered her head – there was *The Night Book* to consider – but that had all been an elaborate fantasy.

It had never crossed her mind to orchestrate her husband's drowning. She hadn't inveigled him into the water that Sunday, had she? She hadn't shoved him under with the bloody boat-hook. She hadn't—

'Oh, come off it, Meriel. You KNEW he'd go after the watch.'

Meriel looked around her, startled, before she realised that the voice she'd heard was her own.

'First sign of madness,' she muttered, pouring the coffee into the plastic cap of the Thermos before taking a bite of her sandwich. 'Get a grip, woman.'

She stared out across the fells, thinking hard.

She'd loathed her husband. What would she have done if, during their evening meal together, Cameron had started to choke? Would she have tried to help him? Or would she have just sat and watched as he lost consciousness and died?

Surely there must be other women, trapped in abusive relationships, who had done that? Or perhaps seen their husbands keel over with a heart attack and left them to their fate. She vaguely remembered a newspaper story about the wife chided by a coroner for not calling an ambulance after her husband had collapsed when mowing the lawn. A neighbour had seen the whole thing – the man toppling to the ground, clutching his chest, the wife staring and staring and staring from her kitchen window, standing stock-still.

The woman had subsequently claimed to be incapacitated; frozen to the spot by shock. No charges had ever been brought.

No. She, Meriel, could not possibly be alone. There must be dozens ⊤ no, hundreds – of women out there who had quietly connived in the death of a husband.

Yes, but you set the process in motion, didn't you, Meriel?

At least she hadn't spoken aloud this time, she thought. But it was true. There was all the difference in the world between passively observing someone dying from natural causes, and deliberately bringing those causes about.

Cameron hadn't just started to drown all by himself. She had deliberately engineered it, hadn't she? If she hadn't thrown his watch into the water, he would be alive today.

And yet, and yet ... Meriel's reasoning became defensive again as she told herself she hadn't *forced* him to go after his Rolex. It had been his decision. He could have let it sink, claimed on the insurance. Anyway, he knew all about that summer's drownings and the underlying cause for them, *literally* the underlying cause; the freezing water that he was well aware lay beneath him.

So he'd been stupid to do it. He'd made his choice and suffered the consequences. She hadn't killed Cameron; he'd managed that all by himself.

Meriel tried her hardest to hold on to this elegantly composed, neatly logical conclusion, but it was no good. She was too intelligent and too honest with herself. The comforting rationale quietly slipped from her grasp like a wet rope.

She sighed. She was right back to square one; the brutal truth that she'd acknowledged to herself at the end of the very day she'd killed her husband. Yes, killed him. She'd told herself then that at least it wasn't murder but manslaughter, and she reminded herself now of its definition.

'The unlawful killing of one human being by another without malice aforethought.'

Meriel finished her coffee and stood up, ready to set out on the long trek back down the mountain.

She wasn't even sure about that, now. There'd been plenty of malice aforethought, all right. She'd written it all down.

If only she could find those *bloody* photocopies.

CHAPTER THIRTY-THREE

Next morning Seb was out early again to get the Sunday papers. By the time he got back to Cathedral Crag with them, Meriel had prepared breakfast and set it up outside on the sunny terrace overlooking Derwent Water.

'Wow,' he said, emerging from the French windows to join her. 'Five-star service.'

She smiled at him. 'Not quite. This is the first time we've had a chance to eat a proper breakfast together and I suddenly realised I haven't a clue what you like.' She gestured towards the Japanese bamboo table with its plates and covers. 'So I've done a bit of everything. Boiled eggs, two each, scrambled eggs – this means we're out of eggs, by the way – bacon, toast, tea, fresh coffee, and orange juice. Is that OK?'

He laughed. 'Not quite up to my Warwick Road standard of a bowl of Frosties and a mug of Nescafé, but I suppose it'll do.' He kissed her. 'Seriously, this is quite something. Breakfast with the most beautiful woman in England, cooked by the most beautiful woman in England, and looking out over one of the most beautiful views in England.'

He flopped down into a chair. 'I know we both want to move somewhere else as soon as we can, make a fresh start and all that, but good God, Meriel, we'll be lucky to find somewhere with an outlook as stunning as this.'

Meriel buttered a slice of toast.

'Mmm. I was thinking about that, actually, a bit earlier on.'

He cocked a finger at her.

'Aha. By "earlier on" I take it you mean around four o'clock this morning. I wondered where you'd got to. I came down to find you but I could see the kitchen light was on and heard the kettle boiling. I figured maybe you wanted to be left alone. Were you thinking about what to do with this place?'

She nodded. 'Amongst other things ... I *do* want to put Cathedral Crag on the market as soon as possible. There's no mortgage on it and it'll fetch a great deal of money. Which means we'll really be able to pick our spot, especially as we won't need a great big rambling place like this. In fact, I reckon we could well end up with a view even better than this one.'

Seb looked slightly uncomfortable.

'Meriel ... there's a lot of things we haven't had the chance to talk about yet. You know, the nuts-and-bolts, practical stuff.' He poured himself a glass of orange juice before continuing.

'You've been under enormous pressure, and obviously and totally understandably preoccupied with the funeral and the inquest and everything ... but perhaps the time's now right for me to tell you that ... well, I have very little money, I'm afraid. I barely earn enough on a reporter's salary to rent my flat and run my car. I have no savings at all. I'm basically a jobbing journo on the make. So when it comes to where we next live ... well, I'm pretty much entirely in your obligation. That makes me feel bad, but I don't see what I can do about it.'

Meriel leaned forward and was about to speak but Seb motioned her to remain silent.

'There's something else I need to get off my chest while I'm at it. Bear with me.'

She sank back in her chair. 'Go on.'

He took a deep breath.

'It's just that I can't get it out of my head that we'll be using *his* money to start our new lives. When you and I planned our future together that incredible night at the String of Horses – a night I'll never forget, Meriel – we never thought for a moment that things would turn out like this, did we? That in the weirdest way possible, he – dammit, I *must* start saying his name: *Cameron* – would be sort of, well, subsidising us. There's a part of me that's finding that really hard to accept.'

Meriel took her time in replying. She stood up and walked to the edge of the raised terrace, looking down on the neatly trimmed lawn beneath. Her eye was caught by a little black and white bird, running up and down the grass. She knew it at once: a pied wagtail. It was searching for insects to feed on. As far as she knew, wagtails mated for life. And she wanted to spend the rest of hers with the man behind her.

She turned to face him.

'All of that does you great credit, but I want you to listen to me very carefully. What I have to say to you is extraordinarily simple.

'First. When it comes to buying our next home, when it comes to buying or owning anything at all – what's mine is yours. Cameron used to say that to me and at first I was foolish enough to believe him. What he really meant was that he wanted to suck me so deep into his world that I'd never get out again.

'But I mean it the way it ought to be meant, Seb. We should share everything we have, *everything* – just as we already share our love for and commitment to each other. No, don't speak, I haven't finished, either.'

She spread both arms wide, as if embracing the house in front of her, and then she turned to do the same towards the garden.

282

'*Second*. All this isn't some sort of subsidy, Seb. None of it belongs to Cameron. Not any more. It belongs to *me* now. It's my inheritance, and it's mine, mine to do with exactly as I choose. And I choose to share it with you. There's no shame or burden in that, none at all. Come here.'

He went to her side. She took both his hands in her own.

'You have nothing to feel even a particle of guilt over. Not now, not in the future, not ever. And neither do I – and believe me, Seb, I've thought about this. But I'm at peace with it now – and so should you be.'

She kissed his forehead.

'So, sit down and tell me about the papers. What are they saying?'

The Sundays, in fact, had barely touched the story of the inquest. One tabloid idly speculated when Meriel Kidd might return to her radio show. Another carried a photo-fashion piece which was in excruciatingly poor taste, headlined: *MOURNING CHIC: HOW MINXY MERIEL WOWED THEM IN WIDOW'S WEEDS.*

An upmarket broadsheet ran a feature on women who had been bereaved young, including an interview with a famous actress who had lost her own husband when she was the same age as Meriel. The banner read: *MY MESSAGE TO MERIEL – YOU'LL FIND LOVE AGAIN.*

And that was it, apart from a couple of stories in the business pages discussing the fate of Cameron Bruton's various business enterprises. The consensus was that his widow would sell the profitable ones and wind the rest up.

'They're right about that,' Meriel told Seb. 'I'm no entrepreneur. I have my own career. And, on that note . . .'

She stood up.

Seb stared at her. 'Where are you going?'

'The office. Lake District FM. It's Sunday so there'll be no one in. I want to have a look at my correspondence, see what needs dealing with right away and what can be put off. Also, today's papers have given me a couple of ideas for phone-ins. I want to flesh them out a bit.'

'But I thought Peter told you to take as much time off as you wanted. I thought—'

She shook her head impatiently. 'I know, and when he said it yesterday I still thought I needed it. But then I took myself up onto the mountain and gave myself a good talking to. And I realised early this morning that it'll do me no good at all mooching around here. I need to get back to work. It's been weeks now since I made a programme.'

'So . . . when do you plan to go back? On air, I mean.'

Meriel considered. 'Well, let's see. Glenda will have

this week's show all prepared, so I suppose it'll be next week. I'll leave notes for Peter and my producer later today telling them, and I can call them tomorrow.'

She smiled at him. 'Gosh, I feel better already.'

Seb returned her smile. 'I must say, you look it. You have done since I got back from Keswick just now. Well ... I suppose I won't see you until much later tonight, then. I'm rostered on the late production shift preparing tomorrow's breakfast show. I'll likely be heading in to the studios around the same time as you're coming back.'

'Probably. Anyway, I'll have some supper ready for when you get home.'

'And I'll clear this lot away.' He suddenly burst out laughing. 'Christ, just look at the two of us, Meriel. We've turned into bloody Darby and Joan already, haven't we?'

She'd been gone for less than an hour when the lights fused. Seb had just finished uncertainly loading the dishwasher – it was the first dishwasher he'd ever seen – but when he switched it on there was a bang and a blue flash from somewhere and the concealed lighting above the kitchen units simultaneously went out.

He jiggled a couple of wall switches. Nothing. It was the same out in the hall. Power to the entire house seemed to be out.

Seb chewed his bottom lip. God knows where the fuse box was. He'd have to find it and change whichever fuse had shorted before Meriel got back. He couldn't leave her to sit all alone in the dark. Of course it was possible that she knew how to fix it but he couldn't count on that.

Fifteen minutes later he was no closer to finding the box. He'd looked in all the likely places on the ground floor – kitchen, cloakroom, downstairs toilet, utility room. That meant the damn thing had to be in the cellar, and that meant finding a torch.

Eventually he discovered one under Meriel's side of the bed and made his way back downstairs to a latched door set at a right-angle to the back kitchen door. He suspected it would open onto the cellar steps.

He pushed the door back on its hinges and peered in. Yup; it was the cellar, all right. Things looked in pretty good order, though; the wooden stairs were free of dust and the stairwell itself had been neatly whitewashed.

Seb kept a firm grip on the narrow handrail as he went carefully down the steps, holding the torch out in front of him. When he got to the bottom he swept the arc of light slowly from left to right. He could see cardboard boxes stacked on top of each other, a couple of old bicycles with completely flat tyres and, incongruously, what looked like most of a car's engine, mounted on thick wooden blocks.

It took him a minute or two to find the fuse box but yes, there it was, a big square wooden cupboard bolted to the back wall of the cellar. He could see thick electrical cables running down into it from the ceiling above.

A shorter man would have needed a stepladder to comfortably open the box but Seb was easily tall enough to do it. Once he'd pulled the little hinged door open he reached inside and began patiently removing the old-fashioned Bakelite fuses one by one from their slots, carefully examining the exposed wire on their undersides.

At the fifth attempt he found the culprit; the little strand of metal inside had completely melted away.

Assorted flat cardboard packets of fuse wire were stacked on a wide shelf above the box, along with pliers and a screwdriver. There was even a little torch, which worked. All very organised.

He found the correct gauge and quickly replaced the fuse, sliding it back into its holder when he'd finished. Immediately, electric light filtered down from the utility room above and he heard the faint noise of the fridge suddenly start to hum. Good.

It was as he was returning the tools and packets of wire to their shelf that he felt it. Something right at the back, pushed hard up against the wall. His fingers explored for a moment, and then he firmly gripped whatever it was and pulled it out.

A thin cardboard tube, like the ones left behind when rolls of kitchen paper had been used up. Except this one felt oddly heavy.

There must be something inside.

Seb turned the tube around so one open end was pointing towards him, and shone his torch directly into it.

It was full of paper. Tightly furled sheets of paper.

He grunted. Probably a wiring diagram of the house – that would certainly fit with everything else he'd found down here in this boy scout cellar: be prepared, and all that. He might as well take a look to familiarise himself in case the electrics blew again.

He stuck his middle finger inside the tube and worked it back and forth until the roll of papers gradually began to emerge. He pinched its leading edge between forefinger and thumb and carefully drew the whole thing out.

It wasn't an electrical circuit plan; he could see that straight away. The outside page seemed to be covered in lines of handwriting, as were presumably all the sheets furled inside it. Was it a letter? Some sort of essay? Whatever it was, what was it doing hidden down here in the dark?

With growing curiosity, Seb decided to take the documents upstairs where he could examine them in daylight. Who knew; maybe he'd stumbled across some kind of story.

He snapped the fuse box closed, and turned back towards the cellar stairs.

The Night Book.

It was definitely her handwriting, there on the first page. Meriel wrote in what used to be known as copperplate, a style based on elegant engravings. She always used a fountain pen when she made her diary entries and the overall effect was old-fashioned and formal.

Seb had unrolled the papers and placed four heavy mugs on each corner to stop them curling back in on themselves. He was intrigued. It looked to him as if Meriel had been secretly writing a novel, and had made photocopies for security. But why hide them away down in the cellar? A bit extreme, wasn't it?

He felt slightly guilty that he was about to read what she'd written. She obviously didn't want anyone else to see these pages. But he was deeply curious. *The Night Book.* What could it be about?

He carefully removed the first few folios from the pile and took them into the garden where Meriel and he had breakfasted together. He sat down in one of the wicker chairs and began to read. Seb noticed at once that although the pages were undated, they seemed to be copies of some sort of diary.

Three minutes later he placed the sheets of paper very gently on the table in front of him and stared, unseeing, across the shining lake.

His voice, when it eventually came, was fluted and strange.

'*Sweet Jesus.*'

And then ...

'*Oh, holy fuck.*'

CHAPTER THIRTY-FOUR

This is going to be tricky. It's important that I use the minimum force required. Too much and I kill him before I'm ready. Or I put him into a coma, which amounts to the same thing. He must be fully conscious throughout it all.

The coal hammer probably weighs at least six pounds. I suppose the thick, flat head is made of solid iron judging by its rusted, pitted surface. I doubt I'll need to use much muscle-power when I bring it down on his skull; the latent weight, combined with gravity, should be enough.

Cameron is sitting in his favourite armchair in front of the television, watching an unspeakably boring business programme he's meant to be appearing on. He won't take his eyes from the screen in case he misses the chance to watch his own precious self, pontificating about some controversial investment scheme or other.

I decide to wait until his moment arrives. How delicious to commemorate Cameron's self-worship by, quite literally, giving him a swollen head. I almost giggle at the thought. Shhh, Meriel. You don't want him turning around. Not now. Not now you are barely three feet behind him, gripping the hammer in both hands and awaiting your moment.

It arrives. There he is on the screen, smirking in self-satisfaction as he tells the world what a genius he is, how he always knew that this particular speculative wheeler-dealer project was a scam. I hear him chuckling to himself as he watches. What's that expression about he who laughs last? This is certainly the last time Cameron Bruton will be making happy noises. Although he most certainly will be making noises, I can guarantee that.

I raise the hammer high above us both, and then swing it down in a steep arc, allowing gravity to do most of the work for me.

There is a loud crunch — not a sickening one, but a deeply satisfying one — and his shoulders rise high on both sides of his head, just like poor President Kennedy when he was shot. Then my dear husband topples sideways over the arm of the chair. He is still breathing and after a few moments begins to mutter something. Good. I managed not to hit him too hard.

But I have no idea how long he will be unconscious for. I must move quickly. I open the top drawer of the Welsh dresser behind me and pull out the long yellow nylon ropes I bought from the mountaineering shop last week. They're thin but strong.

Three minutes later he is neatly trussed to the chair. His

wrists are tightly bound to its arms, and his ankles to the bases of both front legs. I don't care if the bonds are too tight; in due course it won't matter a jot if his circulation is cut off. Cameron won't be needing his hands or feet again. Ever.

He shows no signs of coming round so I go into the kitchen and fetch some bleach. I stand behind him holding the uncapped plastic bottle just under his nose, and squeeze slightly, so that the caustic fumes are forced into his airway.

Cameron responds at once, twisting his head away and moaning. A few moments later he opens his eyes and looks around him. He coughs and immediately groans with the pain that this must have caused him, and then he licks his lips.

'What the fuck's going on? Meriel? Where are you?'

I've done it. I hit him just hard enough. I don't care if he's slowly haemorrhaging under his stupid skull; he only needs to be alive and sentient for a few minutes while I get to work on him.

'Meriel? MERIEL? Jesus, what is this? What are you doing? Where are you? MERIEL!!!'

I step around him and into his field of vision. From the front, he looks pretty bad. Blood is still streaming down his temple and across one cheek, dripping in a sticky pool in his lap. But although down, my darling husband isn't out. At least he thinks he isn't.

'Untie me, you bitch! Now! Or I'm calling the police.

What the fuck d'you think you're playing at? You're in big trouble, Meriel, so the quicker you untie me, the better things will be for you. Do it now!'

They say actions speak louder than words so I don't utter a sound. I just go back to the dresser and open one of the smaller drawers near the top. Cameron follows me with his eyes.

I pull out the little kitchen blowtorch. I last used it to caramelise the tops of some crème brûlées I'd made.

I twist the control ring around to full and press the ignition button. A fierce jet of blue flame immediately erupts from the nozzle.

I turn back to Cameron, and slowly advance. Only now do I speak to him.

I'm dreadfully sorry, Cameron, but I'm going to have to rip that nice shirt off you. I can't be bothered fiddling around with the buttons.

'You see, I'm going to start with your nipples.'

Seb couldn't read any more. Not for the moment. He stood up, swaying slightly, and walked unsteadily back into the house. He needed water, he needed the lavatory – urgently – and he needed time to think.

But five minutes later he was back outside. He was horribly drawn to the breakfast table with its innocent-looking pile of paper, still weighed down on each corner by the jolly tea mugs.

Meriel had written this. *His Meriel*. And what he

had just read was only a tiny fraction of the whole. What other nightmarish, quasi-pornographic fantasies were scrawled across all the other repulsive pages?

Breathing deeply, he picked up the dozen or so photocopies from the table. Thus far he had looked at about half of them.

He realised he simply couldn't bring himself to read the rest. With deep reluctance, Seb slid the very last page from the bottom of the pile, and sank back in the chair with it.

. . . is now completely incoherent. The pleading and begging have stopped and he's now making strange, animal sounds. I don't know how long it will take to sever his penis with the jet of flame but I hope there is enough gas left in the blowtorch. Before he dies, I really want to—

Good Christ. Enough. *Enough.* Seb groaned aloud and threw the page onto the table in front of him.

What did this mean? What did it say about the woman he loved; her marriage; her mental state . . . and what had happened that day out on the boat?

More to the point, what the hell was he going to do now?

CHAPTER THIRTY-FIVE

Seb sat there for a long time, staring out at the lake. He felt paralysed, mentally and physically. Once or twice he tried to stand up but the effort was simply too much for him.

He almost felt bereaved, as if he'd just received the stunning, crushing news of Meriel's death.

Meriel, capable of writing the sickest material he'd ever seen. He simply couldn't take it in. Was she mentally ill, he wondered, did she suffer from some form of schizophrenia? If so, it was deeply buried. Seb trusted his instincts with people and he'd never sensed the presence of such darkness in Meriel. He loved her, for God's sake – or he had done. Now he didn't know what he felt, other than this horrible tight band of pain around his chest.

It was no good. His thoughts were ricocheting around inside his head like a savagely struck billiard ball. He had to focus, work out what to do for the best.

It suddenly occurred to him that perhaps he should try and treat it like a breaking news story. Distil everything down to the essentials; make a conscious attempt to distance himself from this nightmare. Maybe then he could see his way forward.

At last he managed to stand, and walked slowly to his car where it was parked at the front of Cathedral Crag. He fetched his reporter's notebook from the glove box, pulled a cheap ballpoint out of the ring-binder at the top, and went back to the breakfast table. He drew a deep breath. He had to force himself to be logical, methodical, inquiring. It was a story, remember?

'Except I'm a part of it,' he muttered. Suddenly, without warning, a sob shuddered through his body and he dropped his head into his hands, tears spilling from his eyes.

He'd never felt so disoriented, never felt such heartache.

Eventually Seb brought himself under control. He took his notebook from the table and flipped open the pad's shiny cover. The first thing to greet his gaze were his scrawled notes from two days earlier: Cameron Bruton's inquest. He flicked through them impatiently until he found a clean page. After a moment's thought, he quickly scribbled down a series of questions.

Why make photocopies?
Why hide them?
Why hide them in the fuse box?
Where is original manuscript now?
Does M have specific fantasy about C drowning?
(Must read ALL pages to check for this)
M almost certainly lying re C's watch for some
reason. Why? Is there link to 'night book' maybe?

He closed the pad.

This was no news story. This was his life, his love, his heart, his flesh and bones intertwined with another's. His Meriel. *Their* story.

He closed his eyes.

And it had just turned into a nightmare.

'Bob Merryman.'

Seb paused. He didn't have to do this. He could just hang up. Now.

When he spoke, he was surprised by how normal his voice sounded.

'Hi Bob,' he said, 'it's me, Seb. Sorry to bother you in the middle of a sunny Sunday afternoon.'

The news editor groaned.

'You're not bothering me, you're rescuing me. We're having a barbecue. My sister and her husband, David bloody perfect, have been banging on and on about Maggie Thatcher since I put the fucking sausages on. She loves her, he hates her. He says if she's the next prime minister he's emigrating. I'll tell you what, that guarantees Maggie my vote and I've been Labour all my life. David is *such* a prick. Anyway, what can I do you for, Sebbie old chap?'

Seb smiled faintly. Merryman always grounded him.

'Just a sniff of your contacts book, Bob. D'you happen to have the address – that is, the private address – of the county coroner?'

'Timmy Young? Sure. He lives up at Bassenthwaite, doesn't he? Hang on.'

Seb heard his boss's phone banging against the wall as Merryman went in search of his contacts book, an ancient Moleskine, battered and torn and much-repaired with Sellotape, and stuffed full of twenty years' worth of phone numbers and addresses.

A minute later he was back.

'Yeah, here we are. I thought so. Dr Timothy Young: The Grove, Mirehouse-under-Bassenthwaite. Nice place. It's about halfway down the A591, up into the fells below Skiddaw. You'll want the phone number too?'

'Please.'

When Merryman had dictated it, slowly repeating himself to be certain, he chuckled.

'All right. Come on then, Seb. Why couldn't this wait until tomorrow? What's going on?'

His reporter was prepared for this.

'It's nothing really, Bob. It's just that I've been

reading through the Sundays and I started to wonder if there might be a feature in the coroner's angle: what it's like to preside over all these drowning inquests, especially a high-profile one like Cameron Bruton's. I've got nothing better to do this afternoon so I thought I'd—'

'Bollocks.'

'I beg your pardon?'

'Bollocks. You're up to something.'

'Bob, I'm only—'

'By all means talk to the coroner, Seb. About whatever this is *really* about.

'And then, dear boy, you can talk to me.'

CHAPTER THIRTY-SIX

Meriel,

I won't be back here tonight – turns out the breakfast show producer has flu so I've got to do the early shift as well as the late one. I'll probably only get three or four hours' sleep so I'll crash out at my flat in Carlisle. See you tomorrow. Love, S. xx

He stared at the note he'd just written. He *did* love her, still, didn't he? He hated lying to her like this.

But he was in complete turmoil and he needed to get away and think. He'd forced himself to flick through the other pages in the manuscript and from what he could see they were equally as disturbing as the ones he'd first read. He couldn't see anything specifically about drowning – although there was one repellent passage involving boiling water – but without exception they were murderous chapters, steeped in extreme, sadistic violence and undiluted homicidal intent.

And Meriel had lied at Cameron's inquest. He *knew* she had. It was something to do with that bloody watch. The coroner had spotted it too.

Had she crossed the line from fantasy to reality out there on the boat that afternoon? Had she somehow managed to contrive her husband's death? He couldn't think how, but his vague sense of unease after the inquest had now crystallised into an unmistakable misgiving.

Suspicion.

He suspected Meriel. He genuinely did. He believed there was an actual possibility she had somehow murdered Cameron that day. And got away with it.

What if back then the police had somehow got their hands on a copy of *The Night Book*? Their subsequent questioning of Meriel would have been completely different in both tone and direction, that was for sure. They would definitely have organised a forensic search of the boat, too, and probably sent divers down at the spot where Cameron had drowned.

In fact – and Seb started at the thought – that's exactly what they'd do now if they were given these pages to examine. They would see them as potentially circumstantial evidence in a criminal investigation. They'd have no choice.

For the umpteenth time, he asked himself what

he was going to do. He'd got as far as dialling the first few digits of Dr Young's phone number before hanging up again. He just couldn't go through with it. He'd thought that contacting the coroner to ask for an off-the-record meeting might be somehow less significant than going direct to the police, but betrayal was betrayal.

So was murder.

Seb felt like tearing his hair out. He had to talk to someone about this. Someone he could trust. Someone older and wiser in the ways of the world: someone who could tell him what to bloody *do*.

Suddenly, a name came to him.

Of course. *Of course.*

The engineer was in when Seb phoned. He'd been intrigued by the reporter's suggestion that they meet within the hour at a riverside pub near his home.

'This sounds urgent, Sebbie,' Jess said. 'Everything as it should be?'

'Far from it,' Seb replied. 'I'm in a hole, Jess, and I need advice. You've been incredibly kind and helpful to me since I arrived here. I honestly can't think of anyone else I can talk to about this.'

'Blimey. I might not be quite the wise old bird you take me for, Seb, but I'll do my best. Look: we're just about to sit down for Sunday lunch at this end, so I can't quite do the hour. But is three o'clock at the Swan

OK for you? You know, the place down on the Eden near Armathwaite. I know them there, they'll serve us a drink outside hours.'

'Of course. See you there. And – thanks, Jess.'

Seb propped his note to Meriel against a vase of flowers on the kitchen table. Then he carefully furled all the photocopies back into their cardboard tube and locked it in the Spitfire's boot. Five minutes later he was on the road heading for the Eden Valley.

As he drove, he found himself wondering exactly when he would see Meriel again.

CHAPTER THIRTY-SEVEN

Meriel was astonished at the sheer size of her postbag. Peter Cox hadn't been exaggerating; there must be close to a couple of thousand letters, postcards and sympathy cards. There were the inevitable crank ones too, from men who made lewd and sometimes down-right disgusting suggestions about what they'd like to do to her now she was 'free'.

But the vast majority of those she had looked at were kind and thoughtful and she was genuinely touched. There was no way she could read them all, still less answer them personally. She'd have to write a general reply in her next column.

There was hardly anyone else in at Lake District FM today; the place was deserted. All the station's pro-grammes were pre-recorded on Sundays, except for the news bulletins. Even those only went out at the top of every other hour and stopped completely after six o'clock.

She looked at her watch. Almost three. There wasn't much more she could do here. She'd made some notes for future programmes and left them for her secretary to type up. She couldn't be bothered writing memos to her producer and Peter; she'd call them in the morning to tell them she'd be back next week.

Meriel looked around her office. She felt at ease here, and suddenly a profound feeling that everything would be all right washed over her. She really would be able to pick up the threads of her old life. Better than that, she would improve on it. No more Cameron to bully and torment and control her. No more stupid *Night Book*. Just lovely Seb to build a future with together.

They'd have children, she was certain of that. Lots of them. And however their careers developed, she and Seb would always keep a home in the Lakes. They belonged here. They'd discovered each other here.

She walked quickly to the lift. If she hurried, she could probably get back to Cathedral Crag before Seb had to leave for work. There might even be time to make love.

'Christ almighty, Seb, this is *bloody* serious.'

Jess hadn't touched his pint and now it was too late to start: it had been sitting in direct sunshine in the Swan's pretty rose garden and had become so warm it was virtually undrinkable.

He'd listened to the younger man's story with

increasing incredulity, only occasionally interrupting to ask a brief question. For the most part, he simply sat there staring out at the ducks splashing in the slow-moving sunlit river while Seb told his tale.

'I know,' Seb said miserably, wiping perspiration from his forehead with the back of one hand. '*Christ*, it's hot ... I keep wishing I'd never loaded that sodding dishwasher, fused the place, and ended up finding ... *that*.' He gestured at the cardboard cylinder on the picnic table in front of them. 'I wish to Christ I'd never seen the bloody thing, and it was still down there in the cellar.'

Jess gently picked it up, weighing it for a moment in his hand.

'Feels heavy. How many chapters are there?'

'Oh God, I haven't counted ... about fourteen or fifteen, I suppose.'

'Hmm. Well, as it's here, can I take a look at it?'

'Be my guest. Be warned, you might throw up.'

The engineer grunted. 'I doubt it,' he said, easing the tightly scrolled papers from the tube.

A few minutes later he had turned pale.

'Fuck me. She's mad.'

Seb shook his head, almost violently.

'No! That's the whole point, Jess – she's *not*. She's wonderful. Well, I thought she was. She's—'

'How would you know?' Jess interrupted. 'You haven't been together long. You can't possibly know what she's really like, Seb. I've been married thirty years and Sally and I are still finding things out about each other. Although I hope to Christ I never discover anything like this.'

Seb turned his head away, and Jess stirred his hot beer with one finger before continuing.

'You want my advice? OK, here it is. Take this horrible thing straight to the police. They have to investigate what it might signify.'

Seb began to speak but the engineer waved him to be silent.

'Look at it objectively, Seb. Put your reporter's hat on. Here you have a woman whose husband's drowned. Who was the only witness? Her. You yourself say there was something off-base about her testimony at the inquest and the coroner picked up on it.'

Jess gestured at the papers scattered between them on the table. 'Then all *this* stuff turns up. Sadistic death threats hidden away in the dark, like a guilty secret.'

Seb remained silent.

'It may mean nothing, or it may mean something,' the engineer went on. 'Nothing, as in she just happens to be a harmless nutter with a deeply warped imagination. Or something, as an indicator of foul play. It's not for you to sit on this, Seb, it really isn't. You have to come forward.'

Seb pushed his hair back with both hands.

'But I *love* her, Jess. At least, I thought I did. I can't ... I can't go behind her back. I—'

'You already have done. You've shown it to me.'

Seb rubbed his face repeatedly with both hands, and when he spoke again his voice was muffled.

'Maybe the bloke just drowned, Jess.'

'Maybe he did and maybe he didn't. Not your call.'

Seb groaned. 'Jesus, I want all this to go away. I can't bring myself to go to the police and I can't talk to Meriel about it. I wouldn't know where to begin, and anyway I'd probably want to believe anything she told me. I mean ...' his voice took on an almost pleading quality '... she must have *some* explanation for this, mustn't she?'

Jess gave a short, mirthless laugh. 'You might not want to hear it.'

He stroked his chin, thinking.

'All right,' he said at last. 'So you won't go to the police, and you say you can't talk to Meriel.

'So, do neither. Baby steps. Go and see the coroner, like you first planned to. Ask him if you can talk off the record. He's not a policeman; I don't think he has any powers of arrest, although you'd know more about that than me. He's more a kind of civil servant, isn't he? Anyway, it'd be a sort of halfway house for you, wouldn't it? Buy you some time.'

'Would it? What if he tells me I have to take this to the police? Threatens to turn me in for withholding evidence if I don't?'

311

Jess gazed levelly at him. 'You're nobody's fool, Seb. I think that's secretly what you want, isn't it? For someone to tell you what to do. That's really why you've come to me, isn't it?'

Seb didn't reply.

'And I'll tell you something else,' the engineer continued, speaking more slowly now. 'I think you're beginning to wonder if you're actually in love with this woman at all, or if it's really an infatuation. Do you realise that twice in the last few minutes you've told me you *think* you love her?'

Seb chewed his lip for a few moments before replying.

'All right. I honestly don't know what I think any more. Reading that thing was the biggest shock of my life ... and yes, I've probably been kidding myself about this whole coroner business. Of course he's going to ask the police to reopen the case. You're right: I suppose I just want the responsibility for that taken out of my hands.'

Jess spread his arms. 'And there's no shame in that. Anyway, perhaps we're both wrong: maybe this horrible story-book has no bearing at all on Cameron Bruton's death, legally speaking. Then I suppose you could just shove it all back in the cellar and try to work out what to do next. Although personally I'd run a million miles from someone who could even dream up this kind of shit, let alone write it down.'

Seb's voice was infinitely sad. 'I won't need to do

that. When Meriel finds out what I've done she won't want me anywhere near her. We'll be finished.'

Jess leaned forward and briefly squeezed the younger man's shoulder.

'Seb ... I've become very fond of you, you know, since you joined the station. I talk to Sally about you a lot. I've tried to look out for you and I'm ... well, I'm touched you've turned to me for advice like this.

'So let me speak to you now as your Dutch uncle.' He took a deep breath. 'Can you *imagine* what life would be like with this woman if you stayed with her? Married her? Think of the years that lie ahead. No one knows how any marriage is going to turn out. Supposing yours started to go wrong. What if her horrible fantasies became directed towards you? What if you stumbled across something like this, except it was YOU she was writing about? How easy would you sleep beside her in your bed then, eh?'

Seb stared at his friend. These were thoughts he realised he had been subconsciously struggling to push away.

'Go on.'

Jess nodded. Good; he was getting through.

'Apart from all that you'd never be easy in your mind about what happened to the first husband. Be honest with yourself. You're a journalist. You'd always want to know the truth of the matter. It would eat away at you. There. I'm done.'

The two men sat without speaking for some time. It was Jess who finally broke the silence.

'So, Seb? What happens next?'

The reporter sighed.

'First, I'm going to use the phone in the bar there to call in sick. I can't possibly do the late shift with all this going on. Then I'll ring the coroner. If he agrees to see me privately at his house, I'll drive straight over to Bassenthwaite, talk to him this afternoon. And then, whatever happens, I've come to another decision, Jess. I'm going to go back to Cathedral Crag tonight. I've got to tell Meriel what I know, and what I've done.'

He paused. 'And what I suspect, too.'

Jess raised an eyebrow. 'Are you sure that's a good idea? Going back to that house on your own? I'm sorry, Seb, but the woman could be dangerous.'

Seb shook his head. 'I owe her an explanation, Jess. I owe her at least that.'

CHAPTER THIRTY-EIGHT

Miriam Young put the phone down and stared out of the window at Bassenthwaite. Tim was down there now, making repairs to their little sailing boat.

She hated troubling him with work on a Sunday. But it had been such a *peculiar* phone call. She had recognised the young man's voice, even before he identified himself as the radio reporter who covered Tim's last inquest. He had explained that the inquest was what he was calling about.

But this Seb Richmond had been circumspect. All he would say was that he had come across new information which may, or may not, be of interest to the coroner. Something to do with the widow in the case, Meriel Kidd. At this stage it may not warrant a formal approach, but nevertheless a face-to-face conversation was probably in order. The sooner the better.

The reporter had been very polite, but there was something unmistakably insistent about his tone.

The coroner's wife made up her mind.

'Jasper! *Jasper!* Come on, boy – walkies!'

The three-year-old Labrador bounded into the room from his basket in the kitchen, his leather lead already expectantly gripped in his mouth.

'Come along, Jasper. We're going down to fetch daddy.'

'I told him to ring back in half an hour,' she told her husband breathlessly as they climbed back up the hill together from the little harbour where they moored their boat. 'I'm sorry if I've interrupted you unnecessarily, darling, but I just had this ... well, this *feeling* that it was important.'

The coroner squeezed his wife's hand. 'Miriam, I keep telling you – I trust your instincts absolutely. Now, tell me again what this chap said.'

She considered, struggling at the same time to bring her breathing under control. She *must* go for more walks with the dog; she was becoming ridiculously unfit.

'There isn't a lot to tell. It wasn't so much what he said ... it was how he said it. You know, like that Australian chappie off the telly put it the other day: "It's not *what* you say – it's how you come *over*."'

'You mean the columnist ... Clive James.'

'Yes, him, the *Observer* man. Well anyway, this chap – Richmond, he said his name was, Seb Richmond – he was strangely compelling, Tim. I told him you weren't in but he was very clever; he knew how to get my attention. He said one of the reasons he was calling you was that he felt *exactly* the same as you about that missing watch business. That made me sit up.'

Her husband stared at her for a moment and then shrugged. 'It could simply be that he noticed I wasn't entirely happy with that part of her evidence.'

'Yes, but then, as I said, he told me he'd found out something to do with the widow. Something that might shed a fresh light on things, but that he would only discuss it with you. Off the record. He must be clever because it worked and here we are.'

'Indeed.' The house, a 1930s-built wood-framed building that vaguely resembled a ski-lodge, was coming into view. 'Anything else?'

His wife thought for a moment before replying.

'Yes,' she said slowly, 'there *is* one more thing. He sounded sad. Really quite sad. As if he didn't actually want to be talking about it to anyone at all. And yet he seemed almost desperate to come over and see you today, as soon as possible.'

'Most intriguing.' Dr Young felt his pulse quicken, and it was nothing to do with the fact they were now climbing the steep steps that led to the veranda at the front of the house, with its stunning views to the dancing waters below and sunlit mountains beyond.

'The game's afoot, Watson,' he muttered under his breath.

'What's that darling?'

'Nothing. Come on.'

There was no direct road from Armathwaite to Bassenthwaite. Seb was forced to follow a series of winding country lanes that skirted beneath the mighty Skiddaw.

He almost turned back when he was halfway there. Was this all a huge over-reaction? So what if his girlfriend had a taste for extreme fantasy? She'd made no secret of her hatred for her husband, had she? So what if she channelled it in the form of these admittedly gruesome scribblings? Why connect them to Cameron's death? Or interpret her stumble in the witness box as anything other than a completely understandable wobble under pressure? She'd explained it all to him, hadn't she? The business of the watch and those last words?

Seb had a habit of talking to himself when he was wrestling with a dilemma, and he did so now, the wind whipping his words away as he sped, top down, along the dusty back roads.

'That's you thinking like a lover, Seb, or more like a fool in love. Finding excuses. Looking for ways out. Now do what Jess suggested. Try thinking like a journalist.'

Almost at once, all the elements he'd briefly succeeded in explaining away dropped back into their sinister, swirling pattern.

Cameron drowning *the very day* Meriel told him she was leaving him – and barely minutes after he'd threatened her with a very public, hostile divorce.

Meriel withholding any mention of that conversation when giving evidence to the coroner. And then lying to him about something else, something to do with the missing watch.

Meriel composing sick fantasies about murdering her husband.

The certainty of what the police response would be after reading those fantasies: an immediate search of boat and lake bed. What might they reveal?

Seb's mouth set in a grim line. He accelerated, and drove on towards Bassenthwaite.

'You must understand, Mr Richmond, that I can't discuss my thinking about this or any other case with you, other than to repeat what I have already said on the record.'

Dr Young had led Seb into his study as soon as he had arrived; after bringing them both a glass of sherry, Miriam Young had quietly withdrawn and left them alone.

'I completely understand that, sir. I was hoping, though, that we might have what the Americans call a deniable conversation; what we here know as off the record.'

'Only up to a *very* limited point, I'm afraid,' the coroner replied crisply. 'We are not in America.' Then, after a moment, he relaxed a little.

'Look, I don't wish to be difficult. How about this? Why don't I listen to what it is you have to say to me not so much as coroner, but more, shall we say, as concerned citizen? Although I must warn you that if I hear anything I feel should be brought to the attention of the police, I shall do so without hesitation.'

Seb nodded again. 'That's fair enough.'

'Well then, where do you want to begin, Mr Richmond . . . Seb?'

Seb sighed, searching for the right words.

Oh, for Christ's sake, come on. Just tell it like it is.

He drained his sherry in a single gulp.

'The truth, Dr Young, is that Meriel Kidd and I are involved. It's no secret, all our colleagues know about it.' He paused. 'I sometimes stay with her at her house and this morning, after she had gone out, there was a power cut. I had to go looking for the fuse box.'

He paused again.

This was it.

The point of no return.

320

'Eventually I found it – the fuse box, I mean – in the cellar. And when I did … well, the thing is …'

He swallowed.

'I found something else, too.'

CHAPTER THIRTY-NINE

Outwardly Timothy Young had remained impassive throughout Seb's nervous, hesitant testimony.

But his mind was racing. This was dynamite.

Already he had mentally chalked up some crucial questions for the young man sitting opposite, but for now he kept his counsel, merely nodding from time to time in gentle encouragement as Seb's story gradually emerged.

Eventually, in an unconscious echo of Jess a few hours earlier, the coroner asked: 'Can I take a look at it?'

Wordlessly, Seb pulled the papers from their increasingly frayed tube and handed them over.

'Thank you.' Dr Young patted his jacket pockets, found his reading glasses, and perched them on the end of his nose. 'Now then ...'

He read in absorbed silence, carefully placing each

page on the side-table next to him once he'd finished it. At one point he quietly asked: 'And we are quite certain this is Miss Kidd's handwriting?'

'Yes.'

The coroner unhurriedly continued. Unlike Jess earlier that day, he displayed no emotion.

'I see she dates each entry,' he remarked. 'One every few months or so, starting in 1970.'

He glanced up. 'Typically, four or five pages apiece. Quite intense, one might say, all of them. This last one was written in spring of this year. Typical of the entire genre.'

When he'd finished, he looked directly at Seb. His eyes were full of sympathy.

'This must have been extraordinarily difficult for you, my boy. First, stumbling across these documents in the way you described, discovering their dreadful contents, and then making the decision to bring them to me. I assume,' – he cleared his throat – 'I assume you are in love with this woman?'

Seb nodded. 'I was. Now ...' he shrugged, helplessly.

'Yes, *most* difficult, as I say,' the coroner murmured. 'But let me assure you, you have done absolutely the right thing. Absolutely. In fact, the *only* thing. Did you seek advice on the matter?'

'Yes. I spoke to a friend. He said I should contact you. I didn't want to go to the police.'

The coroner inclined his head. 'Yes, yes, I can quite see that ... quite ... but I'm afraid the police *will* now have to become involved. You appreciate that, don't you?'

'Yes. I only wish I didn't.'

Timothy Young stood up, and his next question took Seb by surprise.

'Would you like a cigarette? I'm going to have one.'

Seb looked gratefully at him. 'I gave up a couple of years ago but right now I'd bloody love one.'

The coroner went to a round wooden box on the windowsill and removed two filter-tipped cigarettes and a silver lighter. 'Here we are. Silk Cut, I'm afraid. Cheap and nasty. My secret vice.'

When he had lit both Seb's and his own, he returned to his armchair.

'Now, I'd like to ask you a few questions if I may, Seb. Is that all right?'

'Of course. Go ahead.'

'Thank you.' The coroner gestured to the loose pages. 'These are obviously photocopies. Do you know where the originals might be?'

Seb shook his head, and drew deeply on his cigarette. The unaccustomed nicotine made his head spin. 'No idea, I'm afraid. They could be anywhere in Cathedral Crag. It's a big place.'

The coroner nodded. 'Yes, well, doubtless the police will find them during their search of the property.'

Seb raised his eyebrows. 'They'll search Cathedral Crag?'

The older man looked slightly surprised. 'Oh yes, they're bound to,' he said briskly. 'Not just for the original manuscript, but anything else that might shed light on Miss Kidd's relationship with her late husband.'

He paused to allow Seb to absorb this. Then, speaking more gently, he continued: 'On the question of the marriage ... I presume Miss Kidd confided in you about that, as your relationship with her developed?'

Seb shifted uncomfortably. 'Well, yes. They weren't a happy couple, she said. He used to bully her, emotionally. Badly. A lot.'

'So one can assume that they argued?'

'Yes.'

'Frequently?'

'Yes.'

Seb realised what was coming next. He suddenly felt clammy.

'Miss Kidd will doubtless have told you about events on the day of her husband's drowning. Of their final minutes together.'

'Yes.'

'Did she tell you if they had one of their arguments that afternoon? Out on the boat?'

Seb thought furiously. He'd been so overwhelmed and preoccupied by his discovery of *The Night Book* that it had never occurred to him he might face questions like this. How incredibly naive and unthinking of him. What on earth was he to answer?

The coroner waited patiently.

Eventually, Seb cleared his throat and said: 'That's confidential information, Dr Young. I don't feel happy going into that kind of detail with you. It would feel like I was betraying a source.'

Timothy Young steepled his fingers and rested his chin on them. When he spoke, a more formal note had entered his voice, although his eyes remained sympathetic.

'Mr Richmond. Of course you don't have to answer me, and you'll have exactly that same right when the police question you. But—'

Seb sat bolt upright. 'The police? Question me? Why?'

The coroner carefully tapped his cigarette on the side of the ashtray between them before replying.

'Why? Well, for several reasons. To begin with, they'll want a formal statement from you on how you found those documents. That's more procedural than anything else. But they'll want to garner as much information as they can about Miss Kidd's attitude towards her husband, and in particular her actions on the day he died.'

He took a fresh drag on his cigarette. 'Now, as I'm sure you'll remember from the inquest, there were certain discrepancies in the widow's testimony. She inexplicably failed to mention to the police anything about her final conversation with her husband – the one concerning the time of day – but she let it slip to me. You'll also recall that she seemed distinctly uneasy about the matter of his missing watch.'

He leaned forward towards Seb, speaking now with slow deliberation.

'So, one wonders what else has Miss Kidd omitted from her formal account of what happened that afternoon. It's plain to me she told you they had a row: your discomfort and your refusal to answer my question just now spoke for itself.'

Seb looked hunted. 'If you say so. But as you said, I don't have to answer.'

'No, you don't,' the coroner agreed. 'But what do you suppose a jury would make of such an evasion if you were called as a witness?'

Seb was appalled. Things were going from bad to worse.

'*Me?* A witness?'

'Mr Richmond.' The formality was back. 'Let us be clear. This matter may go to criminal trial. If—'

'I realise that,' Seb interrupted. 'I'd already accepted that possibility when I decided to come here. But why would I be called as a witness?'

The coroner smiled faintly. 'Let me explain. And I'm speaking now not as coroner, but as a former criminal barrister.

'If I were prosecuting this case, and I read in the transcript of your police interview that you refused to say if Miss Kidd told you she'd argued with her husband on the day he drowned – well ... I'd get you into the witness box as quickly as I could manage it. I'd want the jury to watch you prevaricate on the point when I pressed you on it. They'd naturally draw their own conclusions, even if the judge instructed them to disregard your refusal to answer.'

Timothy Young allowed Seb to digest this information in silence before asking him: 'Would you like another sherry?'

Seb grimaced. 'No thanks. I think I might be sick.'

The older man leaned forward, sympathetic again. 'Look, Seb. It's clear to me that you are a highly intelligent and honourable man. A logical one too. You need to apply that logic now.

'You suspect your girlfriend of foul play. Quite frankly, so do I. I was deeply uncomfortable with the whole tone of her testimony at the inquest. Now you've taken the courageous decision to hand over these incriminating documents. Consider why you've done that.

'I would suggest it was because we're talking about a possible murder. The very worst crime there is. *Murder*. Whatever your feelings and loyalties once were towards Miss Kidd, you clearly believe they are overridden by a higher purpose; that it is more important to see that justice is done. And you're right. Therefore it makes no sense to refuse to answer these questions, does it? It doesn't do much good, either, as I've explained.'

Seb shook his head miserably.

'No.'

'So let's try again. Remember why you're here. To help establish the truth of a man's death. Now. Did Meriel Kidd tell you that she'd argued with her husband before he drowned?'

Seb took a long, shivering breath. 'Yes. Yes, she did.'

'And did she say what the row was about?'

'Yes. It was about their divorce. She told him she was leaving him. That very evening.'

'And what was her husband's reaction to that?'

Seb had already crossed the Rubicon; now he deliberately walked away from the riverbank.

'He was furious. He threatened her. He said if she walked out on him he would divorce her in the most public way he possibly could. He told her he would destroy her career. And then ... then he got into the water for his swim.'

The coroner carefully considered his next question. 'What effect did those threats have on Miss Kidd?'

Seb closed his eyes.

'Meriel told me that she hated him. She told me she absolutely hated him.'

*

'Seb? Is that you?'

Meriel laid her book down and looked at her watch. Not yet eight o'clock in the evening; he should still be at the station, putting the next day's breakfast show together.

She heard the front door close followed by a sound she was already learning to recognise, Seb's footsteps crossing the hall. Next moment he was in the room.

'Darling! I thought I wasn't going to see you until tomorrow. Has something happened?'

He stopped a few feet into the lounge, staring at her with an expression on his face she'd never seen before. He looked terrible.

'Seb?' Meriel stood up. 'What is it? What's wrong?'

'Meriel . . .' His voice sounded thick and strange and when he passed a hand across his forehead, she could see it was trembling.

'Seb! Oh Seb, what is it? Tell me!' She crossed the room and reached for his hands. 'You're shaking! What on earth's happened?'

'Meriel . . .' he said again, in the same peculiar, throaty tone. 'There's something I need to tell you. Something we need to talk about.' He gestured to her chair. 'Please . . . sit down.'

'No! Tell me, Seb. Tell me straight away. Now!'

'I will. I need a second. Just give me a second.' Seb pulled his hands free of hers and walked over to the drinks table that stood in the bay window facing

Derwent Water. Dusk was falling and below the house the lake had turned a dull pewter.

He filled two crystal tumblers with whisky before turning round again, a brimming glass in each hand.

She hadn't moved, and was staring at him with enormous eyes.

'I wish you'd sit down, Meriel. Please.'

She stamped her foot in frustration. 'Oh, for Christ's sake, Seb! What in God's name is this about?'

His answer, when it came, turned her blood to water.

'I found your diary.'

CHAPTER FORTY

Once the first shock had passed, Meriel found herself beginning to feel increasingly calm, even fatalistic.

She realised that she had been subconsciously trying to bury her anxiety about where Cameron had hidden the photocopies. Presumably there were others secreted somewhere in the house, but that didn't matter. One set coming to light was enough. And now that had happened, she was experiencing a wholly unexpected sensation of relief.

By contrast, her feelings for Seb, until a few minutes before so warm and vibrant, had now been almost instantaneously deep-frozen. His betrayal was so complete, its likely consequences for her so devastating, that she was experiencing an extraordinarily rapid, spreading numbness in her heart.

She looked with a new dispassion and detachment at her lover. Her former lover, she supposed she should think of him now. He had yet to sit down; Seb had remained standing in the alcove overlooking the lake throughout his ... what? Confession? Accusation? Apology? He was in a dreadful state, trembling and, at one point, shedding tears.

She hadn't uttered a sound, not since he'd told her what he had found, and what he'd done. She'd just sat with her hands folded in her lap, gazing steadily at him as he tumbled through his words.

When it was clear that he was at last done and had no more to say, she spoke in a low, gentle tone that was only slightly tinged with regret.

'I wonder why you felt you couldn't come to me first ... give me a chance to explain. I *could* have explained, you know, Seb. If you'd let me. Afterwards, if you'd decided to go to the authorities anyway, I wouldn't have tried to stop you.'

Seb wasn't prepared for this. He'd expected anger, tears, searing recrimination. Not this serene, almost detached response.

'Meriel ... look ... I didn't have a choice. It wasn't only what you'd written about wanting to kill Cameron ... in all that vile, horrible detail ... it was that I could see, straight away, how that connected with everything else. The way you were at the inquest. How you spoke to me that same night, here at the house.'

'What do you mean?'

Seb ran both hands through his hair.

'Oh, come on, Meriel ... you've been *lying* about something! I just told you that the coroner thinks so, too, and he doesn't even know you! Everyone on the press bench that day felt that either you were lying or hiding something, which amounts to the same thing.'

She looked levelly at him. 'But you always knew that, didn't you? I only ever told *you* that Cameron and I argued on the boat that day. You knew perfectly well I was never going to share that with anyone else, let alone the coroner. You even agreed with me that I shouldn't. So why are you now—'

'*That's not what I'm talking about!*'

She flinched. 'Please don't shout at me, Seb. I had a lifetime of that with Cameron.'

He passed a hand over his eyes.

'I'm sorry. But you *know* that's not what I'm talking about. Look, Meriel. Perhaps I should have said this on the night of the inquest. But I just wanted it all to go away, for us to be happy. So I pretended to believe you.'

'Pretended to believe me about what?'

'About the watch, the Rolex. That business of forgetting to tell the police – and even me – about Cameron asking you the time just before he drowned. The two things are linked in some way, and not in a good way, Meriel. I *know* it.'

She smoothed her skirt with both palms.

'You can't possibly know anything of the kind, Seb.

To begin with, I'm not lying. I have no idea where the watch is. And I genuinely forgot to tell the police about that last conversation about the stupid time. I was in *shock*, Seb, for God's sake. And even if I were hiding something – and I'm NOT – *you weren't there*. No one was. I'm the only person who knows the truth and I've told the truth. And I'll keep telling it. It looks as if I'll have to, after what you've done today.'

Silence fell. It was Meriel who broke it, saying in a small voice: 'I thought you loved me, Seb. I really did. I thought you trusted me, too.'

'I did,' he almost groaned. 'I do ... or at least I ... oh *Meriel*, why did you write such terrible things? Such awful, sadistic things? Why did you make copies? And where are the originals?'

She threw her head back and laughed.

He stared at her in astonishment.

'What could possibly be funny, at a time like this?'

After a few moments, she brought herself under control.

'Oh, I don't know. I suppose it *is* funny, in a way; Cameron still jerking my chain from beyond the grave like this. Jerking yours, too. Maybe it's his ghost's revenge.'

'Meriel, I don't know what you're talking about.'

She smiled faintly. What the hell.

'*I* didn't make those copies. Cameron did. He some-how found where I kept the original manuscript. He was always secretly going through my things, looking for God knows what. When I made up my mind to leave him, I burned it – every single page. But it was too late. He'd already secretly made photocopies and hidden them. I searched everywhere for them but I never thought to look in the bloody fuse box.'

A light began to flicker and brighten in Seb's mind.

'*That's* what you were arguing about on the boat, isn't it?' he asked slowly. 'He told you what he'd done. That's what he meant when he said if he sued you for divorce, he could make things very messy for you. He was going to produce *The Night Book* as evidence of unreasonable behaviour. That's why he said he could destroy your career.'

She gave another, shorter laugh. For the first time her voice was edged with bitterness.

'Oh, I think you achieved that today, Seb. But do you really think I'm going to confirm any of this to you? So you can go running to your new friend, the coroner? You've already shared with him things that I told you in the deepest confidence. Things I thought I was telling to the man I loved, the man I was going to marry and have children with. Things which, for your information, I shall deny I ever said. It'll be your word against mine.'

Seb stared at her, appalled.

'Oh Christ, Meriel, has it come to this? Has it really come to this? Just look at us.'

'No, you look at me, Seb. Look very carefully. You've turned me into a Miss Havisham. Can't you see? You've betrayed me, and now I must harden my heart. I have no other choice. You made yours, and now I'm making mine.'

She stood up.

'From what you told me about your cosy little chat with the coroner, I can expect the police to turn up here at some point tomorrow. So I have a great deal to do this evening, not least calling my solicitor at home. I'd like you to get your things and go, please. Right away.'

He nodded slowly. 'Of course. Of course I'll go. But, Meriel ...'

'What?'

'I had to do it. You must understand. I wouldn't have been able to live with myself if I'd just shrugged the whole thing off, decided it was none of my business. And I'm sorry ... I wouldn't have been able to live with *you*. We're talking about a man's death, for heaven's sake. And it's a suspicious death, whatever you may say.'

He looked almost appealingly at her.

'You still haven't told me, you still haven't explained about the diary. What did it all *mean*, Meriel?'

She sighed. 'It didn't mean anything. They were the outpourings of a very unhappy, very troubled woman. An outlet, that's all. I wasn't proud of any of it. And then, when I thought you had arrived to save me, I burned them. I was ashamed of them. I could have explained all that, if you'd given me the chance. Now I'll have to do that to the police instead. Thank you, Seb.'

'But Meriel ... what about the other things ... the missing watch ... that last conversation.' He licked his lips. 'Fuck it. I'm just going to ask you outright.'

'Ask me what? Did I kill him?'

'Yes. Did you kill him, Meriel?'

'Get out.'

CHAPTER FORTY-ONE

Detective Inspector Mark Thompson was profoundly pissed off.

He had twice been forced to postpone his summer leave this year because of staff shortages. His wife had given him a very hard time about it, and he didn't blame her.

Now, literally as they were packing their bags for a fortnight in Faro – *literally* – the phone downstairs had rung. Clementine answered it and he could hear the ominous lilt to her voice as she called up to him: 'Mark. It's for you. It's your boss.'

She was coming up the stairs as he made his way down and as they passed each other she hissed at him: 'Don't you *dare* let them do this again, Mark, otherwise I promise you I'm going to Portugal on my own. I don't care if it's actually hotter here than it is there. I mean it. I want a holiday. Enough's enough.'

A few moments later he was putting the receiver to his ear.

'DI Thompson.'

'Mark, it's me, Gil. I can't tell you how sorry I am about this, but I'm going to have to call you in.'

'Tell me this is a joke, Gil.'

'I wish. It's a biggie, Mark, otherwise I wouldn't ask. I need my best man. In fact, it isn't even my decision. I've just put the phone down on the assistant commissioner. He won't hear of anyone but you heading this one up.'

'Just hang on, Gil, while I bang my head against the wall.'

The superintendent heard several muffled thuds before his DI's voice came back on the line.

'Why can't Harry handle it, whatever it is? He's a chief inspector now, isn't he? He outranks me.'

His boss coughed in embarrassment. 'I'm sorry, Mark, but Harry's ... well, Harry's on holiday in the States with his family just now. Road trip. Uncontactable.'

'Oh *great*. Lucky bloody Harry, eh? Three more hours and I would've been on a plane myself, to Portugal.'

'And I would have called you straight back the moment you'd landed, I'm afraid.'

Mark drew a heavy sigh.

'All right, Gil. I suppose there's no point me arguing

the toss about this, although fuck knows what I'm going to tell Clemmie. What's the case?'

The superintendent managed to stifle his own sigh of relief.

'It's going to be very high-profile when it gets out,' he warned. '*Very*. You know that Meriel Kidd woman?'

'Not personally but I've heard of her, obviously. The glam radio presenter. Her husband drowned. Coroner ruled it as misadventure, right?'

'Correct. But hang on to your hat, Marky boy, it turns out that just might have been the wrong verdict. Seems we could be looking at murder. With the wife as killer.'

'Holy moley. Why?'

'New evidence. Circumstantial at the moment but it may lead to other stuff. Get your backside in here asap and I'll brief you. Then you'll have to get over to Derwent Water and make an arrest, bring our Miss Kidd in for questioning.'

The DI nodded. 'OK. Give me half an hour. Oh, and you'd better have a crash medical team standing by.'

'Uh? What for?'

'I may need some broken bones setting. My wife's about to try to kill me.'

Tim Young knew the assistant commissioner personally and had phoned him at his desk first thing on Monday morning. By ten o'clock he was driving through the gates of Cumbria police headquarters at Carleton Hall in Penrith, the photocopies of Meriel's notebook safely locked inside his briefcase.

By eleven, the AC had briefed his superintendent and shortly after midday DI Thompson was sitting opposite his boss reading the increasingly dog-eared pages with growing incredulity.

'Meriel *Kidd* wrote this shit? The famous agony aunt, the one with the face that launched a thousand ships? Are we sure?'

The superintendent nodded. 'The boyfriend who gave it to Tim Young says it's her handwriting for definite, although obviously we'll need to get some samples to compare it with. You can do that when you go to the house.'

'OK. How do we know she'll be there?'

'I sent the local uniform over a couple of hours ago. She's at home all right, and the constable told her politely but firmly to stay there until CID arrive. That's you. He's standing watch outside to make sure she doesn't go anywhere. But that's probably unnecessary; apparently she's got her solicitor with her. She seems to have been expecting us. I reckon her boyfriend tipped her off as to what he'd done. I'd have liked to have been a fly on the wall during *that* conversation. Anyway, what's the battle plan, Mark?'

The DI pushed his chair back and stretched his legs out in front of him, deliberating.

'I don't think I need to formally arrest her, do you? Not yet, anyway. I'll just bring her in to help us with our inquiries for now.'

'OK. That's your call.'

'As for the boyfriend, this Seb Richmond guy, he must have had serious motive for doing this. Handing her poisonous scribblings over to the coroner, I mean. Quite a betrayal, wouldn't you agree? What did Tim Young say about that?'

Gil Tremayne held up a forefinger.

'Now. That's where things get even more interesting. Apparently Meriel confided in Seb Richmond that she and Bruton argued that afternoon on the boat, big time. She told her husband she was going to leave him and he went nuts, threatened her with a great big messy divorce, said he'd screw up her career, all of that. Then a few minutes later the man's bobbing up and down in the water, drowned. Doesn't look too good, does it?'

'Not for her, no. Anything else?'

'Yes indeed. Some murky stuff about a missing watch – Bruton's, a Rolex – that came out at the inquest. Young reckons there's something fishy about it, but you'll need to speak to him yourself, I couldn't quite follow his line on that. Anyway, back to today's action plan. Continue.'

Mark had been scribbling a few notes on his police-issue pad while his boss was talking. Glancing at them, he said: 'It's pretty straightforward, really. As I say, first I'll go to Derwent Water and pick Meriel up, bring her back here, and let her cool her heels for a while in one of the interview rooms. I want extra copies of this ordure left in there for her to look at while she's on her own. Concentrate her mind. Meanwhile I'll be talking to lover boy. Do we have a hook on him?'

Superintendent Tremayne nodded. 'Yup. He's at work at Lake District FM up in Carlisle. A reporter there. Covered Cameron Bruton's inquest for them, in fact.'

'Really? While he was screwing the widow?'

The other man shrugged. 'Seems like it.'

'OK. Well, let's send a car for him now and bring him in. Again, no need for the cuffs. He's just a witness at this stage.'

'What about forensics?'

Mark Thompson considered the question.

'Obviously, we need to go through the house at Derwent Water with a fine-tooth comb. Start this afternoon if possible. See if our black widow had any other plans for her late husband. We'll search the boat, too. Where is it now?'

Tremayne consulted a slim file on the desk in front of him.

'A place just outside Keswick. It's in dry dock.'

'Then let's get forensics to give it a dry clean. Now, what about this missing Rolex?'

The superintendent shrugged. 'As I say, you need to speak to the coroner about that. It sounds complicated.' He pushed a white card across the table to the DI. 'That's his number.'

'I'll call him now. Can I use your phone?'

'Go ahead.'

Ten minutes later DI Thompson thoughtfully replaced the receiver on its cradle.

'Well?' his boss asked.

The detective drummed his fingers on the table for a few moments.

'I'm not exactly sure,' he said slowly. 'But, as you say, there seems to be some fog around this. Seemingly Miss Kidd obfuscated in both her statement to us – the one she made on the day her husband drowned – and then later in her evidence to the inquest. Nothing to really get a handle on, but it revolves around her very last conversation with the deceased. Something to do with what time it was, and his watch which subsequently disappeared. Tim Young thinks it could be significant.'

The DI fell silent again, and Tremayne watched his best detective thinking the thing through. He could practically hear the man's brain humming. This was why the AC had been right to cancel the poor bastard's holiday. DI Thompson was a bloody natural.

'Right,' the man opposite him said at last. 'I'll

need to see a transcript of the inquest, that exchange between Young and Kidd about the Rolex. Tell the stenographers it's on either side of the mid-morning adjournment. But whatever, I reckon we'll definitely need divers. I want an *exact* triangulation made of the spot Bruton's boat was in when he drowned. Then we can get down to the lake bed and see what might be there. Can you organise that for me?'

'Consider it done.'

'And you'll bring Seb Richmond in, and make sure those copies of the ... what does she call it?' He peered at the pages in front of him. 'Yeah, *The Night Book* ... Jesus ... you'll get them put on the table in the inter-view room where Kidd can see them?'

'It'll all be taken care of.'

'Good. In that case, I'll get myself down the A66 to this Cathedral Crag place. I just hope her sodding lawyer hasn't advised her to remain silent during questioning. I need this woman to talk. I have to trip her up.'

Maxwell Probus had often idly wondered if his sur-name hadn't in some way predicated his choice of career in the law. Obviously its Latin derivation was significant in itself, but the various English trans-lations – which included 'honourable', 'upright', 'veracious' and (less pleasingly) 'bully' – seemed ideal for someone who had decided to become a solicitor.

He'd spent most of his career in London, specialising in criminal defence work. Probus cut his teeth in the infamous Ruth Ellis trial of 1955 – Ellis was the last woman to be hanged in England – and later acted for two of the men accused of the Great Train Robbery of 1963. But in recent years he had semi-retired to the Lake District, and these days mostly represented drink-drivers, people accused of common assault, and sundry minor malefactors.

Meriel had engaged him three years earlier when she was accused of driving at almost 90mph on the M6 between Carlisle and Penrith. She had stood to lose her licence, which already carried maximum penalty points for previous offences.

Probus had mounted an ingenious defence on her behalf which even she hadn't fully comprehended. Neither had the magistrates, who fined her but were nervous of imposing a ban, such was Probus's Augustan bearing in their court.

Now he was sitting in Meriel's lounge, sipping the repulsive instant coffee she had made him and considering everything she had told him over the last half-hour.

'Very well, Mrs Bruton,' he began, but Meriel held one hand up.

'Please, Mr Probus. I would prefer it if you call me Meriel, or Miss Kidd.'

He bowed his head in acknowledgement. 'Then the

latter it shall be. Now then, *Miss Kidd* ... the facts of this case seem plain enough, as you have described them to me.'

He carefully put his coffee cup on the little table beside him. He couldn't bear to touch another drop of the stuff.

'Your late husband died in a most unfortunate accident. But an accident it was. The coroner's verdict is indisputable. Misadventure.

'These ... shall we say, *diaries*, that you have so frankly informed me you have composed, copies of which are now in the hands of the police ... setting aside questions of – forgive me – taste and decency ... they are works of pure fantasy, are they not? *Private* works, never intended for the eyes of others, still less publication of any description?'

'Yes. I only ever wrote them for myself.'

'Precisely. They may well contain detailed descriptions of Mr Bruton's death at your hands, Miss Kidd, but they are as inconsequential in law as ... well, as are dreams. Private fantasies that simply have no bearing on the circumstances of your late husband's death.'

Meriel swallowed. 'Yes, but they could have a very damaging effect on my reputation and career, Mr Probus, if they were to be made public. I've been very ... straightforward with you this morning. The descriptions in this book are extremely ... violent.'

The lawyer spread his hands.

'But if you are not charged with any offence – and I cannot see grounds for that, based, as I say, on what you have told me – the diaries must be returned to you and the police will have no business in making a single word of them public. And I shall make certain that they do not.'

Probus considered his next words carefully, and when he spoke it was with some delicacy.

'However ... if they were so misguided as to bring a charge or charges against you, based on the pages you wrote, then yes, they would be entitled to present them in open court. That would lead to unfortunate publicity, I'm afraid. But to be frank with you, Miss Kidd, that would be the least of your concerns in such circumstances.'

Meriel nodded. 'And how do you advise me to respond when the police question me later today?'

Probus smiled broadly.

'Let us cross that bridge when we come to it, shall we, dear lady?'

Meriel winced. She supposed she'd have to put up with this crass patronage.

'I will be with you at all times, rest assured,' Probus continued, oblivious. 'If I feel you are being dragooned or unduly coerced, I shall intervene. I am very experienced in these matters, Miss Kidd. You are in good hands, I assure you.'

At that moment there was a heavy knock on the

front door and Meriel crossed to the window that looked out on the drive.

'There's a police car. They're here.'

The lawyer beamed at her.

'Then let them enter, let them enter. You have nothing to fear.

'Nothing to fear whatsoever.'

CHAPTER FORTY-TWO

By two o'clock Meriel was sitting alone in a small room at county police headquarters. One entire wall was darkly mirrored and she was certain it was a singular arrangement, with others able to see into the room from the other side.

Probus, who had offices in Penrith less than ten minutes away, had returned to his chambers, promising her he would be back the moment questioning began. 'I envisage you being home again in time for your evening meal, my dear,' he informed her confidently as he left.

DI Thompson had been formal but polite earlier when he arrived at Cathedral Crag. He explained to Meriel that he had applied for a warrant to search the house, but that everything would be put back the way it was when his officers had finished. He'd asked her for a sample of her handwriting, and she gave him some programme notes she'd been working on. These were carefully placed into a clear plastic evidence bag which was then deliberately sealed in front of her.

Next she had been escorted to the big Rover squad car waiting in the drive, asked to sit in the back, and off they'd set for Penrith, Probus following close behind in his silver Jaguar. Meriel had not been formally arrested. That, she reasoned, must at least count for something.

There were three plastic chairs in the interview room, two on the other side of the table from hers. She'd spotted the fresh copies of *The Night Book* straight away; she could hardly miss them, placed as they were squarely in the middle of the table. It was obviously a crude attempt by the police to throw her off balance, and Meriel decided not to oblige them by looking at even a single page. She was sure someone was watching from the other side of the mirror. She also suspected that later they'd ask her to read some extracts aloud, but hopefully Probus could put a stop to any of that kind of theatre.

Just as she had during Seb's monologue last night, Meriel crossed her ankles, folded her hands in her lap, and sat calmly waiting. In her head she endlessly replayed the same mantra, a comfort blanket of words.

'*I was the only one there. I am the only one who knows what happened. I was the only one there.*'

*

354

Seb insisted on driving himself to the police station. He'd been bullish when the call came from a Sergeant Furness in Penrith, explaining that Seb was wanted for questioning and that a police car would shortly arrive at Lake District FM to bring him in.

As a reporter Seb had had many dealings with the police and he wasn't intimidated by them.

'Forget it, sergeant,' he said. 'Unless I'm a suspect, which obviously I'm not, I don't have to get into one of your squad cars and I'm not going to. Have a parking space ready for me down there. I'll be in a Triumph Spitfire. You can expect me within the hour.'

He'd been delaying having a conversation with Bob Merryman, but now that couldn't be put off any longer.

'A word, Bob?' he called across to the news editor as he put the phone down. 'In private?'

The others in the newsroom looked up curiously. Had Richmond been offered another job? He was certainly the network's blue-eyed boy these days. Maybe he was going to ask Merryman for a pay rise.

When they were alone in a spare studio, Seb came straight to the point.

'Obviously you know about Meriel and me.'

Merryman looked faintly amused. 'No, Sebastian, I had no idea. Whatever do you mean?'

Seb ignored the irony.

'Listen, Bob, this is heavy stuff. Seriously.'

Merryman stopped smiling and frowned. 'Go on.'

'I'm ninety-nine per cent sure that Meriel's been arrested this morning or, if not, she's at least been taken in for questioning. She'll be down at Cumbria Police HQ in Penrith right now.'

The news editor gaped.

'*What?* What the fuck for? What's she done?'

Seb took a deep breath.

'She might have murdered her husband. His drowning may not have been an accident.'

He thought his boss was going to fall off his chair.

'Hold on. Just hold on a minute, Seb. You're telling me Meriel Kidd maybe killed Cameron Bruton and now she's in custody? How the hell do you know all this?'

Seb picked his words with care.

'I found something, Bob. Yesterday. Something hidden at Cathedral Crag. I can't say what it is, but it was . . . incriminating. There's other stuff that I know, or suspect, that if I'm honest with you I've been trying to forget or ignore for weeks. But I simply can't do that any more, not after what I found yesterday.'

Merryman was slowly beginning to recover his poise.

'So you took this thing, whatever it was, to the police?'

Seb shook his head. 'No. I couldn't bring myself to. I took it to the coroner instead. That didn't seem quite so . . . perfidious.'

'*Perfidious?* What is this, Shakespeare?'

'Oh, for Christ's sake then ... *disloyal*. OK? The coroner said he'd hand it over to an assistant commissioner he knows personally, first thing this morning. That's clearly what must have happened because I just had a call from police headquarters. They want to question me as a witness. Now. This afternoon.'

The news editor noisily blew out his cheeks.

'Christ almighty, Seb, what the fuck have you got yourself into here? This is going to be *huge*, and you're right in the bloody middle of it. In fact, it sounds like you could be a material witness. That means I'll have to pull you off the story.' He paused, thinking furiously. 'D'you know if the cops are going to put out a statement of any kind? Announce that they've pulled Meriel in on suspicion of murder?'

Seb stood up to leave. 'I have no idea. If they do, I know she has a solicitor who'll handle things for her. But you don't need to wait for the police to announce anything, do you? I've just given you the exclusive, haven't I? You can run this ahead of everyone else.'

Merryman nodded grimly as he too rose to his feet.

'I suppose you're right there; thanks to you we're ahead of the pack.' He shook his head. 'Jesus ... I'd better go see Peter Cox. Right now. I've no idea how we're going to cover this. Meriel's one of our own. As are you, you stupid bastard. Why couldn't you keep it in your trousers? I warned you, didn't I? I bloody warned you.'

The two men went out into the corridor. 'Seriously, what about you, Seb?' the news editor asked his reporter flatly. 'Do you want us to sort you out a solicitor?'

Seb shook his head as he headed for the lifts.

'No. I don't want to add to the drama of this thing. I can handle it myself.'

'Well, OK ... call me if you change your mind. Don't underestimate the police. They can be tricky bastards. I once knew a – *Peter? PETER!*' The station manager had stepped out of his office a little further down the passage. He spun around, startled.

'Bob? Christ, what's up? Something serious happened?'

'Serious?' echoed Merryman. '*Serious?*' He began to walk towards his boss. 'Peter, you have absolutely *no* fucking idea.'

CHAPTER FORTY-THREE

Unlike Meriel, who remained sitting quite alone – but observed – Seb was questioned almost as soon as he arrived at police headquarters. He was shown straight into an interview room where Mark Thompson immediately joined him.

'Hi, I'm DI Thompson,' he said, shaking Seb's hand. 'This isn't an interview under caution, Mr Richmond, so I'm not going to record it or ask anyone else to be present. We'll need to do a formal interview with you at some point, get a few things on the record, but this afternoon you're simply helping us with our inquiries. OK?'

Seb nodded. 'That's fine. But you'll appreciate how extremely difficult this is for me, Inspector, given my close relationship with Meriel Kidd.'

'Of course. That's one of the reasons I want to keep this as informal as possible. But I really need your co-operation, Mr Richmond. Are you willing to be completely open with me?'

Seb gave a weary shrug. 'Look. I've thought this all through as best I can and I've decided that the only thing I can possibly do now is what I think is right. Dr Young was very useful last night in getting me to see things straight. And call me Seb, by the way.'

The detective sat down opposite.

'Thank you, Seb, I will. Now ... let me be quite frank with you. Miss Kidd is still awaiting questioning here. That's because I wanted to talk to you first. So I'd like you to take me through it all, starting with how you stumbled across this manuscript of hers yesterday.'

Seb had barely finished going through the events leading to his discovery in the fuse box when the door opened and a uniformed constable poked his head into the room.

'Sorry to interrupt, sir, but the officer organising the search at the house is on the line. He says it's important.'

The DI sighed. 'Apologies, Seb, I have to take this. Constable, bring Mr Richmond here some tea, would you?' He left the room.

Five minutes later he was back, thoughtful.

'Well, well,' he said, resuming his seat. 'My men have discovered a second manuscript – another set of photocopies. They were in an envelope taped behind a radiator in the kitchen. It sounds to me as if they're exactly the same as the ones you found yesterday. But I can't understand why Miss Kidd would go to such lengths to duplicate her pages and then hide them. Can you shed any light on that?'

Seb have a short, humourless laugh. 'Yes, I think I can. I had exactly the same question. Last night after I'd left the coroner I went back to Cathedral Crag to see Meriel. Perhaps I shouldn't have, but I felt I owed her an explanation of what I'd done. It was a difficult conversation, as you might imagine. But during it she told me it wasn't she who made these copies, let alone hid them. It was her husband. He did it without her knowledge, after he'd found the originals.'

DI Thompson sat up a little straighter. 'Let me get this right. Cameron Bruton discovered the book and made the photocopies behind his wife's back? When did she become aware he'd done that?'

Seb shook his head. 'I'm not sure. But it was obvious she knew, because she told me she'd searched all over the house for them, without success.'

The detective sat in silence for some time.

'All right,' he said at last. 'We'll come back to this. Meanwhile, what about Miss Kidd's relationship with her husband? You told Dr Young it was a pretty bad set-up.'

Seb went through what he knew about the Bruton marriage. When he'd finished, the DI put both hands behind his head and stared up at the ceiling.

'Right, let's take stock here. So far, we have a relationship gone toxic, a wife so angry with her husband
that she writes vengeful filth about murdering him,
he then discovers it, duplicates it and hides it – and
at some point, tells her what he's done. Where's the
original diary, by the way? Any ideas?'

'Meriel burned it.'

'What? Why?'

For the first time during the interview, Seb looked
distressed.

'Last night she told me that when she realised that
she had fallen in love with me . . . that I'd *saved* her,
as she put it . . . she suddenly wanted to get rid of it.
She said she wasn't proud of what she'd written; in
fact, she said she was deeply ashamed of it. So she
burned it.'

The policeman looked at him with barely concealed
sympathy. 'I'm really sorry, Seb. Truly, I am. I can see
all of this is proving extremely difficult for you. Your
whole world's turned upside down in the last twenty-
four hours, hasn't it?'

Seb stared miserably at the floor.

'You could say that. This time yesterday I thought
I'd found the woman I was going to marry. Now look
at me. I'm helping in a murder inquiry that could see
her jailed for life. And God knows what she's going
through right now.'

He suddenly looked up. 'Is Meriel all right? She must

be in a dreadful state. Christ, I feel awful about this . . . What a fucking *mess*.'

DI Thompson looked shrewdly at the man opposite him.

'I wonder how well you really know this woman, Seb. Far from being in a state, as you put it, she's remained remarkably calm under the circumstances. When I went to her house this morning to bring her in, she was cool as a cucumber.'

Before Seb could reply to that, the detective pressed on.

'Now, I want you to tell me *exactly* what she told you about what happened on the boat that afternoon. Try to remember anything and everything she's said about it.'

Seb nodded. 'All right . . . Well . . . she's always been quite straight about it with me. She said they had a row.'

'So you knew at the inquest that she was lying – lying by omission. Because she never mentioned any such argument to the coroner.'

Seb looked slightly uncomfortable.

'That's right. But I didn't think it was important . . . not at the time, anyway. I thought she was just, well, embarrassed that the last exchange she'd had with her husband was an unpleasant one.'

'OK, Seb, that's fair enough. Do you know what the row was about?'

'Yes, I do. Meriel told Cameron that she wanted a separation, that she was leaving him. He got very angry and threatened her with a nasty divorce. A lot of mud-slinging. Bad PR for her career, all of that. But . . .'

Seb paused.

'Go on. But what?'

'Now I think there was more to it than that. A *lot* more. I think when she told him the marriage was over, he took the gloves off. Revealed to her he knew all about her diary, that he'd found it, taken copies and hidden them. I think *that* was the threat he made: that if she left him, and humiliated him, he'd retaliate, using *The Night Book* as grounds for divorce. The publicity would have been off the scale and it would certainly have finished Meriel's career. She would have clearly understood that.'

'Hmm.' DI Thompson stroked his chin. 'That's an interesting theory, Seb. But why do you believe it was out there on the boat that Bruton told her he'd found the book? Why not at some earlier point?'

Seb leaned forward impatiently. 'Because I would have had an inkling. Meriel told me that very same morning – when we were in bed together – that she was going to ask Cameron for a divorce when she got home. If he'd already threatened her with the book, she would have been far less confident about doing that. She would have said it was more complicated than I

364

realised, or something. Plus, I'd managed to reassure her that the publicity surrounding a divorce wouldn't be all that bad. If she'd known Cameron had found her notebook, she would definitely have argued with me about that. Even if she didn't actually tell me about the book.'

The detective nodded slowly.

'You might be right. In fact, my hunch is that you are. But it's all still entirely circumstantial; actually, it's closer to conjecture. The prosecuting police officer is going to need something a lot more solid to throw into the mix. Which brings us on to the business of the missing watch. Has Miss Kidd said anything to you about that?'

Seb sighed. 'No. Not really. I knew nothing about it until the inquest. Which was odd, because a few days earlier Meriel had sat next to me going through a box full of her husband's personal valuables – gold cufflinks, tie pins, that kind of thing – and she never mentioned the Rolex, or that she'd lost it. Later, when I asked her why she hadn't, she said it was simply because she was embarrassed to have mislaid something so valuable.'

'Did you believe that?'

'No, I didn't. I thought she was lying.'

'Any theories?'

Seb nodded. 'Yes. It ties in with something else Meriel didn't tell me about; her last exchange with

Cameron – you know, that stuff about him asking her the time. After the inquest I asked her about that, too, and she said she hadn't thought it was important.'

'But you think otherwise.'

'I do. I think her reluctance to tell anyone – including me – about Cameron asking her the time, and then her dissembling over the watch, are *definitely* connected in some way. Last night I directly accused her of lying about all of it. In fact, I went on to ask her outright if she'd killed her husband.'

'And?'

'She told me to clear out.'

DI Thompson examined his fingernails.

'An option that won't be available to Miss Kidd when I question her.'

The policeman stood up.

'Thank you, Seb. You've been extremely helpful under difficult circumstances. I'll be in touch.'

Seb looked surprised.

'I can go?'

'For now. As I said earlier, we'll need to conduct a more formal interview with you, on the record. I suggest you have your solicitor present on that occasion.'

'Why? Should I be worried?'

DI Thompson offered Seb what he intended to be an encouraging smile as they left the room together.

'Not specifically, no. But as I believe the coroner may have already said to you, if this matter comes to trial, I think it extremely likely that you will be called to give evidence. In fact, I'm certain of it.'

'Evidence for the prosecution, you mean.'

The inspector turned around in the doorway and stared at him.

'Oh yes. You'll be their star witness.'

CHAPTER FORTY-FOUR

Seb knew the game was up the moment he left the building. Over towards the main entrance of the car park he could see glaring lights, two or three of them, on tall metal stands, and as a marked police car swung through the gates, a few flashbulbs popped.

The pack had descended. Merryman must have broken the story already.

Seb looked at his watch. It was almost three o'clock. If he got to his car quickly he'd catch the bulletin at the top of the hour.

He was just in time. The station jingle was playing as he switched the radio on, and then the voice of one of his colleagues filled the little car.

'*The news headlines at three. Within the last hour Cumbria police have confirmed that they are questioning Lake District FM's Meriel Kidd over the drowning earlier this month of her husband, millionaire businessman Cameron Bruton. Mr Bruton's body was recovered from Ullswater after what an inquest later ruled had been an accidental drowning.*

'*However, this morning police officers visited the couple's home above Derwent Water and commenced a search of the property. Miss Kidd, who has been a familiar voice on Lake District FM since she joined the station in 1973, was driven to Cumbria Police headquarters in Penrith for questioning, although it is understood she went voluntarily and has not been arrested. More from reporter Colin White.*'

Seb bit his lip. Merryman had been quick to hand the story over to someone else. He couldn't blame him: as a police witness he himself had become hopelessly compromised.

White spoke in a soft, Scottish burr and Seb upped the volume.

'*The couple had gone out alone on their motor-boat on the day Mr Bruton died. At the subsequent inquest, his widow told Kendal coroner Dr Timothy Young that her husband had got into difficulties while swimming in the lake and, as a non-swimmer herself, she had been unable to go to his assistance. She said she managed to throw him a lifebelt but he was in no condition to use it. By the time help arrived, Mr Bruton was unconscious and later he was declared dead at the scene by police.*

'*Sources close to this investigation* (that'll be me, Seb thought) *indicate that new evidence has emerged which may cast a different light on events. As well as searching Miss Kidd's home, a former rectory overlooking Derwent Water, the motorboat is to be examined later today.*

'*In a short statement Miss Kidd's legal representative emphasised that his client has not been arrested and is expected to return home later today after fully co-operating with police during questioning.*

'*Colin White, Lake District FM News.*'

Seb turned the radio off and looked over his shoulder at the brick building behind him. DI Thompson had probably started on Meriel by now. Thompson had struck Seb as an extremely intelligent man. Whatever it was Meriel was concealing from everyone, Seb's instincts told him the detective was likely to get to the bottom of it.

He started the car and drove slowly towards the main entrance. Yup, it was swarming with press and TV, both channels. The ITN reporter, an instantly recognisable thirty-something blonde in a turquoise top and matching flares, was recording a piece to camera. Seb caught the words 'suspicious' and 'completely unexpected'.

Merryman had kept Seb's name out of the report but the pack wouldn't be surprised to see him driving out of the police station car park; after all, he'd got the exclusive interview with Meriel the day after Cameron drowned. This was very much 'his' story.

If he'd hoped to drive away without being stopped, he was wrong. As soon as the reporters saw who it was behind the wheel of the car, they surrounded it and he was forced to pull up.

'Seb! Seb!' Flashbulbs popped and the TV cameramen hefted their equipment onto their shoulders and began filming.

'Seb!' It was the ITN girl. 'Have you seen her? Have you seen Meriel? How is she? What's she saying?'

'Come on, Seb!' He recognised the redhead who'd been so rude to him on the morning of the post-mortem. 'Give us a break! We're all in this together, right?'

He cleared his throat and began to lie. 'Guys, I know as much as you do, no more. Of course I haven't spoken to Miss Kidd; she's under interview. I just wanted to find out when she's being released, but no one in there's saying.'

'Oh piss off, Seb.' It was the *Sun* reporter. 'You know more than you're telling us. How come the police let you in there but are keeping us outside?'

'Favour from a friend, a contact, that's all. Much good it did me.'

'Bollocks. Is it true you and Meriel are having an affair?'

Shit. *Shit*. Someone at the station had leaked.

Seb managed to keep his voice steady.

'We're just good friends,' he said. 'Colleagues, too. You shouldn't listen to rumours.'

The *Sun* man sneered. 'From what I've heard it's a lot more than a rumour and the two of you are a lot more than friends. It's all over Lake District FM, for Christ's sake. Come on, Seb, give it up. What's going on here? What's this new evidence they've found?'

Seb shook his head. 'Sorry, mate, but you're barking up completely the wrong tree. I can't help you.'

'You're not kidding anyone, Richmond.' Now it was the *Daily Mail*. The woman, a veteran hack who'd been on the paper for decades, had elbowed her way to the front of the throng. 'How long have you been screwing her? Did it start before her husband drowned? Did he find out? Is that what's at the bottom of all this? Are we looking at a crime of passion here?'

Seb decided the time for politeness was over.

'Fuck off, Barbara. You're talking through your arse, as usual. Now piss off out of the way, all of you. I've got to get back to work.'

He didn't think they were going to let him through but at that point a police car pulled up behind him and briefly sounded its klaxon. The pack reluctantly parted and Seb drove onto the main road and left them all behind, heading for the motorway and Carlisle. He had a lot to discuss with Bob Merryman.

Seb had two principal concerns: the first was whether the station was going to suspend him until all this was over.

The second was where to get himself a good lawyer.

CHAPTER FORTY-FIVE

The interview room was stifling. There was no air-conditioning and the single ceiling fan hadn't worked for weeks after someone left it spinning at full speed overnight.

Great damp patches darkened Probus's suit under the armpits and in a broad band across his shoulders. He mopped his forehead with a white handkerchief, as with his other hand he picked up a sheet of paper the detective had just handed to Meriel.

'I'm sorry, Inspector, but this is completely out of the question. My client is under no obligation whatsoever to read aloud from these pages.'

Probus pushed the document firmly back across the table.

This interview, DI Thompson decided, was not going well. Meriel Kidd was immovable in her account of what had happened out there on the lake. She was calm and unruffled when he'd questioned her about the missing Rolex, too.

'I can only repeat what I told the inquest, Inspector: I've lost it,' she had told him in a quiet, steady voice. 'I placed it in my handbag but it subsequently vanished. Obviously I have mislaid it. Perhaps your men will find it during their search of my home. I certainly hope so. It is worth a great deal of money.'

'But presumably not a lot in sentimental value, Miss Kidd?' It was a low blow, but it hadn't appeared to trouble her.

'None at all, since you ask. It is obvious from these pages you have been given – private items that I should like returned to me at the earliest opportunity, by the way – that I deeply disliked and resented my husband. But I was under no requirement to share that information with anyone, including the coroner. Why should I? It had absolutely nothing to do with his death.'

This woman doesn't need a solicitor, Thompson thought wryly to himself. She's doing very well on her own.

'I should like to hear you read an extract from these diaries, Miss Kidd. Any page will suffice. Perhaps this one.' He handed her a sheet from the top of the pile between them.

It was at this point Probus had intervened, but the policeman pushed the paper for a second time back towards the lawyer and his client.

'I see no grounds for your objection, Mr Probus. I am merely trying to establish—'

'You are merely trying to discomfit my client, Inspector, and I won't allow it. She has not denied writing these chapters. She has no reason to. They are patently fantasy, flights of fancy that bear no relation to reality whatsoever. It is only her wish to co-operate with the police that has brought her here this afternoon. In my opinion she can leave this room at any moment she chooses.'

You're probably right there, you fat bastard, Mark Thompson reflected.

'Very well. We'll come back to this later.'

'We will not. If you ask my client again to read aloud so much as a single word, I shall advise her to leave the police station immediately. This is undue coercion.'

The DI decided to let the point drop.

'Miss Kidd. Why did you fail to tell the police about your final conversation with your husband?'

'I thought I had done so. I was very surprised to learn otherwise. But, as I explained to the coroner, I was in deep shock the afternoon I made my statement. It's hardly surprising I omitted something as trivial as him asking me the time.'

All right, Thompson thought. Let's try this for size.

'You had a very serious argument with your husband out there on the boat that day, didn't you, Meriel? We have a witness prepared to swear that you told him of this. You informed your husband you were leaving him, didn't you? He became very angry with you, didn't he?'

Meriel appeared entirely unperturbed.

'No, and no. No such conversation took place. By "witness" I assume you are referring to Sebastian Richmond, with whom I have just ended a relationship. For reasons best known to himself, he is making this up.'

'Why would he do that?'

Probus leaned forward again. 'I'm sorry, Inspector, but I am going to have to halt this line of questioning. My client bears no responsibility for what this gentleman may have told you. She cannot speculate on the matter.'

Ignoring him, Mark Thompson continued: 'You argued about this book, Meriel, didn't you? Your husband had found it and made copies of it. He threatened you with exposure in any divorce hearing. If your listeners knew you were capable of writing utterly sick, sadistic fantasies such as this, your career would come to an end, wouldn't it?'

Meriel adjusted the dank, clammy collar of her silk blouse before replying. She was drenched in perspiration but when she spoke, she sounded calmer than ever.

'Inspector Thompson. You talk of witnesses. *There were none* – apart from me. My husband and I were alone on our boat. And I am telling you, as the sole witness, two facts. *Facts*, Inspector.

'One. My husband and I did not argue that afternoon. Not about this book and not about anything else.

'Two. I was entirely unaware that my husband had found my manuscript until last night, when Mr Richmond informed me he had discovered a copy hidden in my cellar. I destroyed the original shortly before Cameron died, when I decided that writing it was a silly and unpleasant habit I had to put a stop to. I had no idea my husband had read it and secretly made copies. That has come as a tremendous shock to me, I can tell you.'

The detective looked coolly at the woman opposite.

'I believe Mr Richmond is telling us the truth, Miss Kidd. Which means I believe you're lying to me now. And here's what else I happen to believe. You wanted to kill your husband, didn't you? You wanted to murder him.'

Meriel didn't miss a beat.

'I certainly did. But only in my imagination. I'm sure I'm not the only wife who is guilty of that, Inspector. I see you wear a wedding ring. Perhaps your own wife occasionally harbours similar fantasies to my own.'

You're bloody right there, Mark thought. Clemmie hadn't spoken a word to him since he'd told her they had to cancel yet another holiday. A freelance writer, she had locked herself in her study and the only response when he tried knocking on her door was the steady clacking of her typewriter.

He stood up. 'All right, Miss Kidd. Please remain here with Mr Probus. I'll be back in a few minutes.'

He needed to consult Tremayne. And probably the AC. For the next twenty-four hours, he didn't want Meriel Kidd going anywhere, still less having access to newspapers, a television or radio.

If he found what he was profoundly hoping he would, he expected it to be the bombshell that would blow the widow's defence into a million pieces – provided she didn't see it coming.

And, of course, providing he found it.

'You can't hold her overnight, Mark. You simply don't have cause. What do you think, sir?' Superintendent Tremayne turned to the AC.

'I agree, Gil,' the senior man said. 'Why is this so important, Mark? She's co-operating, isn't she? I'm sure she'll come back in the morning if you ask nicely.'

The DI shook his head. 'I don't want her to find out that we're sending divers down at first light tomorrow.'

'Why?'

'Because if something incriminating *is* down there and we find it, I want to hit her with it stone-cold. The problem I'm having with her is that she's had time to think through all the angles on this. I wish to hell Richmond hadn't gone and told her what he'd done. She's got all her ducks lined up in a row.'

The AC looked pensive.

'Does she know we're searching the boat as well as the house?'

'Yes, and she doesn't seem bothered about it. I don't think we'll find anything incriminating there. But she *doesn't* know we're sending divers down because obviously we don't need a warrant to do that.'

The superintendent frowned. 'But why are you giving her the impression that we need to tell her about warrants? Did you tell her we'd got a warrant to search the boat? You were under no obligation to do that, Mark.'

'Yes, I did, because I want her to feel I'm being completely straight and open with her about the scope of our investigation. I didn't have to tell her about the warrant for the house, either, but I did. I'm deliberately misdirecting her away from the lake itself. As far as she's concerned we're only interested in the house and boat – and the diary, of course. If we find what I think we'll find in the water, I don't want her to have had even a second to cook up a story about it.'

The AC stared at him. 'What *do* you expect to find down there, Mark?'

Thompson looked surprised.

'That's obvious, isn't it? Cameron Bruton's Rolex. It's the key to everything.'

On the AC's advice, Mark Thompson managed to get hold of one of the best prosecution lawyers in the country, a barrister with chambers in Lincoln's Inn. Once the man had been apprised of the situation his advice, delivered over a bad telephone line from the Old Bailey, was unhesitating.

'S'easy, old boy. Tell her you've found something suspicious on the boat. Make something up, you can always withdraw it tomorrow. Say you're arresting her on suspicion of withholding evidence. You think she's doing that anyway, don't you? That means you can keep her in overnight and her lawyer won't be able to apply for a writ of *habeas corpus* for unlawful imprisonment until tomorrow. By the time he's got that sorted, your divers will have popped back up to the surface waving the watch. Easy-peasy.'

The DI frowned. 'Not if I'm wrong and there's nothing there. I'll be the one hauled before a judge, for false imprisonment.'

'Then you'd better keep your fingers crossed, old boy.'

Mark rang off and made his way back to the interview room, collecting a uniformed sergeant along the way.

When they went inside, Probus was up on his feet at once.

'This is unacceptable, Inspector. You have kept my client waiting here for almost forty-five minutes. We are leaving.'

'Be quiet please, Mr Probus.'

Mark faced Meriel.

'Meriel Kidd, I am arresting you on suspicion of withholding evidence. You are not obliged to say anything unless you wish to do so but what you say may be written down and given in evidence.'

He turned to his colleague.

'Take her to the cells, please, Sergeant.'

Probus looked as if he was going to explode.

'This is outrageous. *OUTRAGEOUS!* You have *no* basis whatsoever to make this arrest. I am taking this matter directly before the nearest High Court judge. How *dare* you abuse your powers in this way? This is one of the most *serious*—'

Meanwhile the sergeant had quietly slipped a pair of handcuffs on Meriel and was leading her from the room. She hadn't said a word, and looked unperturbed as ever. Thompson marvelled at her extraordinary composure, even in this insufferable heat. He'd never seen anything like it in his entire career.

He turned to the lawyer.

'Mr Probus. My officers have made a discovery during their search of the boat.'

'Really? What of?'

'I'm not prepared to say for the moment.'

Probus called out after his departing client.

'Miss Kidd, this will not be allowed to stand. I will have you out of this place by lunchtime tomorrow, I guarantee.'

She made no reply, and the door closed quietly behind her.

Thompson ignored the blustering lawyer, who was, as the London barrister had predicted, now promising to bring a writ of *habeas corpus*.

The policeman made a mental calculation. Twenty hours, he decided. He had twenty hours to pull this thing off.

And if he failed?

A long spell of gardening leave awaited. It might even turn out to be permanent.

He certainly wouldn't be short of spare time then to take Clemmie on holiday, would he?

CHAPTER FORTY-SIX

Meriel sat on the edge of the bunk in her cell, thinking. Why had she been arrested? She'd overheard the detective telling her lawyer something about finding evidence on the boat, but that was nonsense. There was nothing incriminating aboard, and nothing back at the house, either, other than more copies, possibly, of *The Night Book*; she had no idea how many Cameron had made.

No, she decided, this had to be some sort of bluff. DI Thompson had tried his best to unnerve her, first by asking her to read extracts from the diary aloud, and then directly accusing her of lying about that final row with Cameron. Only Seb could have told him that – he was bound to have been questioned himself this morning – but all she had to do was continue to deny it. As she'd said to Seb last night (how long ago that seemed now) it was his word against hers; they

385

could prove nothing. Probus had confirmed that to her while Thompson was out of the room.

If the police now thought a night in the cells was going to rattle her, they could think again. It was certainly unpleasant, not to mention extremely boring – she had nothing to read – but she'd cope. They'd have to let her go, probably tomorrow if Probus had anything to do with it.

She lay back on the bunk and put her hands behind her head.

'You're going to be fine,' she said aloud to the white-washed ceiling.

'Keep your nerve, Meriel Kidd. You're going to be just fine.'

Mark Thompson had a bad night. He didn't sleep much and he was up before dawn; he wanted to be at Ullswater before the divers went down. There was nothing he could usefully do at the scene, but he couldn't bear hanging around headquarters waiting for news.

He dressed in the dark, trying not to wake the sleeping Clemmie, and went downstairs to make himself some tea and toast. He switched on the radio in the kitchen in time for the early headlines. Meriel Kidd led the bulletin: yesterday's brief police press statement that she had been arrested and kept in custody had electrified an already sensationalised media.

Probus, damn him, had poured petrol on the flames with an impromptu press conference on the pavement outside police headquarters. He said his client intended to sue for wrongful arrest and would be seeking 'exemplary' damages.

Mark could hear the solicitor's sound bite on the radio now. 'No wonder I couldn't bloody sleep,' he muttered as he poured milk into his mug of tea. 'If I've got this wrong that bastard's going to chew me up and spit me out in pieces.'

He grabbed his car keys from their hook by the back door and went out into the drive. The stars were still out but there was a faint blush along the eastern horizon.

He reckoned the divers could start going down in an hour.

Seb was at the newsagent's less than five minutes after it opened. The newspapers were still in their heavy bundles tied up with baling twine, and he helped the paper boy cut them free and sort them into piles on the floor ready for delivery.

The headlines were predictable.

LADY OF THE LAKE ARRESTED, was the *Daily Mirror*'s. The *Daily Mail* went with *MYSTERY AS MERIEL ACCUSED*. The *Daily Express* offered *MERIEL QUIZZED ON HUSBAND'S DEATH* while the *Sun* had *COPS PUT THE CUFFS ON KIDD*.

When Seb was back in his flat he quickly scanned the stories beneath the banners. They were broadly the same. Meriel had gone voluntarily to the police station, she had co-operated during questioning but had nevertheless been arrested on suspicion of withholding evidence. Her solicitor was saying it was a fit-up – although not in those words – and that heads would roll, damages would be huge, and so on.

There was nothing about him; his name didn't appear anywhere. The police had made no reference to his being questioned, and the rumours about him and Meriel were, for now, unreportable. That would certainly change if and when it all came to court.

Seb was genuinely mystified that Meriel had been arrested so early in the inquiry. He couldn't think why the police had done that, unless this Probus guy was right and it was an attempt to intimidate her.

He wouldn't get the chance to report on it, though – not that he had the faintest wish to – something that had been made clear to him by the station manager the previous afternoon.

'We're not going to suspend you, Seb,' Peter Cox had said during a formal meeting in his office. 'We don't think that's necessary. But obviously you're off the story: you're a witness in what could end up as a Crown Court trial.'

'Of course. Thanks, Peter. For not suspending me. I—'

'Hold on, Seb, I'm not done yet.' His boss shifted uncomfortably in his chair before continuing.

'Bob and I have talked this over and we both think you should come off-air for a while. The fact that you and Meriel had formed a relationship didn't matter two hoots before this, but it most certainly does now.

'Sooner or later the fact you've been questioned is bound to leak. Then the gossip that's been flying around about the two of you will get dragged into the story. When that happens, every time listeners hear your voice all they'll be able to think about is you and Meriel and murder – even if nothing against her is ever proved.'

Seb stared at him.

'How long will I be off-air for? And what do I do with myself here at the station in the meantime?'

The station manager shrugged. 'As to the first question, who knows? Until this thing goes away or until after any trial. By the way, if there *is* a trial, you'll definitely be sent on leave until it's over. Then we can ... take stock of the situation.'

Seb decided he didn't like the sound of that last part.

'As to what you'll do here until then,' his boss continued, 'I'd like you to be a *de facto* deputy news editor, reporting to Bob. Help write scripts, bulletins, news-gather ... just not go behind a mic, I'm afraid.'

Seb let what he had been told sink in. Then he slowly stood up.

'Thanks, Peter. I can see that you and Bob are bending over backwards to help me out here, and I'm grateful.' He walked to the door, where he turned round, his face bleak.

'But my career's in the toilet, isn't it?'

CHAPTER FORTY-SEVEN

There were three divers and by the time Mark arrived at Howtown on Ullswater's southern shore, they were fully suited up. The police launch was about to cast its moorings and head out to the spot where Cameron Bruton had drowned.

Someone must have tipped off the press because there were a couple of photographers and several reporters hanging around the jetty. No TV he could see, but one woman with a microphone. Radio.

As he got out of the car and walked across to the boat, the cameras clicked and the little gaggle of news-men fell into step beside him.

'DI Thompson, isn't it?' It was the man from the *Carlisle Evening News*. 'What's going on here this morning, sir? What will you be looking for out there?'

'No comment.'

'Oh, come on, officer,' another of them said. 'Give

us a break. We've been here since before dawn. You must be able to tell us something.'

'No comment.'

Thank God he'd contrived to keep Meriel locked up. This was going to be on the wires in about thirty minutes, and probably on the next Lake District FM bulletin. She would have been certain to find out and put two and two together.

Mark took the gap between jetty and boat in one leap. As he scrambled aboard the man in charge of the underwater unit gave him a friendly nod.

'Come to see the fun, sir?'

'Yes. I just hope I'm not sending your men on a wild-goose chase, Sergeant.'

The other man shrugged as the idling outboard motor suddenly burst into a throaty roar and the launch surged away from the jetty, leaving the frustrated press pack behind. 'It won't bother my lads if they don't find anything down there. Any excuse for a dive.'

'Well, it'll bloody bother me.'

The sergeant laughed. 'Not to worry, Inspector. If there's anything to be found, they'll bring it up.'

It was still only seven o'clock and although the sun had risen forty-five minutes earlier, it had yet to clear the fells behind them to the east. The lake was glassy-smooth this late-August morning, and with no direct sunlight on it, the water appeared almost black.

Behind them, the wake of the boat curled away on both sides in perfectly symmetrical curving ridges that were lightly foamed close to the boat.

'Looks like we're going through Guinness, doesn't it, sir?'

Mark was distracted. 'I suppose so ... when will we get there?'

'In about thirty seconds. Look – there's the buoy, dead ahead.'

Sure enough, three hundred yards in front of them a small red marker was floating perfectly still in the tranquil water.

'Who put that there?'

The sergeant was already throttling back the engine.

'We did – yesterday. We got down here a couple of hours before dark so there was just time enough to do the triangulation and mark the spot. We based our calculations on what the officers attending the original incident told us, and the witness statements from the civvies on the boat that was first on the scene. I reckon we're accurate to a few yards.'

A few moments later the boat slowed even more and started to perform a lazy circle around the buoy. The sergeant reversed the engine and brought the launch to a full stop, before he cut the gurgling outboard completely.

The divers adjusted their breathing apparatus in the sudden silence, and pulled masks down into position from the top of their heads. Two of them picked up hand-held underwater battery lamps from the deck and switched them on. Even in daylight, they were dazzling. One by one the men perched on the side of the boat, their backs to the water, and gave the thumbs-up.

'Right then, boys,' the sergeant addressed them. 'It's about sixty feet to the bottom. It's ruddy dark down there so stay close and in visual contact at all times. You know what you're looking for – a gold watch. But if you see anything else, anything else at all, bring that up too. Off you go.'

One by one the divers tumbled backwards over the side of the boat and within a few moments, they had disappeared from view.

The sergeant turned to the inspector.

'And now, sir, we wait. Fancy a coffee? I've got some in a flask. It should still be hot.'

DI Thompson shook his head.

Suddenly, he was feeling rather nauseous.

Probus lay in bed while his wife prepared breakfast downstairs. He was confident he could get a judge to sign a writ of *habeas corpus* by midday at the latest. The police had still not offered to share knowledge of what they claimed to have found on the Brutons' boat, and he, Probus, was beginning to think it was an outrageous ruse. They must be mad. What the devil did these blundering idiots think they were playing at?

Privately, he was delighted. The damages his client would assuredly be awarded in due course would naturally inform the fee he intended to charge her. Probus was hardly short of money but a little more – in this case, a *lot* more – was always welcome.

He slid his hairless legs to the floor and went into the bathroom to shave. One's toilet must always be impeccable when going before a judge. He would wear his new Turnbull and Asser shirt – the one with the pink stripes – and that black woollen three-piece suit Diana had bought for him on her last trip to Harrods.

The lawyer sighed with satisfaction as hot water began to gush into the sink. He soaked his shaving brush under the tap before working up a lather in the little soap-dish.

This was going to be a *very* good day.

Probus started to hum to himself.

Mark looked disconsolately at the pile of rubbish that was steadily growing in size on the deck.

Three beer-bottle tops. What looked like the casing of a small penknife, minus the blades. A shard of green glass. A bent and twisted pair of sunglasses, both lenses missing.

No watch.

The water to the side of the boat began to boil and one of the divers surfaced again. He pulled the breathing tube from his mouth and pushed his mask up.

'Sorry, Sarge, I'm nearly out of air,' he called up to his boss. 'Coming aboard. Tom and Dave might have a few more minutes left. We can repressurise and go back down, but I reckon we've pretty much scoured the area. They're just checking out the last quadrant.'

Mark and the sergeant helped the man back up on deck. The DI's stomach was churning; he really thought he *was* going to be sick now. This was looking more and more like a full-on, platinum-plated disaster.

Fuck it. He'd been so *sure*.

'Sorry, sir,' the sergeant said as he helped his man out of his diving gear. 'If it was down there, I guarantee we'd have found it.'

Mark slumped down onto a bench at the stern of the boat.

'Of course you would, Sergeant. Not to worry. Your men did their best. Clearly, my intelligence was faulty.'

The water next to the hull began bubbling and boiling again. Mark looked listlessly over the side.

He would never, ever forget what he saw next.

First, a gloved hand emerging from the water, four fingers clenched against the palm, but thumb extended vertically into the air.

Then a second hand, belonging to the third diver, rising into the slanting rays of the morning sun, shedding sparkling droplets of water.

And holding something between the forefinger and thumb.

A wristwatch.

A gold wristwatch.

A Rolex.

DI Thompson leaned over the back of the boat as far as he could, and threw up.

CHAPTER FORTY-EIGHT

Probus was behind the wheel of his silver Jaguar XJ and about to pull out of the drive on his way to court when his wife opened their front door and called after him.

'Max! *Max!* Stop!'

He wound his window down.

'What? What is it, Diana?'

'It's the police, Max. On the phone. They say they have something they have to tell you about the Kidd case.'

Probus smiled. He bet they did. They must be falling over themselves to back down, now they knew he was applying for a judge's order against them.

'Tell them to wait. I'll be there in a minute,' he called, switching off the ignition.

His smile broadened.

This was going to be enjoyable. Most enjoyable.

Five minutes later Probus was on the phone to his office.

'Justin? Call the clerk to the court ... yes, the *Crown* Court! Tell them I'm suspending my application for *habeas corpus* ... Yes, yes ... indefinitely. No ... no, I don't expect to reapply. What? Oh, just *do* it, Justin!'

He slammed the phone down.

What the fuck had Meriel Kidd been playing at? Why had she lied to him about the watch? What else was she lying about?

And *why*? What in the name of God had the woman done?

As Probus's perfect day was collapsing around his ears, DI Thompson was at police headquarters conferring over a coffee with his superintendent.

'Bloody well done, Mark,' the senior man said. 'An incredible result. You've caught her out in a whopper – she lied to the coroner, she lied to your principal witness, and she lied to you here yesterday. It completely discredits the rest of her evidence. Put it together with her murderous diary and the testimony of a credible witness in Seb Richmond, and I reckon we might get more than a sniff of a prosecution. I definitely think a jury deserves to hear what you've got.'

The superintendent sipped his coffee, thinking.

'And you still reckon she doesn't have a clue what's

coming down the tracks at her? About the watch, I mean?'

Mark shrugged. 'It's hard to know what goes on in that woman's mind, but yeah, I think it's going to be a complete blind-sider, a real body-blow. Yesterday I was extremely careful not to press her on the business of the watch. I barely mentioned it and I didn't ask her any supplementary questions about it. As I said to both you and the AC afterwards, I wanted her to think that my focus is on the diary, the searches of the house and boat, and what Seb Richmond has told me. When I show her the Rolex a few minutes from now, I'm expecting to see her defences crumble.'

There was a knock at the door. The desk sergeant came in and addressed the DI.

'Miss Kidd's lawyer's arrived, sir. As per instructions I've kept him well away from his client and had him taken up to your office.'

'Thanks, Sergeant. I'll be there directly.'

Mark turned to his superior and grinned.

'I'm going to enjoy this.'

'Good morning, Mr Probus. Thank you for waiting.'

'DI Thompson. I would like to see my client. Immediately.'

The policeman smiled. 'Certainly. We shall see Miss Kidd together. Right away.'

'No.' Probus was scowling. 'I need to meet with

her in conclave first. This ... this missing watch you inform me has now materialised ... I must discuss—'

DI Thompson rose.

'You won't say anything about it to her, at least not until I have done so, in your presence. Otherwise you would be seriously compromising this inquiry and interfering in the course of justice. I must present this matter to your client without any prior notice from you. Do I make myself plain?' You pompous, fat bastard, he managed to avoid finishing.

Probus blustered. 'But I should inform her of this fresh information. I must—'

The detective interrupted him again, with finality. 'You must do nothing of the kind. You cannot forewarn your client of our findings, which have been disclosed to you in good faith, Mr Probus. You can only advise her *post eventum*. I have taken legal advice on the point and I assure you I am correct. As I think you actually know.'

The lawyer subsided. It was no good.

'Very well,' he said heavily. 'Then let us proceed, Inspector.'

Ten minutes later Meriel was relieved to see her solicitor entering the interview room behind DI Thompson and a younger detective, who was carrying a small black briefcase. She was certain Probus would have her out of here very shortly. She'd woken up even more convinced that her arrest and detention was a crude attempt to throw her off balance. And it hadn't worked.

She was slightly disconcerted, however, when Probus somehow contrived to avoid meeting her eye as he settled himself on the chair beside hers, and more so when, without a word, the younger policeman switched on the double-cassette tape recorder on the table between them. The red 'record' light glowed.

What was going on?

The senior policeman cleared his throat.

'I am DI Mark Thompson, and I'm accompanied by DC Gerald Watkins. We are interviewing Miss Meriel Kidd in the presence of her solicitor, Mr Maxwell Probus, on Tuesday the thirty-first of August, nineteen seventy-six, at Cumbria Police headquarters.'

He paused for a moment.

'Miss Kidd.'

'Inspector?'

'As you know, we have been conducting a search of your house and your motorboat. I have to tell you that, apart from discovering a second copy of your manuscript at Cathedral Crag, we have found nothing of any significance. Our apparent recovery of evidence on the boat yesterday and your subsequent detention was a grave error, and I wish to wholeheartedly apologise for it.'

Meriel smiled. *That's* why they were recording this.

They'd clearly had second thoughts about the legality of using such obvious scare tactics on her. Probus had them on the run. Now they wanted to demonstrate they'd apologised and backed off at the earliest opportunity. It might limit any subsequent award against them for damages.

'Thank you, Mr Thompson. I note your apology. I assume I am now free to leave?'

Probus coughed. 'Dear lady . . .'

She turned to him. 'Mr Probus?'

Her lawyer inclined his head to the detective. 'There is a little more, I am afraid.'

Meriel faced the DI. 'Please come to the point, Inspector. I want to go home.'

Thompson turned to his junior.

'DC Watkins? If you please.'

The younger man snapped open the clasps of his briefcase and took out a small, opaque plastic evidence bag. He handed it to his DI, who folded it into his palm.

'Miss Kidd.' Thompson fixed Meriel with a calm, steady gaze. 'You have stated to both the coroner and myself, and to my witness, that on the day your husband drowned you placed his wristwatch in your handbag and brought it home with you. And that, subsequently, you mislaid it.'

Meriel's eyes slowly widened and she swallowed twice before replying. Her voice, when it came, was much quieter than before.

'Yes, that's right.'

The DI deftly unsealed the evidence bag and shook its contents onto the cheap Formica table.

Cameron Bruton's gold Rolex skidded across the surface.

'Do you recognise this watch?'

Meriel stared at it. The second hand was still ticking, still moving, wagging at her like an admonishing finger.

She nodded, almost imperceptibly.

'Note for the record that Miss Kidd is nodding her head in the affirmative. Please speak your response aloud, Miss Kidd. Do you recognise this watch?'

'Yes.'

'Whose is it?'

Meriel's entire body seemed to be shrinking in on itself. She had wrapped her arms around her sides and her head and neck were beginning to settle into her shoulders.

'Whose is it, Meriel?'

It was the first time he had called her by her Christian name, and it was a psychologically calculated move.

'Cameron's,' she whispered at last.

'Cameron Bruton, your late husband.'

'Yes.'

'Meriel, can you explain to me why my officers were able to recover this watch from the bottom of Ullswater less than two hours ago, beneath the exact spot where your husband drowned?'

'No, I can't.'

'Speak up, please, Meriel. I can't hear you.'

'NO. I can't explain. I thought I'd taken it home with me.'

'But you didn't, did you, Meriel? You can't have done. Because it's been lying at the bottom of the lake all this time.'

'If you say so.'

DI Thompson almost felt sorry for the woman who was now hunched in the chair opposite. But not that sorry. He moved in for the kill.

'The thing is, you've been lying to everyone, haven't you, Meriel? You lied to the coroner. You lied to your boyfriend. You lied to me, yesterday. Always the same lie. That you'd put this watch into your handbag and taken it home. You never once displayed the slightest doubt about the matter; not once. You never said you *thought* you'd put it in your handbag, or that *maybe* you'd done something else with it. Yesterday, here at the station, you even told me how grateful you would be if my officers found it during their search of your home. It's all been one great big lie, hasn't it, Meriel?'

She said nothing.

Mark Thompson was an experienced interrogator and he knew the value of suddenly changing tone and body language. He did so now, pushing his chair back with both legs and putting his hands behind his head. He contrived almost to look bored.

'Come on, Meriel. You're in a right mess here, aren't you? We can all see that, even Mr Probus there. Just look at his face. Your solicitor doesn't appreciate being lied to, either.

'So I suggest you start straightening things out by telling the truth for once. I've got all day. In fact, I've got all week, if needed. Why don't you begin by telling me what *really* happened on the boat that afternoon?'

Meriel shook her head. 'I have done,' she said huskily. 'I have told you the truth about it.'

The DI laughed quietly. 'Meriel, you've been caught out telling whoppers. Surely you understand how that changes *everything*; puts all the other things you've told us in a deeply questionable light? You're going to have to do a lot better than this, I'm afraid.'

He paused. 'All right. Let's try an easy one. We all know now that your last sighting of this watch was NOT as you dropped it inside your handbag. Because that never happened. So when *did* you last see it? And how did it get into the water?'

She shook her head. 'I don't know ... I don't remember.'

'Oh, I think you do. And your unwillingness to tell me about it speaks volumes. Can you imagine how this is going to come across to a jury, Meriel? All of it? Hmm?'

He let the question hang in the air, before continuing: 'Well ... perhaps I can help you to focus on your predicament a little more clearly. Let me summarise what a future jury would have to consider.'

The DI began to tick off points one by one on his fingers.

'*One*. Far from having the perfect marriage, as you boasted to all and sundry, you had a lousy one.

'*Two*. You hated your husband so much that you wrote gruesome fantasies about killing him in the most foul ways imaginable. I'm an experienced police officer, Meriel, and I can tell you they certainly took *my* breath away. I think it's possible that one or two of the jurors might faint when these chapters are read out in court. That one about pouring battery acid into Cameron's eyes is triple-X.

'*Three*. You embarked on an affair with a much younger man than your husband.

'*Four*. On the *very afternoon* your husband drowned – indeed, only minutes before his death – you told him you were leaving him. Then—'

Probus interrupted. 'That is an allegation made by someone who wasn't even there, Inspector, and which my client vigorously denies. She—'

The DI walked through the lawyer's words.

'Come off it, Mr Probus, my witness is of excellent character and has no reason to lie. It's your client who is the liar, as our discovery of the watch this morning proves beyond doubt. Who do *you* think a jury will be more likely to believe?'

Probus was silent.

Mark turned back to Meriel.

'*Five*. After telling your husband you intended to leave him that evening, the two of you had a fierce argument. You volunteered this fact to your lover afterwards, on a number of occasions.

'*Six*. Your husband discovered your secret, sordid diary. We know this because he made copies and hid them, to guard against you destroying the original when he told you what he'd done. I believe the threats he made against you were specifically about the diary. I believe he warned you that if you left him, he'd make you pay. He'd reveal its existence to the world. Your reputation and career would be destroyed. People would be revolted when they learned what you'd written.'

Meriel had not taken her eyes from the floor. The DI could see her left hand was shaking, and her right was balled into a tight fist.

Probus, who had gone very pale, leaned forward.

'Inspector, my client is clearly distressed. I would like to request that we take a break at this juncture for her to recover her composure.'

And *I* would like you to stuff that request right up your arse, pal, Mark thought. But all he said was: 'Request denied, Mr Probus. We'll take a break when I decide, not you.'

The detective got up from the chair and cocked one

thigh on the table, a move which brought him several feet closer to Meriel.

'And d'you know what, Meriel? We haven't even got to point seven yet.'

Probus, still smarting from the put-down, unwisely asked: 'Well then, why don't you tell us what it is?'

DI Thompson glared at him.

'Be quiet, Mr Probus. Keep your interventions relevant. And your irritation to yourself.'

Probus went from pale to puce in a moment, but managed to swallow back a reply.

'Point seven,' the detective resumed, 'is the part about the watch. You see, not only have you consistently and provably lied through your teeth about that, Meriel, but then there's this curious business of you "forgetting" to mention that your husband asked you the time, just before he died. It's nowhere in your original statement.'

Mark slowly and deliberately rapped the table three times with his knuckles.

'I'd like you to look at me now, please, Meriel. This part's important.'

She slowly lifted her gaze from the floor and stared at her accuser. Her expression was blank, unreadable.

'Thank you. You see, Meriel, from the first moment I was assigned this case, I realised you were hiding something. Something very, very important. Your lies about your husband's watch, and your failure to mention him asking you the time ... they're inextricably connected, aren't they? Last night I read the transcript of your evidence at the inquest and it was absolutely clear to me that you were obfuscating on both points. And that was before we found the watch.'

The DI now held his silence, and Meriel's gaze. It was almost half a minute before he spoke again.

'I think it's clear what happened. Your husband left his watch on deck when he went for his swim, as was his custom. I accept *that* part of your evidence at least, Meriel. Because if he'd been wearing it, it would have still been on his wrist when his body was recovered from the lake.

'When he called out to you from the water, you were seething over the threats he'd just made. You were very worried about them too, and you couldn't think what to do. But suddenly, you saw your opportunity. In fact, I believe that if Cameron Bruton hadn't asked you the time that afternoon, he would be alive today.

'You picked up the watch and you threw it at him. You knew it would sink at once and you knew all about the inherent dangers of the icy water that were just beneath your husband. You hoped he'd go after it – it was a Rolex, after all – and he did. And when he hit the freezing layer, he began drowning, like so many others this summer.

'And then I think you just watched him drown,

Meriel. I don't think you lifted a finger to help him. Not until it was too late.'

He leaned in towards her, until their faces were only inches apart.

'Tell me that I'm wrong, Meriel Kidd. Look me in the eyes, and tell me I'm wrong.'

After a long, exhausted silence, DI Thompson slowly rose from the table and looked dispassionately at the lawyer.

'I'll offer her manslaughter. But I want a full confession and I want it by close of play. If it's not forthcoming then your client will be charged with murder and we'll let the jury decide.'

He glanced back at Meriel as he scooped the glittering Rolex back up from the table.

'You should consider yourself lucky we don't hang killers any more in this country, Meriel.'

He moved towards the door.

'Not much more than ten years ago, you might have swung for this.'

CHAPTER FORTY-NINE

A few minutes after DI Thompson had left the accused and her lawyer in the interview room, a grey-haired middle-aged constable returned with a tray of tea and biscuits.

'The inspector suggests you could do with this while you come to your decision,' he told them, not unkindly. 'I'm to tell you that he would appreciate knowing what that decision is by nine p.m. at the latest.' He quietly withdrew.

Probus had spent the last ten minutes trying to persuade Meriel to talk to him, without success. She sat hugging her knees and staring into space.

Now he poured her some tea. 'Do you take milk, my dear? Or sugar?'

She shook her head. That's better, thought Probus, at least a reaction of sorts. He pushed the steaming black cup over to her.

'Do take care, my dear. It is very hot.'

Meriel nodded, and sipped a little of the tea.

'Thank you, Mr Probus.'

At last. She speaks once more.

The solicitor placed his hands deliberately on both pudgy pinstriped knees, spreading his fingers.

'Miss Kidd … Meriel … you must not be in the least concerned or embarrassed that you have been untruthful with me about certain matters. I assure you it is the commonest thing in the world for clients to be … economical with the *vérité*, shall we say. I am quite accustomed to it and I assure you I have never taken it personally, and certainly do not do so now.'

He paused. 'And I can quite understand why you chose not to mention the matter of the watch. By the way, I assume the inspector's theory concerning that is well founded?'

Meriel spoke for a second time.

'To all intents and purposes, yes, it is.'

'Ah.' Probus sat thinking for a while. Meriel slowly sipped more of her tea.

'Well, that being the case,' he eventually continued, 'I can think of one or more strategems and defences that may be helpful to us. Firstly—'

'No.' Meriel's voice was recovering some of its strength.

'But I assure you—'

'I said *no*, Mr Probus. I am not going to wriggle like

the worm on the proverbial hook. I want this whole business over with as quickly and simply as possible. I've had more than enough of it. I intend to plead guilty to manslaughter.'

Her lawyer hesitated.

'But Miss Kidd, although I can offer no guarantees on the outcome of a criminal trial before jury, I am of the opinion, given the circumstantial nature of the evidence, that a good Queen's Counsel for the defence may well be able to—'

'Mr Probus, with respect, you were of the opinion that you would have me out of this police station by lunchtime today.'

If the solicitor was offended he gave no sign of it and his tone remained polite, even understanding.

'Yes, but also with respect, that was before I knew you were concealing evidence, wasn't it? Forgive me for saying so, but you were perfectly aware where the watch was all along.'

Meriel released her knees and allowed her feet to sink back to the floor.

'You're quite right, Mr Probus. I apologise. I'm being unfair. I know you're only trying to do your best on my behalf, so please listen closely to what I am now going to say to you. I've been thinking very hard for these last few minutes.'

She took a few moments to compose herself before continuing.

'I *did* drown my husband. Not with my bare hands, but by my actions. I truly didn't plan to – the idea to throw his watch into the lake only occurred to me about three seconds before I did it – but I knew perfectly well he'd try and save it. I also knew that would be extremely dangerous given the conditions. And yes, when he eventually surfaced he was in a dreadful state and I did nothing to help him. Nothing at all. I was glad he was drowning. The inspector got one thing wrong, though – I didn't stand and watch Cameron's death throes. I couldn't bear to. I crossed to the other side of the boat and waited there. I could hear him, though. My God, Mr Probus, I could hear him.'

The lawyer was staring at her, his eyes wide.

'And when it was over, when he was quiet at last, and only then, I went back and threw the lifebelt in. Of course, I knew that it was pointless. I was simply covering my back.'

Probus said nothing.

After a heavy silence, Meriel took a long, shivering sigh.

'And do you know what, Mr Probus? *I'm glad*. I'm glad I did it. I'm *glad* he's dead. I'm glad he suffered. He was an utter bastard and he got what was coming to him. I spent years putting up with the most disgusting mental abuse and humiliation, pretty much on a daily basis. Why on earth do you think I wrote *The Night Book*? I'm not mad; I'm not mentally ill, or psychotic. I *know* I'm not. It was my way of letting off steam, and when I thought I'd found a way out in the shape of Seb Richmond, I really *did* burn my pages. I was ashamed of them. And I had no use for them any more.

'And then Cameron tried to blackmail me with the copies he'd secretly made. It wasn't just that he used them to try and stop me leaving him. He said I'd have to . . . let him do things to me. Repellent things. Things in the bedroom. It was disgusting. He wanted to twist my sick imaginings into an even sicker reality – against me. I was terrified.'

She brushed a tear impatiently away from one eye. 'I realise how cynical it sounds, describing Seb as my way out. But honestly, I'd fallen in love, probably for the first time in my life. I think I am still in love, actually, despite what's happened. Although much good it'll do me now. I'll probably never see Seb again. I threw him out when I told him what he'd done, and . . . What are you *doing*, Mr Probus?'

He had quietly taken a slim pad from his jacket while she was talking, and was making notes in it. He glanced up at her; she could see his eyes had begun to shine.

'Miss Kidd. I am not, to adopt the language of your profession, an "agony uncle". I am afraid I see the world in an almost purely legal light. So I am afraid I have little in the way of emotional comfort to offer you.'

He glanced down at his notes.

'However. As your lawyer, I think I can safely say that you have just outlined the case we are going to make for both motive and mitigation. Having heard it from your lips, unprompted by me, I have to say I find it most compelling.'

Meriel stared at him. 'So you agree with me? I should confess to manslaughter?'

Probus nodded emphatically. 'Oh yes. Now I do. Most certainly. Firstly, it is obviously the lesser of the two possible charges, although in any case it is perfectly clear that this case really is one of manslaughter, and not murder. There was absolutely no malice aforethought.

'Secondly, a confession always results in a lighter sentence than if charges are contested and a guilty verdict then follows.

'And thirdly, as I have just said, there are strong mitigating factors here. You suffered a decade of mental cruelty at this unpleasant man's hands. I shall require details, of course, a list of incidents that stand out in your memory.'

Meriel gave a grim laugh. 'That won't be difficult. But I'm not sure what evidence I can produce. That's the thing about mental cruelty, isn't it? No bones are broken or scars left behind. Not visible ones, anyway.'

'Leave that to me. We shall commission and present detailed psychiatric reports.' Probus hesitated.

'However, I must warn you, you will almost certainly be remanded in custody, at least at first.'

Meriel swallowed. 'Will I have to wait long for my trial?'

For the first time that afternoon, the lawyer smiled.

'Oh, there won't be any trial, not now that we are going to make a full confession. No jury, either, nothing like that. There'll simply be a form of hearing where a judge decides what to do with you, taking mitigation into account. And any time you've spent on remand will be brought into consideration, too. But that won't be long – confessions are a fast track to justice. In any event, I certainly don't anticipate that you will receive a long sentence.'

He leaned forward and squeezed her shoulder.

'You didn't plan to do what you did, my dear. You just snapped. Countless women will understand that. They'll even sympathise.'

Meriel shook her head despondently.

'Not when they read what I wrote about killing Cameron, they won't.'

'No, no! Only the judge and one or two court officials will ever see your diary, my dear. Your confession means there's no requirement to present detailed evidence in public. Those copies of *The Night Book* will simply remain on file, gathering dust.'

'Really? *Really?* That would be *such* a relief!'

He regarded her shrewdly. 'In fact, given the tide of

popular sympathy I anticipate, and frankly intend to orchestrate, I'd say that when this is all behind you, you may even be able to resume your career. Perhaps write a book about it all. Go on lecture tours, that sort of thing. You could become a feminist icon for our times; carry a torch for mentally abused women everywhere.'

Meriel looked at him in near-disbelief. 'Mr Probus, I am about to go to jail.'

'But not for long. And in any case, think what a chapter *that* would make!'

He sucked his pen, considering. To her astonishment, he began to hum.

'What is it? Why are you humming like that?'

He stopped abruptly, looking a little sheepish.

'I'm so sorry, my dear. An unfortunate habit of mine. But I was just thinking to myself that with a little luck and a following wind, we might even be fortunate enough to get a woman judge.'

The story was too late to make the early editions. There was nothing about it on the front pages of the national papers that were unloaded off the night train to Carlisle, just headlines screeching that Meriel continued to be interrogated. The *Sun*'s – *KIDD KEPT IN CLINK: THE AGONY GOES ON* – was typical.

But the news had broken in plenty of time for breakfast radio. Seb's wireless alarm switched itself on automatically just before six o'clock and a minute later he was sitting up in bed, staring blearily at the little loudspeaker.

'*In fast-developing news overnight, Cumbria Police have confirmed that Lake District FM's Meriel Kidd has confessed to the manslaughter of her husband, millionaire businessman Cameron Bruton. Shortly before midnight Miss Kidd's solicitor emerged from police headquarters in Penrith, where his client has been held for two days, to make this brief statement.*'

The calm, measured tones of Maxwell Probus followed. Seb thought the man sounded as if he were reading from the telephone directory.

'*This evening my client, Miss Meriel Kidd, accepted responsibility for her husband's drowning in Ullswater earlier this summer. Specifically, she has agreed to plead guilty to a charge of manslaughter, as the police accept that death occurred without malice aforethought. I emphasise, therefore, that this is NOT an admission of murder and neither are the police treating the case as such. Furthermore I believe there are clear and abundant mitigating factors involved, which will emerge in due course. Meanwhile I expect my client to be remanded in custody until sentencing. That is all I have to say at this time.*'

The newsreader's voice was back, but the rest was pure background to the story. Seb switched the radio off and lit a cigarette – that damned coroner had got him started on the bloody things again – and tried to think.

Unless Meriel had had some sort of breakdown under questioning, the police must have made a breakthrough.

And they'd clearly offered her a trade-off – a lesser charge in return for a confession and quick conviction. Case closed.

Seb rolled out of bed and into his clothes. He was due in the office at seven for news-gathering duties, but he'd be free by two and then he planned to drive straight down to Penrith. He was going to see DI Thompson; he'd wait all afternoon if he had to.

And then he would try to talk to Meriel, if she'd let him. They'd have to allow her visiting rights, wherever she was being held.

He was unable to think of any women's prisons in Cumbria. Seb had the depressing feeling that Meriel would turn out to be locked up somewhere a very long way from the Lake District.

CHAPTER FIFTY

The instant Seb stepped outside his flat, he felt it: the change. He came to an abrupt halt, disoriented and confused. What the hell was different?

It took several moments for him to realise exactly what had happened.

The sun had gone. Not half-hidden, glowing palely silver behind an early-morning heat-haze that it would quickly scorch into nothingness, but comprehensively banished by thick, gun-metal-grey cloud that hung heavy and almost motionless across the sky.

It was the first morning in months that he could remember where no dappled sunlight filtered through the leaves of the trees onto the pavements beneath. No sharply defined black shadows of chimneys or lamp-posts slanted obliquely across the road. Everything appeared colourless and drab, a faded black-and-white world compared to the seemingly endless sun-painted days that had, of course, ended, as they were always going to end, slipping away faithlessly in the night to some other land.

It remained hot, but it was no longer the dry heat of yesterday and the hundred days before it. Now the atmosphere was humid and heavy; almost sub-tropical. It reminded Seb of his newspaper days when he was in Ghana, on assignment with the local regiment.

He sniffed at the air. It had an electric tang to it; the unmistakable promise of thunder later.

Even with a sky so dark and threatening, Seb found it almost impossible to consider the prospect of rain, the actual reality of it. As he pulled away in his Spitfire, he realised he'd almost forgotten what rain felt like.

His memory, along with everyone else's, was about to be comprehensively refreshed.

Meriel had been too weary to make her full confession the evening before. Mark Thompson had to be satisfied with her signed statement of intent to do so the following morning. Probus had countersigned it, and the detective supposed that would have to do.

When the DI arrived home he was pretty much exhausted himself. It had been one hell of a day, up before dawn to be at Ullswater in time for the dive, then back for one of the trickiest interrogations he'd ever had to conduct. There was no doubt the case against Meriel Kidd was largely circumstantial. It had been vital to keep her under intense, relentless pressure from the moment he produced the watch in what he admitted to himself was a piece of pure *coup de théâtre*.

But it had bloody worked, he reflected with deep satisfaction, as he fumbled with his Yale to find the keyhole on his front door. Dammit ... why was it so dark out here? The moon had been riding high when he left headquarters half an hour ago.

He looked up at the sky. The stars and the moon had vanished from sight.

The door suddenly opened from the other side and light streamed out from the hall. It was Clemmie.

'What's the matter, Mark? Why can't you open the door? Oh God, you're not pissed, are you?'

She looked so pretty in the soft lamplight and he stepped forwards, took her in his arms, and kissed her for a long time before letting her go again. She smiled at him. 'What was that for? And I apologise, you can't be drunk, I can't smell any booze on you.'

He pushed the door shut behind him.

'No, I'm not. But I will be in about half an hour. And so will you. Because I have good news, my beautiful Clementine: Meriel Kidd has agreed to confess, first thing in the morning.'

He held up one finger as his wife was about to speak.

'Wait, Clemmie, it gets better. This means that as of tomorrow the case is closed. I can legitimately hand over to my DC to wind things up. So, much more importantly, you and I can go on holiday after all. Pretty much right away. Flights to the Med are going begging thanks to the heatwave here; it's a buyer's market. Never mind Portugal: how do you fancy southern Italy and the Amalfi coast? Sorrento, Positano, Ravello ... maybe even Naples? *Sí?*'

She kissed her own finger and pressed it firmly against his lips.

'*Sí*. But you're not to tell anyone at work where we're going. Not a bloody soul, OK? If we get one single phone call from your sodding superintendent or anyone else while we're away, I swear I'll pay the Mafia to drag you behind a mule up Mount Vesuvius and chuck you into the crater. Understood?'

He clicked his heels and bowed formally from the waist.

'*Sí, signora. Comprendo.* Now let's open some wine and take it up to bed with us.'

Meriel made her confession verbally in the presence of DI Thompson and a woman officer she hadn't seen before.

Although the little room had windows overlooking a small courtyard, all the ceiling lights were switched on and a standard lamp had been dragged in from somewhere and placed next to the table. It was growing steadily darker outside, even though it was mid-morning. Occasionally a faint rumble of thunder muttered in the distance.

Probus sat at her elbow, murmuring an occasional suggestion concerning the phrasing. As well as being recorded on cassette, a police shorthand secretary scribbled it all down at incredible speed and when she was finished, bore it away to be typed up and copies made.

Less than an hour later, Meriel was reading through the neatly typed pages before she carefully signed each one at the bottom. They were a fleshed-out version of what she'd told Probus the afternoon before. There was no attempt at mitigation; her lawyer told her that was a separate matter and something for later. This was just a straightforward laying out of the brutal facts.

She felt oddly detached and dispassionate as she reviewed what she'd just said. She'd been unable to sleep in her humid cell the previous night, wondering what effect seeing what she'd done set down in black and white (well, black and sepia, actually; the confession forms had a distinctly nineteenth-century look about them) would have on her.

But she needn't have worried. It was almost as if she were reading about someone else. Someone she knew vaguely and felt rather sorry for. Someone who'd got themselves into an awful lot of trouble, by the look of things.

She signed the final page and sat back in her chair. She felt remarkably calm, everything considered.

'There. What happens now, Inspector?'

'Thank you, Miss Kidd.'

There was another rumble of thunder, louder than before. Mark took the pages and slid them carefully into a cheap cardboard file. 'What happens next is that the custody sergeant will come in to explain where you are to be taken to from here. There'll be a short remand hearing here in Penrith and then you'll be making quite a long journey in a prison van, I'm afraid. Everything will be made clear to you on your eventual arrival, and Mr Probus here will be in touch in a day or so, won't you, sir?'

The solicitor nodded. 'Yes indeed, Inspector, but I have already explained to Miss Kidd how matters will unfold. I think she was asking you how much longer she will be held here in Penrith.'

Mark got to his feet and glanced at his watch.

'About ten minutes, I should think,' he said shortly. He turned to Meriel.

'Thank you for your co-operation, Miss Kidd. It will count in your favour with the judge, as I am sure Mr Probus has explained. The next time we see each other will be at the hearing to determine sentence. Goodbye until then.'

He swiftly left the room.

Meriel leaned back in her chair and stared listlessly

at the ceiling while Probus quietly made notes on his yellow legal pad.

'I must say, Mr Probus,' she said at last, 'I had no idea events would move along quite so quickly this morning. If I'd realised, I would have taken it all a bit slower. Do you know . . . I don't think I'm going to get any lunch.'

Whatever Probus began to say in reply was completely drowned out by a colossal bang, apparently coming from directly overhead. A brilliant flash almost simultaneously filled the little room with pure white light and there was a second, ear-splitting explosion, followed by a tremendous rattling from the window panes.

They turned to see enormous hailstones pounding the glass in a furious assault, almost as if some godlike entity was trying to smash its way into the little room. There was a third thunderclap, even louder than the first two. It sounded to Meriel as if giant tree-trunks were being violently split apart just above them.

She turned to her lawyer.

'Oh well, I suppose there's one comfort,' she said, almost shouting so that her voice could be heard above the angry drumming at the windows and yet another shivering thunderclap.

'At least it looks like I'm going to be kept safe and warm in the dry for a while, doesn't it?'

*

Meriel was long gone when Seb arrived at police head-quarters soon after three o'clock. He'd phoned ahead before driving down from Carlisle and Mark was expecting him. The reporter had been delayed by the huge thunderstorm – roads were awash in places – and he was shown straight into the detective's office.

'Seb.'

'DI Thompson.'

The policeman smiled. 'You can call me Mark, now, Seb. The Meriel Kidd case is closed. We won't be needing you any further.'

Seb stared at him in surprise. 'But I thought you wanted me to make a full witness statement. That's one of the reasons I'm here.'

The other man shook his head. 'It won't be necessary. We're able to keep your name completely out of things. Miss Kidd made a detailed confession this morning – the argument on the boat, the reasons for it, how she lured her husband to his death.'

'All because of what I told you she said to me?'

'Up to a point. But – and I'm telling you this strictly off the record, Seb – it was mainly because we found the watch.'

Seb was electrified.

'I *thought* that was why you must have sent the divers down yesterday. So that bloody Rolex *did* have something to do with it all.'

Mark nodded. 'Yup. You were completely right about

that. We found it at the bottom of the lake, directly under the spot where Cameron Bruton drowned.

'You were right about a lot of things, actually, Seb,' he went on. 'About Bruton threatening Meriel with exposure over *The Night Book*. And about the connection between the missing watch and him asking her the time just before he died.'

'What exactly happened there?'

'When he called up to her she threw the watch into the lake, just out of his reach. She admitted hoping that, when it began to sink, he'd go after it and would get in difficulties when he hit the icy layer beneath the surface. And when he did precisely that, she simply stood back and let him drown. It's true Meriel can't swim but she delayed throwing him the lifebelt until she knew it was too late.'

'Christ. *Christ*. I think I suspected something like that all along, but hearing you say it out loud ... well ... and she's admitted all this, has she?'

'Yup.'

Seb sat in silence for a while, before asking: 'What will happen to her now?'

The DI considered. 'Personally I think even a top silk might struggle to get a charge of murder to stick, so we decided to go with manslaughter, especially as she was willing to confess to it. Keeps everything neat and tidy. She'll—'

'No, no,' Seb interrupted. 'I mean today. What'll

happen to Meriel today? Can I see her, assuming she'll want me to?'

The DI shook his head.

'I'm afraid not. She was remanded in custody by local magistrates a couple of hours ago and by now she should be snug as a bug in jail, assuming they kept ahead of this storm. I think they've taken her to Low Newton women's prison. It's just outside Durham, about an hour and a half from here. She won't get visiting rights for a while yet.'

He hesitated. 'You can always write to her.'

Seb looked despondent.

'She'll probably send my letters straight back unopened. Even if she *had* still been here at Penrith, I didn't hold out much hope that she'd agree to see me. She must hate me.'

Mark Thompson looked at the unhappy young man opposite, and came to a sudden decision.

'Here's something else I shouldn't be telling you. But I can't see the harm.'

He weighed his next words carefully.

'I had quite a long private chat with Mr Probus – he's Miss Kidd's solicitor – after her confession this morning. Incidentally, I must say it sounds to me as if she'll have some pretty strong grounds for mitigation. But Probus also made reference to you, in passing. To be precise it was something his client said about you. You might be surprised to hear it.'

Seb lifted his head.

'Why? What did she say?'

The DI slowly and deliberately pointed a finger at the reporter.

'Meriel told Probus she thinks she's still in love with you.'

CHAPTER FIFTY-ONE

JANUARY 1977

He took the whole day off on the morning she was due to be sentenced. He couldn't bear to be in the news-room, listening to all the gossip and sensationalised chit-chat as details of the hearing clattered in on the teleprinter in dribs and drabs.

He went fell-walking, far away from radios and televisions and early-edition evening papers.

Seb had only had one letter from Meriel since she was remanded for reports, and he hadn't replied to it. She'd made it clear she'd send anything he wrote to her straight back to him, unread. He had understood.

Staring out high above little Buttermere, which wasn't much bigger than the brave puddle nearby that called itself Rydal Water, he pushed the memory of that lonely letter away.

Forty miles to the north, in a dusty Carlisle court-room, Meriel was learning her fate. He'd find out what it was soon enough. For now, it was enough to think of her as he sucked the freezing air into his lungs, the wind up here kicking up tiny blizzards in the powdery snow that settled into miniature snowdrifts around his feet.

Maybe he and Meriel would come up here together one day – a good day – and he could tell her how he had stood here, thinking of her, on a very bad day a long time ago.

The winter sun was beginning to set over Ennerdale over to the west.

It was time to go back down.

He saw the newspaper hoarding on the corner of Warwick Road, its banner a silent scream into the darkness of a midwinter's evening.

DEATH BY ROLEX – BUT
MERCY FOR MERIEL.

He stopped to buy a special edition of the *Carlisle Evening News*, but he didn't want to sit alone in his flat reading it so he went to the pub instead. There, over a pint of Theakston's and a stale ham sandwich, Seb learned what had befallen the woman he had loved, and then betrayed.

FIVE YEARS FOR MANSLAUGHTER – BUT JUDGE SAYS MERIEL A VICTIM TOO

By our special correspondent

Fallen radio star Meriel Kidd is tonight beginning a five-year sentence for the killing of her husband, millionaire businessman Cameron Bruton, who drowned last summer in Ullswater.

It is only now that the full facts of a death previously shrouded in mystery have come to light, and a gold Rolex watch emerged at the centre of the lethal drama.

After submissions this morning from both prosecution and defence counsels, Judge Susan Sladen said she accepted Kidd's plea of guilty to the lesser charge of manslaughter, rather than murder.

Bruton drowned while swimming close to the couple's boat. In a formal admission made by her QC, The Rt Hon. Crispin Bocage, Miss Kidd said she had deliberately thrown her husband's expensive watch into the water in the hope he would dive after it. She said she was fully aware there had already been a spate of accidental drownings in the Lakes during last summer's heatwave, when swimmers encountering icy water just below the super-heated surface got into serious difficulties.

Judge Sladen said it was clear Miss Kidd had hoped the same thing would happen to her husband. But she continued: 'Nevertheless, this was not a premeditated act. The accused was acting on a momentary impulse, and there was no certainty of what the outcome would be, hence my decision to accept a plea of manslaughter.'

Turning to motive, the judge said three separate psychiatric reports into Miss Kidd's state of mind on the day of the killing showed 'beyond doubt' that she was under severe stress.

'Mr Bruton had made specific threats of a sexual nature against his wife, threats which one could almost say were akin to blackmail, and she was extremely upset. I have seen documentary evidence for the basis of these threats and I believe they were serious and credible.'

Judge Sladen went on to say that despite public appearances to the contrary, the Brutons' marriage was 'deeply toxic' and the couple had not slept in the same bed for months. She added: 'I also accept that Miss Kidd's husband was a profoundly controlling individual who sought to dominate every aspect of his wife's daily life, checking up on the most minor of expenditures. Again, I have seen documents to support this; bank statements peppered with question marks, exclamation marks and highly critical comments over what were clearly innocent and modest transactions.'

In summary, Judge Sladen said that Meriel Kidd had 'snapped when she was unable to take any more'.

However, attempting to induce her husband to drown was 'completely unacceptable'.

'That is what the divorce courts are for,' the judge told her.

Meriel Kidd is expected to be transferred in due course from the remand wing where she is currently being held near Durham to an open prison in Kent. Legal commentators say that although she has been sentenced to five years, she is likely to be released on licence after serving three.

Her former employers, Lake District FM, refused to comment after today's hearing.

Seb folded the paper and drank what was left of his beer.

Three years.

He would wait for her.

If she'd have him.

CHAPTER FIFTY-TWO

Dear Miss Kidd,

I hope you don't mind me writing to you like this, but I felt I finally had to after reading about the outcome of your case in the papers last month and seeing on the news what you have been through. As a matter of fact I don't believe your 'crime' should have come to court at all, and if it did you should have been let off.

I am sure I am not the only woman who does not blame you for one second for doing what you did. I too am married to a horrible, domineering man who loves to bully and humiliate me at every opportunity. I too wish my husband were dead. We aren't rich enough to own boats or expensive watches but if I had been in your shoes that day, I would have done exactly as you did.

The other night Hugh was drunk and I had to help him up to bed. Far from being grateful he insulted me and was foul to me all the way up the stairs. I don't mind admitting when we got to the top I was of a mind to just push him back down again and hope he'd break his stupid neck at the bottom. I would have been glad if he had. I only just managed to stop myself, I can tell you.

You are far from being alone.

Yours sincerely,

Jane Smith. (Not my real name because maybe one day I really WILL do something I shouldn't. Or rather SHOULD.)

Sitting on her bunk bed in the cell she shared with a quiet alcoholic convicted of arson – the woman had burned down her employer's office after being sacked for poor timekeeping – Meriel was surprised they'd let that last letter through. Her post wasn't particularly heavily censored, but the ones that contained threats against husbands or boyfriends usually had such references blacked out with thick felt-tip pen. A friendly warder had told her that the most explicit ones were destroyed – usually after spending a few days pinned to the staff canteen wall, where they met with general approval and were toasted in mugs of tea.

She slid another from its envelope. There were a lot that morning – a couple of dozen at least.

Dear Meriel (if I may presume to call you that),

I run a women's discussion group in Plymouth and I can say hand on heart that I cannot remember a subject that has so unified us as has your plight.

The papers are saying that the judge was lenient with you partly because she was a woman, but actually we all thought she should have let you go free after hearing what you'd been put through for so many years. Yes, it is wrong to kill, but you didn't exactly hold the swine under, did you? At the end of our discussion I asked for a show of hands to the question: 'in the same circs., how many of you would have done the same?'

I'm not saying it was unanimous but you got a clear majority, Meriel. I think if you'd gone before a jury, you might well have got off.

Chin up. There's a lot of support waiting out here for you when you get out.

With warmest wishes,

Zelda Manning, chair, Plymouth Women Against Abuse.

Meriel sighed. Maybe she *had* been wrong to confess to manslaughter. Perhaps she should have fought her corner in open court in front of a jury of her peers.

443

There were usually more women than men on juries. And with a woman judge ...

There was no point agonising about it now. She reached for another letter.

Dear Miss Kidd, or should I say Miss Bitch?

I think what you did was despicable and my wife concurs wholeheartedly with me. She agrees that it is better I write this letter as I am considerably more fluent with words than she is.

Five years inside for being a murderous bitch? What a joke. You'll be out in three, unless another bitch in there sticks a knife into you, which I definitely think they will, and so does my wife.

We both hope you rot in hell.

Yours, from someone who thinks we should never have got rid of the rope. (My wife concurs wholeheartedly with me on this also, you bitch.)

PS Do you sign autographs? In which case please send one to above address, made out to Henry and Tabitha. Thankyou. SAE enclosed.

Meriel smiled. There had been a few like that. Not many, but far from unsettling her, bonkers hate mail cheered her up for some reason. Something to do with the theatre of the absurd, perhaps.

Outside, above the walkway that ran along the

length of the cell block, an electric bell rang loudly. It meant that in five minutes it would be time for free association. Meriel had only been transferred to this jail a week ago but already she was something of a folk heroine. Most of the other prisoners wanted to hear her story and yesterday one had confided that, years earlier, she had calmly watched her first husband choke to death 'right in front of me at the kitchen table'.

'It was a bit of brisket got stuck,' she whispered. 'I suppose I should have whacked him between the shoulder blades but as I'd never dared hit him back after one of his beatings, I didn't see why I should start now.'

Already Meriel was beginning to assemble accounts such as this, and the letters that arrived every day, into the rough shape of a book. Probus had been right. Judging by the support she had received already, there really might be a way back for her when she eventually rejoined the outside world.

The one letter she yearned to receive more than any other was from Seb. It had yet to arrive.

But that was entirely down to her.

She'd kept a copy of the one she'd sent to him, shortly after she had been remanded to Durham. Meriel dug it out now from her foot-locker.

Seb
   I want you to know that I forgive you for what you did. I have thought a great deal about it and I can see that

you genuinely believed you had no other choice, and strange as it may sound, I respect you for it. It must have been extraordinarily difficult for you to decide what to do.

I am only sorry you felt unable to come to me first, but I truly understand and accept that the shock of reading the things I had written would have been devastating. When I think back to some of the descriptions on those pages I can scarcely credit that I was the person who wrote them. You must have been in turmoil as you read chapter after chapter after chapter. And of course, your instincts about what I had done (remember asking me outright if I'd killed Cameron?) were absolutely right.

Of course now I wish I had told you everything, right from the start, right from that night when you first came to Cathedral Crag after Cameron had drowned. But I was terrified of two things: being found out, and losing you.

And now look at me. Both those things have happened. Clever old Meriel, eh?

The one thing I never lied about, Seb, was that I loved you. And I think I still do, however hard that may be for you to believe.

But whatever your feelings are for me, please, please don't come here. Don't ever, ever visit me in prison. I couldn't bear it. And please don't write, either. I'm in a very strange place (I don't mean this horrible remand wing, I mean in my mind) and I need to rediscover myself. Sorry if that sounds ridiculously Californian.

Perhaps we shall see each other again, my love (see: I

DO still love you!) but not until all this is completely over and I am certain of myself again. Although to be honest, I'm not entirely sure that I ever will be. That's another of the reasons I can't see you, at least for a very long time.

Look after yourself.

All my love (there we are again!)

Your Meriel. x

PS I mean it, Seb. Please don't reply to this. I'll only send it back unopened. M x

EPILOGUE

He cursed his MGB roadster – an upgrade from the Spitfire – as it hurtled around a corner, almost on two wheels, before lurching back onto all four and fish-tailing dangerously. A flat battery at the start of the drive here and then an even flatter tyre. Great! Thank you so *bloody* much, God.

He was late. The dashboard clock showed him it was now seven minutes past eight and she'd been due to be released on the hour, after an early breakfast and then signing for the return of her few possessions.

East Sutton Park women's open prison was outside Maidstone in Kent and he'd planned to leave Carlisle shortly after midnight to be sure of getting there in plenty of time. That was before the delayed jump-start from the AA and then the blowout on the M1.

449

He saw the signs for HM Prison on his left and swerved violently. He just made the turn, and skidded to a halt almost directly outside the gates of the jail.

Almost, but not quite. A large silver Mercedes was parked on the single yellow line in front of the automatic barrier that controlled access in and out of the place.

There were two men inside it, sitting in the front seats. They were in dark suits and the one behind the wheel was smoking a fat cigar.

He slowly pulled past them. He'd never seen the driver before but he recognised the passenger. It took him a moment to place him, and then his memory engaged. Of course. Probus. The lawyer.

Seb's heart missed a beat, partly from relief – he obviously wasn't too late, after all – but also from a sudden, gnawing anxiety. What were they planning on doing? He pulled up again, this time just in front of the executive saloon.

He began drumming his fingers on the steering wheel. When Meriel emerged, which car would she choose to get into?

'Here she comes.'

David Weir started the Mercedes' engine and punched Probus lightly on the shoulder.

'It's payday, Max.'

The agent stepped out of the car and folded his arms

on the roof, so that he could face Meriel as she walked through the barrier and down the last few yards of the prison drive that led to the main road. She was wearing the same suit she had on in her last appearance in court – black jacket, cream blouse, black pencil skirt and black heels – and she was carrying a black leather holdall.

'Meriel! Over here! Welcome back to the world, honey. Look who's with me! Boy, have we got a champagne breakfast lined up for *you*. I've booked you a suite at Claridge's so you can sleep it off – you can't have had a drop of anything stronger than coffee in the last three years. And then this afternoon we've got some seriously big meetings scheduled. I want to—'

He stopped. His client wasn't even looking at him, still less listening to what he was saying.

Meriel Kidd was staring at the man sitting squarely on the bonnet of a sports car parked directly in front of the Mercedes.

He wore faded jeans and a brown leather flying jacket with a fur collar.

He had dirty-blond hair and three days' worth of stubble.

He was smiling at her, shyly.

'Hello, Meriel.'

'Hello, Seb.'

'Can I take you somewhere?'

'I'd like that.'

David Weir smacked the roof of his Mercedes with the flat of his hand.

'Meriel! Hey! For Christ's sake! *Hello?* Where are you going? Who is this scruffbag? Probus and I need to—'

She appeared to notice him for the first time.

'Oh, hello, David. Not today, I'm afraid. Not tomorrow, either. Not for a while, actually.'

The agent exploded with irritation.

'I asked you a question! Where do you think you're going?'

She looked at him in genuine surprise as Seb opened the door for her, took her bag and tossed it onto the tiny back seat.

'Isn't it obvious? But since you ask, David . . . About as far away from men like you as it's possible to get.'

She slid into the passenger seat and Seb climbed in beside her. He started the engine and pulled away. The furious agent's bellows faded swiftly behind them.

They drove in silence for a long time. It was Seb who spoke first.

'You opened my letter.' It was a statement, not a question. 'The one I sent last week.'

'Yes. How did you know I'd read it?'

'Because you didn't send it back. I've been in agonies every morning since I posted it, wondering if it would

452

drop through my letterbox. I've had that bloody stupid song "Return to Sender" running through my head for days.'

She smiled.

'Where are we going?'

'Cornwall. I've rented a cottage.'

His left hand was resting on top of the gearstick. Very slowly, Meriel placed her hand over his.

He glanced at her.

'You should put your seatbelt on. They're getting really strict about it these days.'

'Sorry.' She clicked the clasp into place.

'I waited,' he continued in the same matter-of-fact voice. 'I waited for you, Meriel. There's been no one else.'

She pressed his fingers with her own.

'I know. I could tell, the moment I saw you.'

'God, is it that obvious?'

She laughed softly. 'Only to me. You look exactly as you did that summer day by the river, when you stared across the lawn at me, and I thought: "Oh, *there* he is." And then later that night, when you woke up after we'd made love for the first time. The look that tells me you're making a promise.'

Seb lifted his fingers so they intertwined with hers.

'A promise to do what?'

Meriel smiled.

'To restore me with your love.'

She managed to blink back the tears that suddenly threatened to overwhelm her.

'And the thing is, my darling Seb, that's exactly what you've done.

'You've restored me.'

Acknowledgements

Grateful thanks to my editor Suzanne Baboneau for her iron-fist-in-velvet-glove technique of keeping me to deadline, and my literary agent Luigi Bonomi for his iron-fist-in-iron-glove alternative. Without them none of my novels would have got past their prologues.